TWAS THE BITE BEFORE CHRISTMAS

ELLEN RIGGS

BOUGHT-THE-FARM
MYSTERIES

FREE PREQUEL

Rescuing this pup could bring Ivy a whole new life... if it doesn't kill her first.

Discover how big city executive Ivy meets Keats, her crime-solving sheepdog, in A Dog with Two Tales. Ivy Galloway doesn't know how desperate she is to escape the big city and her soul-sucking corporate career until she meets a sheepdog in need of rescue, too. This short prequel to the laugh-out-loud Bought-the-Farm Mystery series is a page-turner for lovers of animals, humor and spunky amateur sleuths. Join Ellen Riggs' author newsletter at **ellenriggs.com** to get this FREE prequel.

Twas the Bite Before Christmas

Copyright © 2020 Ellen Riggs

ISBN 978-1-998742-00-4 Paperback - D2D
ISBN 978-1-990613-20-3 AudioBook
ASIN B08F4JR4JF Kindle
ASIN B0CGYV94NR AudioBook

Publisher: Ellen Riggs
www.ellenriggs.com
Cover designer: Lou Harper
Editor: Serena Clarke
2501220919

CHAPTER ONE

W e were standing on Main Street outside Hill Country Designs when Keats suddenly collapsed onto his side, let out a steamy puff of air, and then closed his eerie blue eye. He lay silent and unmoving in a circle of light cast by one of Clover Grove's old-fashioned streetlamps as the first fine snow of the season sifted down and speckled his bushy black tail and ears. Then he released a high-pitched, heart-wrenching whine.

I stepped over the prostrate dog and turned to my best friend, Jilly Blackwood. "Can you believe this?"

She pushed up her green wool hat, freeing tendrils of curly blonde hair, and then shook her head. "This isn't like him at all," she said.

"Oh, it's totally like him." I gave the dog a little nudge with my boot. "All business when a killer attacks and all drama when a bath's been drawn. He's been picking up some performance tips from Mom."

"Keats, come on," Jilly said. "This isn't the time to play dead. It's a big night. We're about to witness the town's first Christmas tree lighting in decades."

Our friend, Teri Mason, switched off the neon "open" sign

inside the store and then stepped through the door. When her eyes landed on Keats, she screamed.

"Oh no, what happened?" She rushed over and dropped to her knees in the slick film of snow. "Keats, what's wrong?" Her voice had a note of hysteria and she looked up at me. "Ivy, *do* something. Why are you just standing there?"

The dog lifted his head and turned to gaze at Teri with his warm brown eye. Then he flicked a blue glare at me and flopped onto the sidewalk again.

"That's why," I said. "He's throwing a tantrum and I don't want to indulge him."

Teri ran her hand over my sheepdog's sleek head and the white tuft of his tail gave a feeble twitch. "A tantrum? Are you sure?" she said. "He seems to be suffering."

"He's suffering all right... from a bad case of the winter coats." I rolled my eyes. "His pride took a near-fatal hit when Jilly pulled it out of the shopping bag."

Jilly laughed and Keats cracked open his blue eye to wither her. "Keats, be reasonable," she said. "It's just a coat and you look so handsome in it."

The dog found his voice and gave an indignant grumble of protest. A month ago I'd bought a basic black coat from Grub, the farming supplies store. After a chilling altercation with the owner, however, I didn't want the visual reminder and donated the coat to my favorite dog rescuers. Today Jilly stopped at The Hound and the Furry pet boutique and picked up the only coat left in Keats' size. It was a puffy yellow parka complete with a faux fur trimmed hood, that was better suited to the high life than herding. My sheepdog had crumpled instantly when I put it on, forcing me to carry him to the truck.

Good thing I hadn't added the matching boots that completed the ensemble.

"Keats, I'm sorry," I said. "But unless you're working around the barn, you can't be outside for long without proper gear. This is hill country. Winters pack a wallop here."

"They sure do," Teri said, getting up off her knees. "By January it's so bleak I close up shop for a month and head to Key West."

That explained why some of Teri's paintings and designs had a tropical theme. In fact, the bohemian caftan she wore tonight under a pink coat was covered in matching hibiscus. You could always find Teri in a crowd.

Jilly shivered and then shrugged. "I'm no fan of the cold but it beats last Christmas in Boston."

That was true but also setting the bar pretty low. A year ago, Jilly and I were successful executives and worked through Christmas, just as we did every other holiday. It was a point of pride that also allowed us to avoid our families and difficult memories. We'd become family to each other in college and had our own rituals, which basically amounted to Jilly trying new gourmet recipes and me enjoying every bite. It was enough then. If anything, we were smug about our independence and commitment to our careers. Traditional celebrations were for regular people.

When we moved to my hometown of Clover Grove to launch Runaway Farm and Inn, however, our priorities shifted completely. Thanksgiving had blended my crazy family, our boyfriends, and our new "found family," which included people like Teri and more than 50 rescue animals. It was the best holiday of my life and Jilly said the same. But we hadn't exactly become "regular people." The series of murders on or around the farm since our arrival slammed the door on that possibility yet made me very thankful indeed for all that I had.

Especially the theatrical border collie now on strike at my feet.

Rescuing Keats was what started it all. When I met him as a desperate, neglected pup, he'd been so sweet and eager to please. Now he was a true working dog with a farm to manage and a side hustle of crime-solving. He had strong opinions that he expressed with his posture, strategic use of his mismatched eyes, mumbles and grumbles, and the occasional flamboyant protest. Normally I let him have his way. Keats had repaid me many times over for risking my life to save him. He was also bred for livestock management, which certainly didn't come naturally to me, a former human resources executive.

On top of everything else, Keats was simply an incredible companion. Last Christmas, Jilly had been my only friend. Now, I was surrounded by my boyfriend Kellan Harper, five quirky siblings, a diva of a mother, many new friends and an expanding community. Yet the bigger my circle grew, the more I seemed to need the anchor of my dog. I blamed my anxiety on the concussion I got saving him, combined with some savage attacks since our move. A big city girl sticking her nose into small-town murder investigations needed a canine partner in crime-solving.

Still, I had to draw the line somewhere. Sometimes I had to be the leader.

"Get up, Keats," I said. "Do it on your own steam or I will carry you into town square and rock you like a baby. If you want your heroic reputation to take a public beating, that's your choice."

"She'll follow through, Keats," Jilly said. "They didn't call her the grim reaper of HR for nothing."

He opened his blue eye and I could tell he was starting to relent. Now it was time to give a little.

"How about I get you another coat?" I said. "Maybe this one's too puffy. The hood is a bit much and the yellow is kind of... garish."

He mumbled something that sounded like, "Ya think?"

"He matches Buttercup," Jilly said. "I think it's cute."

Buttercup was the ancient yellow jalopy I'd inherited from my mom when her license was seized over repeated collisions with stop signs. It was impossible to flit around unnoticed in a car that color and Keats probably felt the same about the coat. Whether he was herding or sleuthing, he liked to keep a low profile.

Teri went back to lock the door of her store. By the time she rejoined us, Keats was on his pins. His ears were flat and his tail down but he was mobile.

"Cheer up," I said. "You're about to witness something huge. Clover Grove is embracing the miracle of Christmas."

"I can't believe the town's never had its own Christmas tree," Jilly said. "In the movies, that's a small-town tradition."

"They did in olden days," I said. "Before Dorset Hills stole our thunder."

Our larger, more prosperous neighbor was more commonly called Dog Town because it was the destination of choice for dog lovers. They had the budget to go all out for holidays, so Clover Grove had started bussing people over there to enjoy their events and decorations.

"No one does holidays better than Dorset Hills," Teri said. "But it irks the heck out of me that people do their shopping in Dog Town instead of supporting our local businesses. How can we ever grow that way?"

"That's what the Clover Grove Culture Revival Project is all about," Jilly said. "We're going to turn this town around."

Already I could see signs of progress and we'd only been trying to raise awareness for a month. The stores along Main Street had made an effort with their festive displays and there were so many pretty lights the streetlamps were hardly needed. It looked quaint and inviting, something I never recalled from my youth. In fact, I couldn't get away from this town fast enough and worked hard to get a scholarship for college so that I never needed to come back.

While I was gone, homesteaders had taken over with their back-to-the-land movement that prioritized canning over culture. Our team was behind a recent whirlwind of activities like book clubs, wine appreciation nights and sessions to learn about music, theater, the arts, gourmet food and far more. Even a cynic like me could smell change in the air.

Or perhaps it was just the cinnamon in the hot apple cider that Mandy McCain, the ace baker and owner of Mandy's Country Store, was serving free at the entrance to the town square. She grinned when she saw us. "Oh my gosh, Keats looks—"

"Don't say it. He's very sensitive." I accepted the cider she offered, downed it in one scalding gulp and held my cup out for more. "Got any bourbon to chase that? I need something to get through the mayor's speech."

Mandy laughed and offered me gingerbread cookies instead. They were all cut in the shape of Christmas trees but the decorations varied so I had to make the right choice. Finally I selected one and just as I was about to take a bite, a big hand circled around and snatched it.

"Hey!" I turned to see most of the cookie disappearing into my brother's mouth.

"What's yours is mine," Asher said, spraying cookie crumbs. "Always has been."

As the last of six, the sibling "tax" system meant that everyone but Daisy, the eldest and our unofficial matriarch, would take a bite of my treat until there was barely a morsel left. Tonight, Asher offered me the trunk of the gingerbread tree and I took it, even though Mandy quickly offered me another cookie. Old habits died hard.

"Oh, Asher, you're terrible," Jilly said. The lilt in her tone said the opposite—that she was finding him more amusing and delightful by the day. Many powerful men in sharp suits and status cars had tried to elicit that lilt with wining, dining and glittering gifts. Instead, my cookie thief brother in his faded jeans and pickup truck was stealing her heart crumb by crumb. His dazzling good looks had less to do with that than his decency, loyalty and endless good cheer, which police work hadn't managed to erode.

Kellan Harper, Asher's tall, dark and handsome boss, offered me his cookie with a courtly little bow. I accepted it, layered it back to back with mine and took a big bite.

"See how it's done, brother?" I said, spraying crumbs back at Asher. "Gallantry and class."

"For a classy lass," Asher said, grinning as he pulled Jilly's arm through his. "Keats, buddy, I feel for you in that prom dress. Don't let Ivy emasculate you completely."

Keats wilted even more at his tone.

Jilly pulled Asher away. "I chose that coat in case you're wondering."

"Oops." He grinned over his shoulder. "You look dashing, Keats. Dashing, I say."

"I like it," Kellan said, staring down at the dog. "Now I can see him coming."

Keats enjoyed herding Kellan, and for a cop, my boyfriend was surprisingly oblivious to ambush. If he didn't see Percy, my marmalade cat on the prowl, he likely wouldn't see Keats in his buttercup parka, either. Maybe Keats had the same thought because his tail and ears perked up. There would be even more sport in stalking the chief with such an impediment.

Kellan dropped an arm around my shoulders and we followed the others. He was normally reserved at public events—always the chief of police, even off duty—so the gesture gave me an extra thrill. We'd had a quiet month without a homicide or any of the clashes that resulted when I overstepped his professional boundaries with my sleuthing during investigations. It felt like our relationship had reached cruising altitude, a mere 10 years after we'd crashed and burned in college. Christmas was only a few days away and life was sweeter than this gingerbread.

"Doesn't Jilly feed you?" he asked, as I mowed through both cookies like a woodchipper.

"As an only child, you can't possibly understand," I said, washing down the last mouthful with cider. "I learned to get while the getting's good. Besides, these are the best cookies I've ever tasted. It's no wonder the town's Secret Santa has been delivering them into mailboxes by night. It's given everyone a thrill."

He wrinkled his handsome nose. "They're too spicy for me. Practically burned my tongue off."

"Well, this evening will be plenty bland now that the mayor's involved. Why has she surfaced suddenly?"

"Smelled opportunity," he said. "That's how politicians work. You've been building community spirit. I'm guessing she wants to ride that train right into new branding."

"And it all starts with a single Christmas tree." I looked up, way up, with a smile. "And what a tree it is."

The 20-foot fir completely dwarfed our town square, which was never much to look at, especially compared to Dorset Hills' Bingham Square, with its massive bronze German shepherd statue. Both town halls were built from the same yellow brick, but ours was dull and blackened by time, whereas Dog Town's had been sand-blasted till it glittered like a fairy-tale palace.

Letitia Smart, a florist, had worked with a scant few dollars from town council to decorate on a shoestring. Discount baubles and plenty of lights went a long way to spruce up the square. The snowflakes fluttering down did the rest.

"Isn't it pretty?" I asked, sliding a boot under Keats' belly. Tension crept up the leash as the dog contemplated another showdown.

"Very." Kellan didn't move his arm, despite my squirming. In fact, he pulled me closer so that I wouldn't fall over with Keats. "It's a shame they can't just flip a switch, let us all gasp in awe and leave it at that. But no, they need to stick a pill into our candy."

Clover Grove's mayor walked up the stairs to the makeshift stage. Meryl Martingale had gone to school with my mother but she'd made a wiser choice in husbands and lived a life of leisure until her midlife foray into politics. A few years ago, she'd transformed quite suddenly from a mousey woman into a highlighted lioness. The town's high-speed gossip grapevine said her husband Larry, the town's only accountant, had an affair and this was the price tag for her keeping it quiet. I didn't put much stock in the grapevine but Larry was the one looking mousey standing behind her now.

Meryl cleared her throat, tapped the mic and said, "Good evening."

"Wait! Wait!" There was a flurry across the square. The crowd parted to reveal a small woman in a hooded Dr. Zhivago style coat. "Meri, darling, don't start without me."

As far as I knew, no one called Meryl "Meri" but that didn't stop my mother from bellowing out the schoolyard nickname.

"Dahlia," Meryl said over the mic, giving Mom the grand entrance she craved. "The ceremony waits for no one."

Mom waved one red leather glove and called, "Just let me find my children so that I can hear their gasps of awe when the lights go on."

Meryl gave an exasperated sigh, also over the mic. "Galloways? Hands up for your mother."

I didn't make a move, nor did my four sisters. Finally Asher's glove rose jerkily, propelled by Jilly's mitten.

"Oh, *there* you are darlings," Mom said, wedging herself into our midst. "It's so chilly I need the welcoming warmth of my offspring. Such as it is."

Poppy snickered first but it caught on like the nice little flame Mom wanted. Sometimes, Mom had enough self-awareness to laugh at herself. It was her saving grace in my eyes. In Keats' eyes, blue and brown, she needed no such grace. He adored Mom and his tail lashed for the first time since the yellow coat came out of the bag.

Mayor Martingale cleared her throat. "It is my very great honor to welcome you tonight to our first tree lighting event in over forty years. I'd love to take credit for the idea but it goes to a few good citizens who are working to revive some of Clover Grove's old traditions. Let's give a hand to Hazel Bingham, who knew this town when it was the belle of the ball in hill country, as well as Letitia Smart of Flora to Fawn Over and Mabel Halliday of Miniature Mutts."

Everyone clapped but a few people turned to see my reaction at being overlooked. Jilly and I had done most of the grunt work on the Clover Grove Culture Revival Project to date and everyone knew it. The mayor was likely snubbing Runaway Farm and Inn because of the bad press the murders brought to the town. I was afraid those incidents would overshadow any good work we did forever.

A red leather glove shot up and snapped soundlessly. "Meri, darling? I think you've forgotten about Ivy, Jilly and me. We've worked tirelessly to bring attention to this movement."

There was another snuffle of laughter among my siblings. Mom's primary role in the "movement" had been to brag about it. She wasn't a worker bee but she was never shy about taking credit.

"You're right, Dahlia," the mayor said. "Ivy and her friends have played a role. I'm glad they're willing to step up to help when needed." Her eyes sought me out. "As a matter of fact, Clover Grove needs you now, Ivy. Are you willing to serve?"

I glanced down at Keats for my answer. His tail gave a reluctant swish, as if to say, "There's no getting out of this one."

Then Jilly elbowed me as a reminder that the inn was always in need of promotion.

"Of course, Mayor," I called out. "How can we help?"

She gave a dramatic sweep of her arm and then held her hand to her ear. "Do you hear what I hear?"

"Uh, not really." The square was quiet except for whirring of gears as the gossips recorded everything for later delectation. "I don't hear anything in particular."

"Exactly. We're celebrating Christmas as a town for the first time in ages. Where's the caroling? We need a choir. Immediately."

"A choir?" I said. "Well, okay. We'll look into that."

Asher raised his hand over the crowd, once again propelled by Jilly's mitten. "What?" he said, and then, "Right. A call for volunteers, please."

Gloves and mittens rose. Teri, Mabel and Letitia were the first of many women to come forward. Finally a few men joined them, all of them clients at Bloomers, Mom's unisex hair salon. Naturally the red glove shot up then, too. The rest of the family groaned. We knew she was totally tone deaf.

"Show of hands, Galloways," I said. "Show of voices."

Every hand went up except Asher's and there was a little tussle as Jilly tried and failed to pull the strings. Surely Jilly and my four sisters would be enough to help drown Mom out and stop us from providing further fodder for civic amusement.

"Wonderful," the mayor said. "We've already posted rehearsal dates, leading up to the showcase on Christmas Eve. It's going to take our breath away, just... like... this!" With a flourish, she switched on the tree lights. Thousands of colorful sparks lit up the noble fir, making everyone gasp in childlike awe. Everyone except Kellan and me. It's not that we didn't feel it. He squeezed my shoulder and I squeezed his free hand. We felt the awe but his police training and my decade in HR had taught us to lock things down with a nosy audience.

Maybe Kellan also felt the vague sense of foreboding that suddenly washed over me. Keats certainly did. The dog's ruff puffed around the yellow hood and his tail stiffened. That's when I remembered what had happened on Thanksgiving. Percy had intentionally knocked over some figures in the gorgeous ceramic replica of Clover Grove that Mabel Halliday created. One tiny figure had toppled in town square and the cat had scraped imaginary kitty litter over the "body." At the time, I'd taken it as a harbinger of bad luck for one citizen this festive season. But as weeks passed I'd forgotten about it. Looking around now, I wondered if someone had a target on their back.

Kellan leaned over and whispered, "He was just toying with us. Like cats do."

I wasn't surprised that he'd read my mind or that he dismissed what he'd seen that day. While he occasionally admitted my pets knew more than we did, his logical mind usually prevailed.

"You're probably right," I said, looking back at the tree. "But if someone has to go, I'm glad we gave them a glorious send-off."

CHAPTER TWO

Jilly came out to join me on the porch and linked her arm through mine as a van containing the mayor's brother and family rolled up the twisty lane at Runaway Inn.

"Our civic sacrifice has already paid off in spades," she said. "I'd sing my lungs out year round if Meryl Martingale would keep sending us guests. There couldn't be a better endorsement than one from the town's highest official."

"The early reward surprised me," I said. "And we've sacrificed more for this farm. But choir really isn't my thing, Jilly."

"You have a beautiful voice," she said. "I hear you crooning to Alvina and she loves it."

"Easy crowd, and private performances only. Our new choirmaster will likely be harder to please."

She fluttered dismissive fingers. "It's a Christmas choir. All voices should be welcome, including your mother's."

"So you say now. You'll change your tune when you hear her later."

"You're all so tough on Dahlia. I'd feel pretty lucky to have a mom like her."

Her arm dropped from mine and I knew she was thinking of her own family. Close as we were, I knew little about Jilly's family. Her inner repression machine rivaled mine and there had been no concussion to unleash her thoughts and tongue. I never pried because *she* never pried. Some day I'd meet these people and I'd try to be as welcoming as she was of my family.

Daisy came out of the house, wearing her ever-present rubber gloves. There was a spray bottle of cleanser sticking out of her apron pocket. "Oh good, they're here," she said.

"Gloves and apron off, sis," I said. "You'll look like maid service instead of co-manager."

Hiring Daisy was a recent decision made possible by a cash infusion from heiress Hannah Pemberton, the previous owner of the farm. Hannah had been subsidizing the start-up of the inn since the beginning but this month's deposit had brought tears of gratitude to my eyes. I had no doubt the Rescue Mafia—a group of vigilante dog rescuers from Dorset Hills—had put in a good word for me as thanks for taking on an emu "temporarily." The large bird was still here a month later, sharing a pen with Alvina, the alpaca. The Mafia probably also kept Hannah informed about the farm's other challenges, specifically the rash of crimes that made it difficult to attract guests.

My goal was to become self-sustaining, of course, but launching an inn in a small community like Clover Grove would have been difficult even without murders following me like a plague. The additional funding said Hannah didn't blame me for what had happened. That she knew my intentions were good. So, I'd keep the emu if I had to, along with every other rescue animal the Mafia wanted to "launder" through the farm before finding other homes. There was plenty of space, although Charlie, the farm manager, was working harder than ever to fence off land and had dropped hints about building a second barn. He needed help, too. While I loved hard labor, other commitments kept pulling me away. Like crime-solving. And now choir, of all things.

Keats trotted ahead of us to greet the guests in his yellow parka. His boycott had ended after I placed a rush order online for a simple, black coat befitting a hardworking farm dog. He would suck up the embarrassment till it got here. An ambassador needed to compromise.

The van's doors all opened at once and a family of six spilled out. The driver, a tall man with silvering hair, was Meryl Martingale's brother, Bill Stout. He shook our hands, and then introduced his wife, Reyna, and their kids, who ranged from 13 to 19. All the teens looked distinctly unimpressed with the farm. The charms of a small-town Christmas would be lost on them, just as they were on Daisy's two sets of twin teenage boys. I was counting on her to help wrangle this crew, because I had virtually no experience with young people. Give me a belligerent pig over a truculent teen any day. At least you could nudge the pig with a poker if it got mouthy, as my sly sow Wilma did regularly.

Once the introductions were out of the way, I offered the grand tour of the barn and pastures. I loved showing off my animals and witnessing the grudging smiles that inevitably followed.

Today, the guests started moving en masse toward the house. All four kids asked at once, "Do you have wifi?"

"Oh yes," Daisy said. "Plus there's a huge TV and a good selection of my sons' video games."

The smiles that spread around after that weren't grudging at all.

Jilly heaved a sigh of relief. "I'll help Daisy get people settled while you check in with Charlie. Let's leave for choir practice in half an hour, okay? Can't be late on our first day."

I gave her a gloved salute and headed toward the barn with Keats. Percy appeared out of nowhere and the two streaked ahead of me, bright flashes on a dreary day. It was overcast, with dark clouds threatening snow. The townspeople were excited at the prospect of a white Christmas. To me, that just spelled more work.

Charlie, the silver fox who was a proud member of Mom's

casual dating "rotation," walked me through the day's updates. It was like a teacher accounting to the principal about who'd bitten or kicked whom in the schoolyard. There was always bickering among the animals when Keats wasn't around to police them. My city girl delusions of peace in the barnyard had vanished with the fall leaves. These were rescues who mostly came from neglectful, abusive backgrounds. Despite the abundance of food we supplied, they had a scarcity mindset and mealtimes created frenzied competition. Charlie had recently gotten a blacksmith to create more pokers with iron hooks on wooden poles, so that we had options. The original had come in handy in murderous assaults from humans, as well.

I texted Jilly to meet me at the truck in five minutes. The car would have been my first choice, but it was time to conquer the truck's standard transmission once and for all. Buttercup was a fair-weather car. In the time it took her to warm up we could walk to town and our boots had better traction. The pickup, on the other hand, was toasty warm and could get through anything, especially now that the chains were on. I'd rather persevere with the stick than end up a popsicle in a ditch in Buttercup. Besides, I owed a smooth ride to Keats and Percy.

The furry twosome stopped kibbitzing in the barn, puffed suddenly and then bolted out the back door. Charlie and I exchanged a quick glance before racing after them. Outside, we saw the youngest guest, Bronwen, climbing the fence to the pasture that held Alvina and the emu.

"Get down right now," I shouted. "It's not safe."

Keats leapt at the girl's leg, caught the cuff of her jeans and hung there like a bright yellow anchor.

"Let go," she said, trying to thrash him off. "Ow ow ow."

The screaming started when Percy landed on her head and squatted like a living fur hat. The more she swiped at him, the harder the cat clung with his claws.

It was enough to stop her from going over the fence but she

managed to unlatch the gate before I got there. It swung open and the cat and dog released in the same moment to prevent a breach. The nameless emu dodged around Alvina, leapt lightly over the dog and cat, and ran like the wind. In what seemed like seconds, she became a mere dot in the fields. Keats set off in pursuit but I called him to come back. Fast as he was, he couldn't keep up with a bird that could clock 30 miles per hour.

"Satisfied?" I asked Bronwen, as she climbed down, rubbing her head. Her staticky brown hair had become tumbleweed thanks to Percy's styling intervention. "Now that poor bird may die of frostbite."

"I just wanted to see the alpaca dance." Her shrug and her smirk said otherwise, and both Keats and Percy circled her, waiting for permission to strike again.

Jilly and Daisy came running down from the house and I pulled out my phone while telling them what had happened.

"I'm so sorry," Daisy said. "She's as slippery as my youngest two."

"We'll put a tracking collar on her," I said. "The one that gives electric shocks."

Bronwen backed right into Daisy, who grabbed her hood with the rubber-gloved hands of experience.

"I hate it here," the teen said. "You all suck."

"Extra shock for the lip," I said, pulling off my glove so that I could text. "Bronwen, fair warning. I'm only nice to animals. And only nice to *nice* animals. Right now, you are a mean animal who deliberately set a helpless bird free in winter."

Jilly ran a mitten across her mouth as a signal to zip my lips. "Are you calling the police?" she asked.

"No!" Bronwen said. "I'm sorry."

Now Jilly couldn't help chuckling. "I meant to catch the bird."

"I should get the cops over here to deal with the kid," I said. "But they're no match for an emu on the run." I stared at my phone.

"This is Cori Hogan's fault. She shouldn't have dumped the world's second largest bird on a novice."

"So you're asking the Rescue Mafia to corral the emu?" Jilly looked at her watch. "We're going to be late for choir practice."

"People can start singing without us." My breath billowed from my mouth in quick puffs of steam but slowed when I heard the roar in the distance. "Help's on its way."

Keats ran out to greet my neighbor, Edna Evans, as her ATV bumped slowly through the field. The emu trailed behind on a rope. Her text said she'd managed to lasso it without difficulty when it stopped under her bird feeders for a snack. Securing it hadn't fazed her either. As a prepper for the apocalypse, she knew every knot going and could make a hammock from a ball of yarn, or so she claimed.

"Honestly, Ivy," she said, hopping off and leading the emu toward the alpaca pasture. "Why am I always returning your animals? You take the name 'Runaway Farm' too literally."

Her tone was harsh but she was gentle with the big bird, who followed meekly. I noticed my crotchety octogenarian neighbor had switched to winter fatigues. The material was heavier but lighter in color to blend into the bare trees and dry grass.

When the gate was latched, she walked over to Bronwen, who shrank back against Daisy. "Are you up to date on your vaccinations, young lady? I used to be a school nurse and I always keep a hypodermic on hand in case of toxic encounters with young people."

"Now, now," Jilly said, eyeing the teen. "I'm sure Bronwen has learned her lesson. Am I right?"

The girl shrugged, still defiant. It said a lot that her parents and siblings hadn't bothered to come down to see what the fuss was about. I knew what it felt like to be at the end of the sibling lineup. Maybe I'd have pulled attention-seeking stunts like this without Daisy to watch over me when Mom couldn't or wouldn't.

"I'll speak to her parents," Daisy said, frogmarching the teen toward the house. "They signed waivers, so if she's trampled it's not on you, Ivy."

Daisy must have been truly angry—or scared—because she was the most restrained of the Galloways.

"We'd better get going," Jilly said. "Thank you, Edna."

"That's it? All I get is a thank you for roping this bird when you two are clearly going off on a fun adventure? Dagnabit, I deserve a grapefruit martini."

"It's not even noon," I said.

"Grapefruit makes it the breakfast of champions," Edna said, grinning.

"Consider yourself lucky you don't need to come with us," I said, as I walked away. "We're going to choir practice. To pay the mayor back for sending us some much-needed guests."

"You mean spies," Edna said. "They're here to report on you. It's a test."

The thought had occurred to me. Everything was a test now, it seemed.

"The only test I'm worried about now is auditioning for the choir," I called back. "The new choirmaster is cranky, the mayor said."

Edna tossed her rope to Charlie and walked ahead of us to the truck. "Well then, you'll need backup from someone even crankier."

CHAPTER THREE

"It may surprise you to hear that I'm a fine alto," Edna said when we reached the truck. "I expect you'll need me to drown you out. You've embarrassed yourself enough in town already."

"I can carry a tune, Edna," I said. "Mom's another matter."

Jilly bent over beside the passenger door and unzipped what appeared to be a padded purse. Percy did a figure eight around her boots and then she slipped his paws into a yellow jacket that matched Keats'. The cat didn't mind his coat at all, no matter how silly it looked with the orange fluff exploding around it. He stepped into the bag without hesitation. My friend zipped it, and straightened, pushing the strap up over her shoulder.

"You're a genius," I said. "I never thought of that."

"Percy's an important member of the team," she said. Glancing at Keats, she added, "Notice how cooperative he is with his parka."

"Critter couture?" Edna said, trying to push me out of the way and get into the driver's seat. "You two are nuts."

"Not nuts enough to let you drive my truck in broad daylight when there are cops around." I jabbed my elbow into her rib cage and yelped when it connected with a bulletproof vest. "When you get yourself licensed again, maybe. In the meantime, zip it on the insults. I stall more when I'm flustered."

That was true, but I didn't stall at all on the way into town despite Edna's continual lobbing of shots from the passenger seat. I deliberately lurched once just to cut off her commentary, but Keats' paw landed on my shoulder between the seats to remind me that the innocent suffered, too.

We parked near town square in a spot smaller than I would have liked. It was a good opportunity to show Edna—and myself— that I was making headway with my handling. Parking the truck in front of bystanders in town was a recipe for trouble, but today I did it efficiently and Keats mumbled what sounded like praise.

A good-sized crowd had gathered in the square by the time we arrived. There were many familiar faces, including Teri, Mabel, Letitia and the Langman sisters, Heddy and Kaye. My own sisters, Poppy, Iris and Violet, waved from the back row. Mom was nowhere in sight and I hoped she'd decided to give choir a pass. Daily rehearsals in cold weather would be too much like work, which normally wasn't her strong suit.

Jilly and I circled the crowd with Edna to introduce ourselves to the choirmaster. Our job was to see to planning and administration —the grunt work—while our musical leader worked whatever magic he could in just a few days before the grand performance on Christmas Eve.

When we reached the old man I took to be our choirmaster, Edna gasped. She grabbed my coat and hauled me backward so hard I nearly fell.

"You didn't tell me Felix Milloy was involved," she said. "Dagnabit, I thought he was dead."

The old man was wearing a long gray frock coat and a raccoon hat complete with tail. He came toward us now, swinging a metal cane. "Well, if it isn't Edna Evans," he said. "I thought you were dead. At least, I hoped so."

"Ditto," Edna said. "You could have had the decency to stay gone till you passed, Felix."

Despite her feisty words, my neighbor slid behind me, making me a human bulletproof vest to top off the regular one.

There was a titter through the crowd as people realized a simple choir practice had potential to provide excellent fodder for the rumor mill.

"You broke up with *me*, remember?" Felix said.

"Any woman would have done the same in my position. You're lucky they let you leave town at all." Edna turned to me. "What was the chief thinking in letting Felix back into Clover Grove?"

I shook my head. "I don't know anything about Mr. Milloy except that he's trained some of the best vocalists in the world. The mayor invited him back."

"*Bribed* me back." Felix's grin revealed a snaggle of yellowed teeth. "She rolled out the red carpet, Edna. I was happy to come until you showed up looking"—he eyed her up and down—"like an army commando. Or the bride of Frankenstein."

"Now, now," Jilly said, stepping forward. "Edna is a very good friend of ours, Mr. Milloy. We can't allow you to insult her."

"I consider it a compliment, Jillian," Edna said. "Besides, I have bigger things to worry about than my appearance. Like the end of the world. Needless to say, Felix wouldn't last an hour in any bunker of mine."

Felix stared at her, perhaps pondering her mental status. Then he shook his head and turned to appraise Jilly. "You look like a lady. Please tell me that isn't a cat in your purse."

"Meet Percy," Jilly said. "The purse cat. He's a very good friend of ours, too. Ivy Galloway and I are your managers, and Keats, the sheepdog, is our deputy."

Felix's already-puckered mouth laced up tight in disgust. "The whole town's gone crazy. I was wise to stay away as long as I did." He turned and brandished his cane. "Enough chitchat. Split into three groups, everyone. Sopranos over there. Altos there. Bass there. If you don't know, just stay where you are till I tell you."

I didn't like being parted from Jilly but she moved into the ranks of the sopranos. My sisters joined me in the alto section. It wasn't surprising that we all sang in a lower, darker register. We'd led an alto sort of life. Edna stayed behind me, and I turned to whisper, "Surely an old boyfriend can't scare a warrior like you."

"I'm not scared, I'm disgusted," she said. "Some old trash you just want gone forever. Like my sister, remember?"

"Silence," Felix shouted, making us jump. He sure knew how to use his vocal training. "We only have a few days until the concert and I won't allow gossip to sully my reputation. Do you hear me?"

"It was sullied beyond repair six decades ago," Edna muttered behind me.

Most of the crowd murmured, "Yes, Mr. Milloy."

"Who does he think he is?" asked Beverly Roxton, the veterinarian's wife. She looked like most middle-aged women in town, with her fringe of gray hair under a sensible hand-knitted hat, with matching scarf and mittens. But Beverly's blue eyes and tongue were sharp and she'd cut me with snarky comments during my visits to the vet's office with Percy. "I didn't take time off work to get yelled at by a rude old has-been."

"Being old doesn't make him a has-been," Edna said. "But he's definitely rude."

Keats mumbled something that sounded disrespectful and his mouth opened in a cheeky pant.

"What was that?" Felix asked.

"Just my dog," I said. "Choking on a hair ball."

"Well, tell him to stop it. We're about to begin." He pulled a pitch pipe and a small baton out of his pocket. "Silent Night, everyone." He blew a note and we all hummed. Counting out three beats, he gave a sweep of the baton and we launched into the carol.

To me it sounded pretty good and I was surprised when the

baton came crashing down so soon. Before Felix could say a word, however, there was a clatter of heels over cobblestones and a voice rang out. "Wait for me, darlings!" Mom joined the rest of the Galloway Girls in the alto section. "Ready, Maestro."

Felix directed his baton at her. "I do not tolerate tardiness, Miss Fancy Pants. Let your first warning be your last."

"Excuse me?" Mom said. "I do not tolerate chauvinism, Mr. High-and-Mighty. My son-in-law is the chief of police and—"

"Mom, be quiet." My face turned into a furnace. Kellan and I had barely managed a dozen official dates and there was certainly no wedding on the horizon. "Be silent. Or sing Silent Night."

While I'd shown up wanting Mom to keep quiet, now I realized her smart mouth was better deployed in song than bickering with our honorary guest.

The baton came up and we sang again. Mom delivered her performance with such tuneless gusto that she threw me entirely off key. Poppy's shoulders started shaking and infected Violet and then Iris. Daisy had stayed at the inn so there was no one to squelch us. Even Edna, rattled as she was by ghosts of boyfriends past, snickered.

After the second verse, Felix snapped off the song with his baton and used his cane to part the crowd. "You five. I can see you're related. Each of you looks like a cheap knockoff of the others, ending with little Miss Fancy Pants."

Mom drew herself to her full five feet. "You, sir, are no gentleman."

"And you, ma'am, are no alto. In fact, there's no category for that noise." He flicked his baton. "All of you to the back. You're relegated to mouthing the words."

"You can't stop us from singing," Mom said. "We're tax-paying citizens of this town, unlike you, whoever you are."

"He's the mayor's special guest," I said, signaling Keats to herd my family to the back row.

Felix followed me and when I turned, he reached out and touched his baton lightly to my throat. "*You* may use your voice, Ivy, until I tell you otherwise. You too, Edna. It surprises me to admit you can carry a tune."

I didn't get a chance to react before Mom attacked. "Don't you dare threaten my daughter. Drop your weapon or I'll be forced to—"

"Mom, no!" This time four Galloway Girls chimed in harmony.

Turning, Felix smirked. "All right. The rest of you girls can sing, too. Fancy Pants can keep a lock on it."

Mom sang anyway during our next rendition of Silent Night, albeit more quietly. By the end of the second verse her voice was drowned out completely by a louder one behind us. It sounded like a rhythmic combination of screeching and bellowing. As someone with farming experience, my first guess was braying. Actual braying, not my mother's singing. Soprano, alto and bass, all at once.

I turned to see a donkey standing a couple of yards behind me. It was larger than my own three donkeys and its eyes looked hollow... perhaps even haunted. Keats went over of his own accord to sniff the animal. The white tuft on the dog's tail rose to half mast and he mumbled something to me. He was worried, not threatened.

Joining them with my hand outstretched I touched the donkey's neck and then its side. "Oh no, he's starving," I said, pulling a handful of biscuits out of my pocket that I always kept for my critters. He accepted them greedily, lifting floppy lips to expose big yellow teeth.

"Ms. Galloway?" Felix's voice carried nicely on the chilly breeze. "Can you feed the wildlife *after* rehearsal? I'm a busy man."

I went back to my sisters, and as the choir began singing again, so did the donkey.

When we stopped singing, so did the donkey.

"Cut that out, beast," Felix shouted. "You sound worse than Fancy Pants, and that's saying something."

"Don't expect a free shave at my salon," Mom muttered.

"One word about your straight edge and I'm marching you out of here," I whispered.

Felix swept off his raccoon hat by the tail and swung it in a circle. "People! Let me tell you how this is going to go. We need to put on a show. That's a promise I made to the mayor. A show requires bodies. So your bodies will be here, even if your voices are banned from the performance."

"What's in it for us?" Poppy called. "We're here to sing."

"What's in it for you is that we only need a few good voices to make this choir stupendous. If you lip-sync, everyone will think you're talented and the mayor will be happy. How does that sound?"

I caught Poppy's arm and whispered, "If the mayor keeps sending guests I can afford to hire you part-time at the farm. Just play along for once, Pops. Please."

It took a lot for Poppy to back down but she was also the most underemployed among us now that Mom was thriving at her salon. Finally she called, "We Galloways support you, Mr. Milloy."

"You're disrupters, all of you. But let's find out how well you can actually sing. We'll give Silent Night another battering and this time, when I tap your shoulder, you stop."

All five of us started singing Silent Night. It was impossible to hear who was in tune and who wasn't, because the donkey threw back his head and brayed like his life depended on it. Maybe it did. There was a fierce intensity to the sound that made my own donkeys seem like amateurs. I caught Keats' blue eye and confirmed my suspicion. That donkey had come for a reason. He was trying to tell me something.

Felix tapped my shoulder and I stopped singing. The donkey instantly stopped braying.

"Pray continue, Miss Galloway," he said.

I'd barely sung a note when the braying began again. Felix tapped me. I closed my mouth, and the braying stopped.

Jilly glanced from Keats to the donkey and back to me, while her padded purse wriggled. We all understood that this donkey had come to me to solve his problem, whatever that was. I couldn't and wouldn't let a starving creature down. Not for all the Christmas carols in the world.

"Miss Galloway, I'm sorry," Felix said. "Or rather, I'm sorry to give up an alto with promise. But obviously you can't sing with us until your donkey dilemma disappears."

"You can't fire my daughter," Mom said. "The mayor assigned her to run the choir."

"It's okay, Mom," I said. "I'll find out where the donkey belongs and join in next time."

The donkey brayed over my words and it was unlikely anyone heard me. Still, it sparked a smattering of applause off to one side of the square. I turned to see Mayor Martingale and two town councillors. Other people had stopped to watch as well.

"Felix," the mayor called, "The Dorset Hills choral society can sing us into the ground. But do you know what they *don't* have?"

"Me," Felix said. "They don't have a world class choirmaster who's worked with the greats."

"True," the mayor said. "They also don't have a singing donkey. And we do."

"Meryl!" Felix was aghast. "You cannot be serious."

"She is," Mom said. "That's her serious face. Look at the lines on—"

Iris cut Mom off with a sharp tug on her sleeve.

"Felix, I know it isn't what you planned," the mayor said. "But things like this happen for a reason. So the donkey stays." She waved in my general direction. "Ivy will take care of everything."

CHAPTER FOUR

"Ivy will take care of everything," I said in a singsong voice as I drove down Main Street. "Of course I will. If I can take out a few killers for the town, being the agent and handler of a stray donkey should be a cakewalk."

"It'll be fine," Jilly said, reaching through the seats to pat my shoulder. Her hand landed on Keats' paw, which had been parked there since we finally pulled out. It had taken an hour for Asher to find a friend with a trailer and come over to hitch it to the truck. The trailer was bright yellow. What were the chances? "You would have helped the donkey anyway," she added. "You know that."

"How are we going to find his owner?" I said. "No one in town knew anything about him and donkeys are a dime a dozen in hill country."

"The same way we find anything," Jilly said. Keats gave a mumble and she added, "Exactly. Keats will know."

"Oh, Jillian," Edna said. "You put too much stock in this dog's so-called magic. He's smart, but a dog nonetheless."

"Edna, I know you're upset about running into your first love," I said, "but if you're going to diss Keats, you can ride in the back seat."

"I never loved Felix Milloy," she said, shuddering. "Far from it.

He had a terrible crush on me in tenth grade. I finally let him take me to a school dance, where he turned into an octopus."

"What happened then?" Jilly asked. "He seemed pretty upset about it."

"When he grew eight hands, I used two hands and one knee. Even then I was trained in self defense, you see. I left him immobilized on the school lawn, and in a cast for two months." She turned, grinning. "His conducting arm healed just fine."

"Wow," I said. "Totally tough even at fifteen."

"Felix was on the wrong path," she said. "I knew how tempting that was because we both had trouble at home. My sister had tried to steal him but he was one of the few who could tell us apart and preferred me."

"Then he couldn't have been all bad," Jilly said.

"He got worse before he got better, always clashing with the law. Petty crimes, mostly." She shook her head. "I was surprised he achieved so much in his career. I wonder why he came back now."

"Perhaps he'll crack open his heart when you invite him for dinner," I said. "Jilly can make her Fall-in-Love Beef Stroganoff."

Edna turned to stare at the side of my head. "Why wasn't I invited to your wedding with Chief Hotstuff? I'd expected to be named bridesmaid. Was it something I wore?"

I laughed as I eased onto the shoulder just outside of town. "Touché, Edna. Now, switch places with Keats, please. He needs to ride shotgun."

Her bifocals slid down her nose. "I will not. Age before canine, Ivy Rose Galloway."

"It wasn't really a request, Edna Hortense Evans."

Her jaw actually dropped. When I was researching Edna's family during a crime, I'd discovered her middle name and waited for just such an occasion to use it.

She crossed camouflaged arms. "I refuse to yield my seat to that dog."

"Fine," I said. "Keats?"

He shot through the seats and into Edna's lap before she had a chance to block him. That was saying something because her reflexes were stellar for a woman of any age.

"I don't want to be covered in dog hair and dirt." She tried to wrangle him back but Keats planted his white paws on the dash and dusted Edna's face with his tail.

After rolling down my window, I checked my mirrors and pulled out again slowly. It was like piloting a parade float. My dream of owning a sweet compact car with an automatic transmission was being mocked by fate. Instead, my vehicles just kept getting larger and more challenging to manage. Now on top of everything, I had live cargo in tow.

"Just simmer down, Edna," I said. "Keats and I need to focus. I'm assuming the donkey lives close by if he walked into town." I gave my dog a quick pat. "Buddy, do your thing."

Keats' head swiveled as he scanned the barren fields with his blue eye. His ears came forward to catch any aural clues. Finally he lifted his muzzle to draw in the smells from the open window. If the donkey had taken this route into town, he'd have left a scent trail and Keats' nose rivaled that of any hound.

After a few minutes, white paws danced on the dash. We were coming up for a turn. He looked left and mumbled a command that made me turn the truck slowly onto a secondary highway.

"You don't really believe he knows where the donkey lives?" Edna said, as Keats signaled another turn.

"He knows something," I said. "It's not an exact science. One thing leads to another." I turned into a lane that was even more twisty than the one at Runaway Farm. Maybe that's what made it feel foreboding, but the day was also dreary and the fields dull. Silence fell over us and Keats' tail drifted out of Edna's face and into her lap.

I'd expected a derelict farm to appear when the lane ended,

but the house was well-maintained and there was a newish white van parked out front. A couple of large pots of orange chrysanthemums that should have been dead by now still bloomed on either side of the yellow front door. The paddock outside the small barn held a couple of ponies, two white cows, and a donkey smaller than my passenger. All looked well fed and content. Turning off the engine, I mirrored Keats' position, head cocked, listening for clues. My animals usually bellowed greetings when someone arrived, but the formerly chatty donkey in the trailer kept his opinions to himself.

A woman who looked to be in her sixties came out onto the porch and stood between the pots of 'mums. She was wearing an apron and a red kerchief around her gray hair. From her frown, I guessed the mat under her clogs didn't say "welcome."

"Carmina Prescott," Edna told us. "I was there when ol' Doc Grainer delivered most of her nine kids." She gave a little sniff. "Some people just don't know when enough's enough. Now they've multiplied all over hill country and none of them amounted to much."

"Maybe you'd better stay in the truck," I said. "I might have to use my HR skills and I don't need you making little digs."

Edna was already opening the door and shooed Keats out before jumping down. "We're here to talk to a lady about a donkey, Ivy. It's not exactly high stakes. No need to treat every conversation like a murder investigation."

I got out, too. "In my corporate experience, it made sense to treat every conversation like a potential investigation. Saved time later. Right, Jilly?"

"That's how I approached headhunting," Jilly said, joining us with Percy slung over her shoulder. The cat purse was quickly becoming her trademark accessory. "No one ever tells the full story, do they, Edna?"

Edna looked slightly sheepish over having hidden her backstory from us, thereby dragging us into grave danger. Shaking it off, she charged ahead of us to the stairs, calling out a greeting to Carmina.

That gave Keats a second to nose Percy's bag as a signal for Jilly to release him. She unzipped it and the two were gone in a flash. I didn't wait to see where they went before following Edna up the stairs. She was more of a liability than either of the pets.

Carmina didn't take the hand I offered, which was just as well since hers was covered in flour.

"What can I do for you, ladies?" she said. "And Edna?"

Edna had made plenty of enemies as nurse to the only doctor in town, as well as head of the school vaccination program. She'd changed since her recent brush with death, but few knew that. Even those who did were waiting for the other shoe to drop. Jilly and I might be the only ones to believe her transformation was the real deal. We'd seen enough false ones in our work to know. Still, we kept our eyes wide open. The only people we trusted 100 percent were each other, plus Keats and Percy, who were now people to us.

I stepped forward and gently eased Edna back a little. "Mrs. Prescott, I'm Ivy Galloway and we ran into a little trouble at choir practice earlier today."

She tried to hide a grin and failed. "I heard."

"Already?" Jilly said.

I laughed. "My friend is still surprised at the speed of the town grapevine."

"My daughter sent me a video," Carmina said. "I had to turn the sound down. That loudmouth donkey was getting the animals all worked up even from inside the house."

Gesturing to the yellow trailer, I said, "So the loudmouth donkey isn't yours?"

She shook her head quickly. Too quickly and too assertively. She knew something.

I looked around for Keats, who was normally ready to confirm my first impressions, but he was still doing reconnaissance.

"Why would you ask? Who sent you here?" Carmina twisted her apron in her floury hands.

"No one sent me. I just heard you had a donkey and I'm checking with anyone in walking distance from town who might be missing one."

"The only donkey I own is in the paddock," she said, practically wringing the apron. "And you can see he's secure and well cared for."

"That does look like a happy donkey," I said. "Unlike my skinny new friend."

Keats trotted around the corner with Percy and his tail was at half mast. He wasn't thrilled with the place, but he wasn't on high alert, either.

"What were they doing?" Carmina said, scowling at the dog and cat. "You can't just let your pets run around a stranger's property, Ivy. You never know what could happen."

"True," I said. "Stay, boys."

Edna stepped forward, evidently fed up with my slow and steady approach. "Carmina, we don't have all day. You saw the video. What do you know about the donkey?"

"Why would I know anything about a stray donkey?" The apron-wringing increased. "Just because these two girls are dating the police doesn't make them cops."

"Possibly married," Edna said, smirking. "Ivy's mom said so."

"I heard that too," Carmina said. "You're putting the cart before the donkey, Ivy."

My face warmed up but I didn't fall for the diversion. "The stray donkey is starving, Carmina, and I can see that wouldn't happen here. So if you're aware of someone who isn't treating animals well, I'd like to do something about it."

"That's not your job," Carmina blurted, before pressing her lips together.

"Caring for rescued animals is my job," I said. "And my calling.

I'll do whatever it takes to help any creature I find in poor shape." I pulled out my phone. "Besides, it's my legal obligation under the county's Animal Services regulation. Subsection 3.24, to be specific. Anyone failing to report neglect or abuse risks a fine and loss of their own animals." Glancing down at her paddock, I added, "I don't know about you but I'd never ever take that chance. I've had Animal Services pestering me before and it was super annoying. Have you met field officer Tess Blade?" I gave an exaggerated shudder. "If you're willing to take her on, you're a braver woman than I."

I beckoned the others and started walking down the stairs. I thought Carmina would fold quickly because her hands must have ached from all the wringing. But I was already opening the truck door when she called out, "I might know something."

CHAPTER FIVE

"You just made that up, didn't you?" Jilly asked from the back seat as we headed out to the highway again. "The whole Animal Control regulation blah-blah."

"Call it wishful thinking," I said, throwing her a grin over my shoulder. "There *should* be a regulation requiring people to report animal neglect and abuse."

"Agreed. But why is Carmina so worried about this Vinnie guy that she'd try to shield him?"

"Because Vincent Swenson is bad news," Edna said. She was in the passenger seat, evidently preferring Keats' muddy paws to taking a back seat with Jilly. "The Swensons have always been involved in criminal activities. Vinnie's grandfather, Frank, was smart enough to avoid getting caught but the gene pool's deteriorated with each generation and Vinnie has a rap sheet dating back to his teens."

"But the Swensons are one of the town's founding families," I said. "I thought they were pillars of the community."

"You thought that about the bridge club, too, didn't you? Look how that turned out." Edna patted my arm. "Poor naïve Ivy."

Jilly snorted at that. It had been a long time since anyone called either of us naïve. In fact, we'd taken considerable pride in our cynicism back in Boston. Somehow quaint Clover Grove had managed to shock me a few times.

"So this Vinnie's a dirtbag and possibly an animal abuser," I said. "That means we'll need to convince him to surrender ownership of the donkey. What's our best strategy, Edna? Jilly's charm, my logic, or your intimidation?"

She sighed. "As much as it pains me to say it, I never intimidated Vinnie, even in my school nurse days. He took those vaccinations head on. Stoic. Unlike your brother." Glancing back at Jilly, she added, "I'm still shocked Asher made it onto the police force."

"He's won awards for courage in a crisis," Jilly said. "Lots of them."

It was sweet to hear Jilly defend my brother before I could.

"Car crashes and crane rescues," Edna said, waving a camouflage glove. "Not real crime, like a real cop."

"Asher's been involved in some terrifying, grisly incidents," I said. "What's more, Kellan says he volunteers when others don't."

"No need to get defensive," Edna said. "He's a decent man, and I don't say that lightly. But you're naïve and Asher is a yokel."

"My brother is not a yokel."

"Fine, then. A bumpkin," Edna said.

I dared to take my eyes off the road. "Look, Edna, you're fully capable of hitching a ride home or hotwiring a car. So if you want to keep dissing Jilly's boyfriend, I'll drop you here."

"You two fascinate me." Her glove wagged back and forth between us. "You're more loyal to each other than your own families."

"Jilly is my family," I said. "As are Keats, Percy and the animals. The Galloway crew falls more in the community category. At least, so far."

"Fine. I'll spare Jillian's tender feelings." Edna was clearly enjoying herself. "I think she could do better, but the pickings are mighty slim in this town. Always were."

"We can't all be so lucky as to land a catch like Felix the octopus," I said. "How about doing a seminar to show the yokels how it's done?"

"Maybe I will accept your challenge to hotwire a car," she said. "I stashed a go-kit in the back of the truck in case of emergency."

"There had better not be weapons in my truck, Edna."

"Spank me now, thank me later," she said. "When you meet Vinnie you'll be glad of a firearm."

"I'll never be glad of a firearm unless there truly is a zombie uprising. Weapons can be used against us, and worse, catch animals in the crossfire."

She shook her head. "You're becoming a mouthpiece for Chief Hotstuff. Kellan has a stronger constitution than Asher, but he's no match for Vinnie for sheer guts."

Keats mumbled something that sounded like, "Would you two quit bickering? We've got bigger fish to fry."

"You're right," Edna said. "We should stay focused."

I turned in time to see her sallow cheeks flush. "Aha! Edna Hortense Evans, you just answered my dog."

"She sure did," Jilly said. "How does that humble pie taste, Edna?"

"About the same as your apple pie at Thanksgiving," Edna said. "Surprisingly bland and decidedly soggy."

"Bold move to diss both Jilly's boyfriend *and* her cooking," I said. "You want her out, bestie?"

"No way," Jilly said. "Not when we're going to pick a fight with this Vinnie over a donkey. Let's have some compassion for Edna, instead. Her pride's taken some hard knocks today."

Keats mumbled again and this time Edna was direct. "You're right, Keats. Pity *is* worse than mockery."

I turned into the Swensons' lane. Most lanes on the old farms were long but this one went on forever. As suspense built, the jokes fell away and by the time it spit the truck into the parking area, I was anxious. A quick glance at Keats told me I was right to be. His ruff was up, his ears flat, and he snorted in what seemed like disgust.

On first glance the place didn't look too bad. In fact, the red brick farmhouse was in good shape and a cute weathervane with pigs on it twisted slowly. There was a brand new four-car garage behind the house with a van parked outside. The gray barn, however, was dilapidated. Some boards were missing and there was a hole in the roof. Clearly Vinnie took better care of his vehicles than his animals.

As if to confirm my opinion, the donkey began braying in the trailer. It wasn't the raucous song we heard in town square earlier. Now the notes were longer, lower and decidedly doleful.

"If he's home, he's not happy about it," Jilly said. "Poor thing sounds brokenhearted."

Keats let out a mournful howl, too. Even Percy moaned in his carrier.

"This isn't good at all," I said. "We're going to have to tell Vinnie the mayor wants the donkey to come home with us. How can he argue?"

"Vinnie Swenson could argue the sun into rising from the north," Edna said. "Then he'd probably take bets on it."

It wasn't like Edna to be so negative about her powers of persuasion. She was normally confident to a fault.

"We'll think of something," I said. "We always do."

None of us jumped out of the truck quickly this time. Not even Keats, although I opened the door and gave him permission. He didn't like the vibe here any more than we did.

"Okay," I said at last. "Shall we get this over with?"

Edna mumbled an agreement and probably wouldn't have appreciated knowing how much she sounded like Keats.

We all slid down from the truck and gathered in front, facing the house. Keats circled me and pressed in to let me know he preferred starting with the barn. Meanwhile Percy mewed to be set free, and then headed off to the biggest pasture.

"Vinnie must be out here," I said, staring around. "No wife or kids, Edna? It doesn't feel like a family home."

She shook her head. "He had a nice young blonde for a while but couldn't get it to stick. No wonder."

The main pasture was empty, which wasn't unusual at this time of year. Even with their shaggy hill country fur coats, most livestock preferred to spend time inside.

I turned to go into the barn, but Keats signalled for me to follow him to the gate instead. Percy had beaten us there and climbed the fence to paw at a broken lock hanging from the metal hook. Jumping down, he picked his way over the inch or two of snow that had fallen the night of the tree lighting ceremony. He let out a plaintive meow and then hooked the other half of the lock out of the snow with his claws. There were no tracks other than Percy's. Had the donkey been on the lam that long?

Edna held Jilly back to wait for me so that we could go into the barn together. We'd become the five amigos. If this kept up, she'd need to start bringing her favorite cat, Panther, to balance things out.

"Ivy, are you sure you don't want me to get my firearm?" she asked.

"Quite sure." I moved in front of the others. The donkey had come to me, so I'd better take the mission head on.

"Crossbow?" Edna tried again.

"Definitely not. You promised to keep that locked away."

"It is locked away... in my go-kit in your truck."

Finally she pulled a can of pepper spray out of her coat pocket. I rolled my eyes but was secretly glad she had it.

There was a smaller pen closer to the barn. Keats went into a point to show me another broken lock. Percy trotted along the top rung of the fence and then swatted the gate open, as if to punctuate Keats' point.

"Carmina said Vinnie had sheep, goats and cows as well as a donkey," I said. "Where are they? And why is the only noise we hear coming from the trailer?"

"That's quite a dirge," Edna said. "I've never heard a sadder donkey."

"Maybe his friends have all run away," Jilly said. "It looks like the place was vandalized."

"We should call Kellan," I said.

"Yes," Jilly said, quickly. "Let's."

Edna straightened her shoulders. "We're not calling Chief Hotstuff until we have more to tell him." She held up the pepper spray and tried to get ahead of me.

I switched on my phone light and slipped into the lead again. It was dim inside and I had no idea where the barn's light switch would be.

"Mr. Swenson?" I called. "Vincent?"

I didn't expect an answer and I didn't get one.

Well, unless you counted the answer Keats was pointing out. In a small pen, a large man lay face-down on the manure-encrusted floor. His face was submerged in a metal water trough. It had been full when he fell but the water was frozen now. The hair poking out from under his black wool hat was bright red.

"Vinnie?" I asked Edna.

She nodded. "Red hair on a guy like him always takes you by surprise. But it looks like he's the one who got taken by surprise this time."

CHAPTER SIX

We walked out the front door of the barn and came to a standstill on the driveway near the truck. I reached up to adjust my hat and managed to hit both Jilly and Edna square in the eyes with the beam of my phone light. They squinted at me, looking as stunned as I felt.

"Well," Edna said. "At least this issue has nothing to do with you or the farm."

"That part's a relief," Jilly said. "Right?"

I nodded uncertainly. "And yet, here we are. Somehow the ones to find Vinnie."

"Just bad luck," Edna said.

"Wrong place, wrong time," Jilly added. "Coincidence."

"Except not really," I said. "That donkey came to find us."

Me. That donkey came to find me, very specifically. I was sure of it. My reputation as a crazy rescuer who understood animals was apparently circulating through the livestock community. Maybe they had their own grapevine. *Problem farmer on your hooves? Call Ivy.*

I had to fight a very inappropriate giggle. A man had died here. Vincent Swenson may not have been a good man but he was the product of his upbringing, just like all of us, and he deserved better than my hysterical laughter.

"Don't let your imagination run away with you, Ivy," Edna said.

I rolled my eyes. "Says the prepper who's always imagining things."

"Things that may very well come true in my lifetime," Edna said. "Unfortunately."

"That donkey was singing his sad song to me and everyone knows it. Unfortunately."

Taking off her fleece-lined camo hat, she rubbed a hand through her staticky perm. "A donkey walking into town square isn't that rare. Cattle are even more common."

Keats whined and I looked down. His ruff had settled and his ears were up and twitching. Throwing his head back, he sniffed. Then his tail gave a sudden swish. He'd picked up an interesting scent, but it didn't appear to be dangerous.

Meanwhile, Percy was traveling the fence highway around one paddock after another. His orange flag of a tail was not only down but swishing. The cat and the dog were reading different things into this situation.

"I know how it sounds, Edna, but I believe that donkey came to me because it wants something." I tipped my head toward the trailer, where the donkey was still braying mournfully. "That's why he only screeched when I was singing. I don't speak donkey, but I have to assume it's about what happened out here."

Jilly came over to stand beside me. "I've seen too many strange things happen between Ivy and animals to believe that was an accident. At the very least, the donkey sensed an animal lover who'd try to help."

"I suppose it's possible," Edna said. "Either way, Vinnie's been dead a few days by the looks of things and that donkey is more than a few days skinny. If he belongs here, Vinnie's been neglecting him. The livestock caught a lucky break, if you ask me."

"But if Vinnie was such a jerk, why would the donkey be so sad to lose him?" Jilly said.

"Home's home," I said. "He probably doesn't know better. *Yet.* I'll make sure that donkey lives out his days in comfort."

"Of course you will," Jilly said, and for once she didn't sound disapproving of my new acquisition.

"Maybe the donkey's arrival wasn't about Vinnie, per se," I said, keeping my eye on Percy. "I bet he's worried about his friends. While we've been talking, Percy's explored every pasture and flipped each lock to the ground. I think the livestock were deliberately freed."

"Stolen, more like," Edna said. "Taken out of county where they can be retagged."

I shook my head. "Doesn't make sense that someone would steal skinny, unhealthy animals." Then an idea hit me. "Rescue, maybe?"

Edna and Jilly exclaimed in unison. "The Mafia!"

"Let's get them on the phone," I said.

"Shouldn't we call the police first?" Jilly stared at me. "I mean, we all know we should."

"Another couple of minutes isn't going to help Vinnie," I said, pressing the number for Cori Hogan, my main Mafia contact. "The clues are frozen in time."

"Hey," Cori said, when she answered. "Can I get back to you? I'm kind of in the middle of something."

"It's a rescue 911," I said. "Or at least I think it might be."

"That's different," she said. "Go on."

I put the phone on speaker so the others could hear her huffing and puffing. The tiny dog trainer was either working out or staging a tough rescue. Climbing was her forte. I'd seen videos of her scaling trees and buildings and rappelling into yards to save pets in need.

"So, I'm out at Vinnie Swenson's right now," I began.

"Vinnie the criminal?" Cori asked. "Hasn't Chief Hotstuff managed to lock him away yet? We've given him plenty of ammo. If

Vinnie weren't so well connected to the hill country underworld, we'd have gotten those animals out of there by now. Best we could do was dead drops of food and medicine."

"Did Vinnie have a donkey?" I asked. "A big one?"

"Yeah. At least he used to. It's been MIA for months and that worried us." Cori was fully focused now. "Why?"

"We found a stray and someone thought it might belong here."

"No sign of Vinnie?" she asked.

"Off the record?" I said.

"Everything's off the record with us. Otherwise I'd be dead by now."

"Well, since you used the 'd word,' let's just say Vinnie won't be neglecting animals again. Ever."

"Murdered?" Cori's voice dropped to a whisper.

"Unclear. No visible signs of foul play."

There was a long pause and then the huffing and puffing started again. "If my hands were free I'd applaud. It was probably just a heart attack because his body finally realized he didn't have one."

"Probably," I agreed. "Although it sounds like he has enemies."

"No shortage of those but it would take guts to tackle Vinnie. Even Tess Blade is afraid of him. And Lloyd Boyce, her predecessor at Animal Services, was taking graft to keep quiet about the situation there. Vinnie was on the road a lot and never bothered getting someone to care for the livestock."

"That's awful." I had to shout the words because the donkey's braying was getting louder by the second. I looked up to see him trotting toward me with Percy by his side. The cat was a master of latches and had clearly released the animal. That took some talent.

"What's that racket?" Cori said. "Is Edna with you?"

"Very funny, young lady," Edna said. "That's all the thanks I get for blowing up that—"

"Never mind," Cori interrupted. "There are things Mrs. Chief Hottie doesn't need to know."

I stared at Edna. "Are there explosives in my truck right now?"

"See?" Cori said. "Total overreaction. You've got to stop braying, Edna."

"About the braying," I said. "This donkey interrupted our choir rehearsal in town square and—"

"Wait, wait," Cori said. "I want to savor that picture for a minute."

"One thing led to another and we ended up here." I watched the animal trot briskly into the barn and out the side door with his orange sidekick. All the while, he kept up a constant stream of unearthly screeches. "He definitely knows the place."

"What's bugging him? He should be glad someone offed Vinnie. Now he and his buddies can find good homes."

"That's the problem. The buddies are gone."

There was another long pause on Cori's end. "Gone where?"

"Well, I thought you and your crew may have... you know."

"Not us." She was moving again now. "I wish I could take credit."

Cori was plenty capable of evasion when animal welfare was at stake, but HR had given me a good ear for it. She was telling the truth.

"Are there others like you?" I asked.

"No one skilled enough to handle an extraction like that," Cori said. "What does Keats say?"

I looked down at the dog and found he'd gone into a point.

"Oooh boy," I said. "Now we're in trouble. He's pointing in the direction of the hills, Cori. I'm afraid the animals are on the run. Possibly for a couple of days. There are no tracks in the snow."

"Okay, stay calm," Cori said. "I'm on my way. We'll round them up. I know exactly what Vinnie had on site and they've likely found shelter together to stay warm."

Relief coursed through my body. Witnessing death didn't faze me as much as it should anymore, but recovering livestock running wild in the hills sure did. "I need to call Kellan though. Obviously."

"I suppose. Just tell him we'll stay out of his business if he stays out of ours. Like I want to waste time figuring out what happened to that scumbag Vinnie anyway."

"Kellan will think it's all his business," I said.

"Give him a choice then. Would he prefer to round up over twenty head of livestock or let us do it?"

I tried to answer but the donkey came over, leaned into the phone and gave a raucous bawl.

"Tell that whiner to settle down," Cori said. "I'm moving as fast as I can. And if he plays his cards right he and his friends can live in the lap of luxury at Runaway Farm forever."

Jilly finally spoke up. "We do not have space for over twenty head of livestock, Cori."

"Wah wah wah," Cori said. "Who's whining now?"

KELLAN'S TEAM were all over the property when we herded the livestock back up the lane to Vinnie's. The truck moved slowly as Cori directed two dogs—Keats and her own highly skilled border collie, Clem—to bring in the stragglers. The sheep, goats and cows were all antsy and probably starving, but they resisted the drive. It seemed like they preferred the wilds to coming home, or at least this particular home. Edna was behind the wheel while Jilly and I spread out in a wide arc at the rear with half a dozen Rescue Mafia members, including Bridget Linsmore, Remi Malone and Evie Springdale. We were all cold and windblown, yet they looked as exhilarated as I felt.

The two dogs had never met, and while Keats was normally indifferent to other dogs, Clem became an instant pal and mentor. Cori's dog was a herding prizewinner who'd also trained with her on a ranch. Seeing her work with the two dogs was both exciting and terrifying. The goats had retreated to high, craggy outcroppings, already seeming as feral as their wild ancestors. Clem and Keats outclimbed them and forced them down from above.

Edna waited below to round them up in my truck. She drove like a maniac, bumping over the hilly terrain until my head ached. But there was no denying she knew how to control a vehicle.

The police grumbled and moved aside as we herded all the animals into the large pasture where they could potentially trample on evidence.

"What else are we going to do?" Cori said, flipping her black gloves with their orange middle fingers. "Pack them up in our cars and take them home?"

Kellan came out of the barn, frowning. "They're evidence, too," he said.

"They're starving animals first," Cori said, resting her expressive gloves on her hips. "Paws before laws." She glanced at her Mafia pals. "Or clues before hooves. What do you think?"

"I think we should listen to what the chief has in mind," I said.

"Notice I didn't ask you?" Cori said, flashing some glove at me. "You're biased."

Kellan's frown eased a bit, perhaps relieved I took his side against the Mafia. At least some of the time. "Did you get them all?" he asked me.

"I hope so," I said. "They moved pretty fast."

"We got them all," Cori said. "According to the dogs, anyway. I've never known a sheepdog with a nose like Keats has, and he stopped pointing after the goats came down."

My hand fell to my dog's black ears. I was incredibly proud of him. With little formal training, he had really outdone himself with a pro trainer and her pro dog. "You were amazing, buddy," I said.

Keats responded with what sounded like a humble-brag, and everyone laughed.

Even Kellan smiled, and it looked like it cost him. Turning to Cori, he said, "Thank you, Miss Hogan. There's no way we could have done that so quickly and efficiently."

"Or at all," Cori said. "It's important to know your limits, Chief." She paused for a second. "Do I have to call you Chief if I live in another jurisdiction?"

"Cori, quit while you're ahead," Remi said. She was the most soft-spoken of the team but frequently willing to risk the sharp edge of Cori's tongue. "Remember that—" She stopped abruptly.

"Remember *what*?" Kellan said. "Do you have more information about what's happened here?"

They all shook their heads at once, as if it had been staged.

"That looked Cori-o-graphed," Kellan said.

"Not at all," Cori said. Her smug grin turned to grudging admiration. She wanted to hate all cops, I knew, but Kellan kept defying her expectations. "We know nothing about what happened to Vinnie Swenson."

"Nothing," the rest of the Mafia echoed.

"But we won't pretend we're sad to see him go," Cori continued. "He was on our hit list."

"Excuse me?" Kellan said. "We don't have hit lists here."

Remi raised her hand to request permission to speak. "She just means Vinnie was on our rescue radar for his ill-treatment of animals. Obviously there was nothing we could do about that, since it isn't in our purview."

"Plus he was a known criminal," Evie said. "We do have *some* common sense."

"Very little," Cori said. "It's a point of pride."

"Our job requires a certain amount of blind faith," Evie told Kellan. "A belief that good will prevail."

"So does mine," he said. "And you were wise to step lightly around Vinnie."

"If you don't mind my asking," Cori said, "who stepped *on* Vinnie?"

"I do mind." Kellan frowned. "This is an open investigation. Obviously."

"We just did your heavy lifting," Cori persisted. "At least you could tell us if he died of a heart attack."

"Heart failure," Evie said. "Failure to have a heart at all."

"Good point," Cori said. "Or did someone finally take him out for that?"

Kellan sealed his lips but his very silence confirmed it was the latter and we all knew it. If he thought Vinnie had died of natural causes he'd have said so, just to put an end to speculation. In my case, speculation opened the door to investigation, and he knew it.

"I've got business handled here," he said. "But I'd appreciate your ideas about handling the livestock, Miss Hogan."

"Chief, it would be my pleasure to help," Cori said, grinning.

He sighed. "I know it will cost me. And it'll probably cost me even more if I ask you not to dump them all on Ivy."

"Who am I talking to here?" Cori asked. "Chief or boyfriend?"

"Cut him a break, Cori," I said. "You know I can't handle or afford another twenty head at Runaway Farm."

Cori glanced around at her friends and then nodded. "We'll deal with it." She beckoned with both hands, and her orange middle fingers flared back at Kellan. "You'll remember this, right Chief?"

He turned and walked back to the barn, shoulders slumping slightly. "As if you'd let me forget."

CHAPTER SEVEN

"Just let me drive," Edna said from the passenger seat of the truck as we drove into town for choir practice the next day. "I've more than proven myself."

"You have proven you could handle a tank in the apocalypse," I said. "Or an untamed bronc."

"Or even a llama," Jilly added from the back seat. "Possibly a kangaroo."

"Color us impressed," I said. "Where did you learn all that?"

"Stunt driving school," Edna said. "Yesterday's conditions weren't really a challenge. Most of the foliage was already gone and there wasn't much ice. It barely took an hour."

"The cows and sheep were pretty eager for a good meal," I said. "They came when Bocelli called."

"Bocelli? You named that donkey after an opera star?"

"Pop opera. Our newest choir member is no diva. He's accessible."

"If you've named him that means he's staying," Edna said. "Isn't that how this works?"

"He found me, so how could I turn him away now? It's not like the emu, which I haven't named. I'm willing to part with Big Bird."

"Big Bird's still a name," Jilly said. "But at least Cori found someplace else for all the others. I don't think we could handle those lunatic goats."

Keats, comfortably ensconced on Edna's lap, mumbled a protest.

"*You* could, of course, Keats," I said. "But we can't afford more mouths to feed. Hannah's been so generous but we need to have a brainstorming session with Evie about marketing in the new year."

Evie Springdale was a talented PR person, as well as videographer, and she'd offered to give us a hand finding new guests.

"Marketing in the face of murder, she called it," Jilly said. "And here we are dealing with another one."

"Like you said, it has nothing to do with Runaway Farm," I said.

"Only yesterday you were pointing out your ethereal connection to this donkey," Edna said. "Seems like you want to play both sides."

"Well, obviously I don't want to investigate murders at random, Edna. That's Kellan's job. I only wanted to protect the animals, and with that covered, we can go back to our regularly scheduled programming. Specifically, getting a Christmas performance ready."

"I'd rather investigate the murder than deal with the choir," Edna said.

"We've got enough on our hands," I said, although I secretly agreed with her. In fact, I'd offered to help Kellan check a few things out. To say his response was on the wintry side was being kind. He barely tolerated my meddling in police work when it implicated my farm or family. Now he could shut the barn door firmly in my face, which is exactly what he did before we left the Swenson place. Chief Harper wasn't nearly as respectful as boyfriend Kellan.

"Felix Milloy is harder to handle than a killer," Edna said. "I can't just lasso him or run him down." Jilly started to protest and Edna raised a glove. "Joking, Jillian, joking. Do not let your sense of humor languish if you intend to spend your life with Asher Galloway. You need to laugh at him, not with him."

I tossed her a quick glare. "Don't go thinking you can diss Jilly's boyfriend just because you're an octogenarian cowboy. Your current mission is to keep Felix's huge ego in check. No one is more capable than you, Edna."

"Don't waste your flattery, Ivy." Edna's shoulders straightened a little as she accepted the challenge. "I knew that already. Why do you think I wore a nice coat today? The Bride of Frankenstein look isn't going to keep his old trap shut."

"I wondered if you were having second thoughts about Felix," Jilly said. "It might be nice to have company in the bunker on a cold night."

"Please. What's that old songbird got to offer our brigade? The last thing we need in a bunker is a choir."

"The last thing we need in Clover Grove right now is a choir," I said, trying to find a parking spot long enough for the truck and the trailer. That spot simply didn't exist on the main drag, especially during the Christmas rush, so I took to the side streets. Unfortunately, that meant I had further to walk with a donkey on a rope. Adding Bocelli to my lineup was going to fan the flames of gossip, especially after the initial furor over Vinnie Swenson died down.

Edna snickered all the way to the square. I lifted my chin and pretended not to notice the stares. At least Bocelli was more docile than my regular crew of donkeys. Traffic and noises didn't faze him at all. He nuzzled my hood and then let out a big gust of steamy breath. It smelled like the hay he'd been munching constantly since his cronies had been found. I'd expected him to be distressed over parting with them but he was quiet now. Maybe he wouldn't even "sing" anymore. His story had been told and ended more or less happily. Maybe Bocelli would get fired and could stay home.

Something yanked me backward suddenly. Twisting, I saw that

the donkey had grabbed my hood with his big yellow teeth. He gave it another sharp tug and a little twist.

"Let go," I said. "I got the message."

"What message?" Jilly asked, sounding anxious.

"My service to Bocelli isn't done, apparently. He has more to say."

The donkey released my hood and Edna shook her head. "You really are a character, Ivy."

"Drop it, Edna," Jilly said. "We're here."

The crowd in the square was far bigger than it was the day before. Either everyone wanted to sing, or everyone wanted an excuse to gather and hear the latest gossip—straight from the donkey's mouth.

"Nice of you to join us," Felix called, as Jilly moved into the ranks of the sopranos and Edna and I took our places in the last row of altos.

The old man looked even more cantankerous today. His long black scarf was looped around his neck so many times it appeared to be strangling him and his face was flushed. Steam puffed out of both nostrils and his mouth, like the dragons in movies.

He stumped over to me leaning more heavily on his cane than he had the day before. The prospect of coaching a donkey had no doubt bruised his ego, but he pressed on. Like Edna, he was a still a firecracker. Clover Grove bred survivors in their day. Hazel Bingham was a strong woman, too.

"What's wrong with you, Felix?" Edna asked. "You look even closer to death than you did yesterday."

"I am closer to death than yesterday, and so are you," he said. "This choir is going to finish me off faster. I should never have come home."

"That's what I said." Edna grinned. "If you leave now, I'll take over the choir."

His back straightened. "You always had an inflated opinion of yourself."

"Takes one windbag to know another," she said, still grinning. "We've probably both exceeded our expectations."

"Excuse me! Have you forgotten the rest of us, Mr. Milloy?" someone called from the soprano section. "I'm freezing, and we're doing the solo auditions today."

The woman with big aspirations was Beverly Roxton, the veterinarian's wife. As much as I liked her husband, I'd never taken to Beverly. She ran the practice like it was her personal kingdom, just as Edna had done at old Doc Grainer's office. The two women grated on each other because of their similarities.

Felix turned and stumped back to the front of the group. Meanwhile, the mostly female crowd began whispering about Vincent Swenson's passing.

"I heard he was found under a pile of manure," someone said.

"I heard he was run through with a pitchfork," said another.

"Riddled with bullet holes, mafia style," a third said.

"Run over with his own tractor..."

"Sliced up in the combine..."

"Trampled by livestock..."

Beverly's voice cut through the muttering. "It doesn't matter how Vinnie Swenson died. What matters is why. And who did it."

"And whether or not the killer will stop there," said Letitia Smart, the florist. "Vinnie ran with a bad crowd."

"Someone saw him on Gertie Rhodes' property last week with a metal detector and a shovel," Mabel Halliday said. "Apparently."

"Not again," Beverly said. "That old myth about the treasure never dies."

"But the people who look for it do," someone said, causing a general chuckle.

"That was decades ago and never confirmed," Beverly said. "Let's not start up old rumors again."

"For once I agree with Beverly," Edna said. "Let's start up new ones, instead."

"Edna, don't stir the pot," Jilly said. "We're here to sing."

"Everyone else is here to speculate," Edna said. "Probably because they want you and Ivy to pass ideas along to your uniformed boyfriends."

"You mean Ivy's husband," someone whispered—loud enough for me to hear but quiet enough that I couldn't pinpoint the source. My face hadn't fully cooled off since walking the donkey through town, so it was easy to stoke up the fires again.

"Ladies, enough," Felix said, coughing so hard he nearly choked. "Let's start with Silent Night again and for pity's sake, stay silent otherwise."

The baton came up, the hushed frenzy died down, and voices rang out on the frosty air. For the entire first line, there wasn't a peep out of Bocelli. But when I chimed in with "shepherds quake at the sight," the donkey threw his head back and let out an ear-splitting screech. Today it sounded less like mourning and more like a warning. I looked down at Keats and found him bristling all over. He heard an alarm in that sound, too.

Felix slashed his baton across his throat. "Can't you train that thing to keep quiet till needed?"

"It's awful," Beverly said. "The sound sends shivers down my back."

"I can't train him in a day," I said. "Donkeys are tough to train anyway. But if I keep quiet, he'll probably stop. Carry on."

Mom clicked into our midst in high-heeled boots. "Don't worry, darling. The girls and I have you covered."

"The donkey's easier on the ears than you, Fancy Pants," Felix called. "That's why I asked you to mouth the words. Your voice could kill a man."

"If only it were that easy," Mom said, with a bright smile. "Let's see if it works. The mythical sirens could do that, right Ivy?"

"Ask Iris," I said. "She's the cultured daughter."

Felix worked his baton and the next version sounded wonderful, with the notable exception of the braying coming from my mother.

"Let's try a quartet," Felix said. "My ears need respite." He pushed through the crowd, looking even more unsteady, and jabbed Jilly, Beverly Roxton, Heddy Langman, and finally, after a long hesitation, Edna Evans. "You're our best and brightest, from what I can tell in all the racket."

We all simmered down as the four sang O Come All Ye Faithful. Their harmony lifted my heart and chased away the horrible image of Vinnie from the day before. I stared at the Christmas tree, still gorgeous in daylight without its sparkling cape of lights. Then, as if on cue, the skies released fat, feathery flakes. By the time the quartet had repeated the carol, we were all covered in a light dusting.

"Adequate," Felix said. "Decidedly adequate, which is better than I feared." Leaning on his cane, he gave a half-hearted poke of the baton in my direction. "Let's move on to the farce."

I sighed and then straightened. "All right. Which carol, Mr. Milloy?"

He shrugged. "Choose your poison."

"Fine. Hark the Herald Angels Sing. Please count us in."

It almost seemed as if the baton had become too heavy, but he did it. Sucking in a deep breath, I launched into the song. Bocelli let loose and drowned me out entirely. My early fears of being heard and judged for my singing had certainly taken a strange turn.

Felix looked as stricken as the donkey and I blundered on. What a comedown from his former glory to be conducting a circus act like this. My voice choked off abruptly, however, as the donkey stopped braying, grabbed my hood again and jerked me backward. I sat down hard on the cobblestones, but he didn't stop there. There was a tearing sound as he used my hood to haul me away from the crowd.

"Keats!" I called as my butt thumped over the cobblestones. "Help!"

The dog who'd saved me from far worse assailants followed but he didn't intervene. It was Mom who came to my rescue, brandishing her purse at Bocelli until he released my hood.

As she helped me up, the crowd parted to reveal Felix staggering backward, too. He fell over, with both cane and baton stretched to the sky.

"Oh dear," Mom said. "Have we really killed him?"

The choirmaster thrashed several times and then lay still.

"Look," Letitia said. "He's made a snow angel."

Edna stared down at the man and shook her head. "Felix was no angel," she said. "But I do hope there are choirs wherever he's gone."

CHAPTER EIGHT

Daisy, Jilly and I gathered on the inn's front porch that afternoon as the police SUVs drove down the lane. Kellan had called ahead to say they were coming, ostensibly to avoid upsetting the guests. He needn't have worried as the Stout family had left after lunch to enjoy the greater Christmas spectacle Dog Town could offer. From Thanksgiving straight through to the new year, Dorset Hills held a festive event every single day. It was Pioneer Christmas today at the old Dayton Estate, which was new and sure to be a big draw. Their events committee didn't rest on old faithfuls when there were new old things to explore.

"What's up with Kellan?" Daisy asked. "He looks so glum." She was armed, as usual, with rubber gloves, a spray bottle and a roll of paper towels. We had a professional cleaning service, but no one could meet her exacting standards. I'd feared the extra work at the inn would be too much, but she'd scaled back her other part-time jobs and embraced the new challenge. No doubt escaping all the testosterone at home had some appeal.

"That's his cop face," I said. "He's here as Chief Harper. I think he likes to signal that for me straight away with frowns and scowls."

Daisy laughed. "Meanwhile, there's Asher grinning like a fool. I could never get that boy to be serious."

Her voice had a note of motherly pride. After our deadbeat father left, Mom cycled through menial jobs, leaving Daisy to shoulder the burden of raising the rest of us. My sister tried hard not to play favorites but it was hard to avoid with the golden boy. He slid under and around barricades like a sunbeam. Daisy not-so-secretly considered him her first and best son. Luckily her boys were too busy wreaking havoc to notice. Sometimes I wondered if she drained her maternal energy tank on her siblings before her own kids came along, because she'd always let them run wild.

Jilly smiled, too, but the fondness was mixed with worry. The Chief of Police glower didn't bode well for the quaint Christmas she craved for our guests and ourselves.

The only one unfazed by Kellan's negative vibe was Keats. Freed of his yellow parka, he slunk out of the barn to lurk in the shadow of the SUV. He waited till Kellan was about halfway to the porch before charging. Percy popped out from under the car and joined him. I called out a warning a little too late. Kellan lurched forward as the two animals bounced lightly off his butt. The cat continued around the house, but Keats circled back and started worrying Kellan's uniform cuffs.

Jilly and I laughed, and Asher fought a grin, too. Only Daisy gave the chief the respect he deserved.

"Keats, stop that," my sister said. "Right now."

Keats considered commands from anyone but Jilly and me to be strictly optional, but Daisy had a better rate of obedience than most. It was as if he knew she was the voice of reason in Galloway chaos.

The dog fell back and Kellan thanked Daisy before giving me a baleful glance. He knew I'd let the ambush happen to take the wind out of his "chief" sails. It was using an unfair advantage, I supposed. Keats put more effort into his herding assaults when Kellan was acting all chiefly, probably to give me a fighting chance at the upper hand.

"Really, Ivy?" Kellan said. "Do I have to depend on your sister for protection?"

"Why not? The rest of us do." I snapped my fingers to bring Keats to my side. "What's wrong, Chief? Did Vinnie Swenson totally steal Christmas?"

"Quite possibly," he said. "The preliminary reports are back and it seems Vinnie was poisoned. Someone likely waited for him to collapse in the barn before cutting the locks to release the livestock. Nothing was taken from the house as far as we can tell, although the back door was unlocked."

"I assume you have a list of suspects," I said. "Edna said Vinnie was always in trouble. And Cori said he'd disappear for stretches and the Mafia would feed his animals."

Kellan's scowl deepened. He didn't like being beholden to the Rescue Mafia because of their "paws before laws" mentality. But he'd also gotten some good intel from them recently that helped protect our community. It left him in the awkward position of practically endorsing their antics. I could see it pained him now to ask, "Did they have a camera on the property?"

"I don't know," I said. "It's a reasonable assumption since they knew when to swoop in. Do you want me to ask for you, Chief?"

He rolled his eyes. "I can sell my own soul to them. Again. The question is what will that information cost me?"

Braying started up in the new pasture Charlie had partitioned off for Bocelli. We'd tried introducing him to the camelid pasture that contained two llamas and three donkeys, but Drama Llama and the Thugs had shown their gang colors. Mild-mannered Bocelli would likely be a better fit with Alvina, the alpaca, and her unnamed emu pal. Negotiating the personalities of the livestock was more complicated than managing the inn's guests.

"Bocelli says it's worth the price," I told Kellan.

"Oh?" He raised one dark eyebrow. "You're speaking donkey now, too?"

"Not well enough. He has plenty to say around this whole situation and I only understand a bit of it."

"I'm sure Bocelli wants everything to be wrapped up by Christmas," Jilly said. "We were just starting to generate some community spirit when this happened."

"And now Felix Milloy, too," I said. "At least his death was from natural causes."

Asher cleared his throat and scuffed the light snow on the driveway. Kellan silenced my brother with a look but all that got him was another ambush from Percy. The cat launched at Kellan's midriff and climbed quickly to his shoulder, then turned to face us.

"Percy," Daisy said. "That is so rude."

The cat started licking his paws and washing his whiskers.

"I saw that look between you guys," I said. "What was that about, Asher?"

Kellan shook his head. "Officer Galloway knows better."

I decided to try the direct route. "Chief Harper, was Felix Milloy poisoned too?"

Percy must have flexed his claws because Kellan gave a yelp that sounded more like yes than no.

"Why on earth would someone poison Felix?" Jilly said. "He's only been back in town for a week, and at the special request of the mayor."

Kellan's exaggerated shrug was probably intended to unseat Percy but it didn't work. He'd have to drop and roll to pull that off, because this cat was an expert clinger.

"I have no idea," Kellan said. "Yet."

"Maybe you could use some help," I said. "Wait... is that why you're here? To ask me to team up with you?"

"That won't happen until Clover Grove freezes over," he said.

"It *has* frozen over," Jilly said, grinning too. "Kellan needs our dream team on the case, Ivy. Percy, Keats... grab your parkas. To the Batmobile."

"I don't think he's joking," Daisy said, aiming her spray bottle at Jilly and then me.

"Thank you, Daisy," Kellan said. "It's nice to have one Galloway on my side."

"I'm on your side, Chief," Asher said. "Especially on company time."

"Then maybe you could tell your sister and the so-called dream team not to get involved."

"Ivy," Asher said, "The Chief doesn't want you to get involved. He wants you—and especially Jilly—to stay safe."

The braying down in the pasture got louder and more strident.

"Bocelli takes the opposing view," I said. "He came to me for a reason and I can't let him down."

Kellan ran bare fingers through his wind-ruffled dark hair. I found myself wanting to do the same so I glanced down at Keats to stay focused. The dog was staring at the screeching donkey, ears flicking back and forth, as if taking in the details of the discordant song.

"The donkey wandered into town square at the right moment, that's all," Kellan said.

I shook my head. "It's more than that. Yesterday he tried to keep me out of harm's way when Felix collapsed. Practically ripped my hood right off."

"She's right," Jilly said, pressing closer to me as a proof of loyalty. "You really had to be there to understand."

"All I need to understand is how you ladies ended up at the scene of the Swenson crime with Edna Evans. And why, before calling me, you enlisted the rescue vigilantes."

I kept my eyes down because I felt guilty about that. "There was nothing to be done for Vinnie," I said. "So we focused on helping those who needed us more."

"After trampling evidence," he said. "I bet you've started asking questions, too."

"I haven't had a chance, what with rounding up livestock, tending to guests, and choir practice. But I do have a few that are bursting to get out."

Kellan placed his glove on his chest in a plea. "Ivy, come on. One murder is bad enough, but now it's a double homicide. You really need to be careful. The killer may already know you were at the Swenson farm because you have Vinnie's donkey."

"It's not my fault the donkey singled me out, Kellan. And I certainly didn't want to be part of a ridiculous caroling act with him." I turned to Jilly. "Hey, we can cancel the show now, right?"

She shook her head. "People are going to need a pleasant distraction more than ever."

"But it feels insensitive to be singing with a dead man's donkey," I said. "Don't you think?"

She moved away so that she could stare at me. "I think you're using this as an excuse to wiggle out of a commitment to the mayor, whose family is staying with us. Think about the much-needed vote of confidence she's given the inn. And then get ready to bust a lung with Bocelli."

"Whose side are you on?" I grumbled.

"Yours, same as always, but the show must go on." She gave me a little wink. "I'm afraid that means more rehearsals with nosy people."

I caught her meaning. Rehearsals would be an opportunity to poke around and hear the scuttlebutt. Somebody always knew something if you listened carefully.

"Well, okay," I said. "But only because it will help bring Christmas joy to Clover Grove."

Kellan's eyes moved from Jilly to me. I tried not to smile as Percy started licking his cheek with a raspy tongue. The cat's breath wasn't sweet, as I knew from my own close encounters. Today it made the tough detective wince.

"I know what that look meant," he said. "You're not even going to pretend to stay out of this, are you?"

"Wouldn't it be worse if I pretended?" I asked.

After pondering, he nodded. "Yeah. But can you at least try to stay safe?"

"I always try, Kellan. It just doesn't work out the way I want some of the time."

"Some of the time?" he asked.

"A lot of the time, I guess. I could do with less excitement in my life."

His sigh came out on a gust of steam. "And yet you pursue it. In fact, you stampede after it on the animal of the moment."

I laughed. "I'll make a New Year's resolution to go on an adrenaline diet."

Keats slipped down the stairs and circled Kellan to bring him closer. The cat leapt lightly onto the railing and then onto my shoulder.

"I'd like to spend a nice Christmas with you, that's all," Kellan said, and his eyes softened. "Is that too much to ask?"

"That's what I want, too," I said. "But we've also got to think about the big picture."

"And in your opinion, that is...?"

"Community, just like you've said before. We're trying to create a new Clover Grove that's filled with camaraderie and good cheer instead of gossip and backstabbing. How can people relax and come together with two murders hanging over the holiday? They'll be worried they could be next. So we need to get this figured out fast."

Kellan turned to Daisy and shrugged. "I've done my best, and now I leave this situation in your capable rubber gloves. And by the way, I understand your mother made remarks to Mr. Milloy that could be construed as threatening."

Daisy pushed strands of hair away from her forehead with one glove. "What else is new?"

"Far be it from me to defend Mom," I said, "but Felix was threatening my jugular with his conductor's baton. There were plenty of witnesses."

"Witnesses who also say she wished him dead."

"That was just Mom being dramatic. He said the donkey sounded better than her."

"Truth," Asher said, speaking up again. "Someone revoke her choir license."

Daisy directed a stream of cleanser at Asher and he dodged it. "I'll do what I can, Chief," she said. "But keeping this town safe is probably easier than managing our family."

"Don't I know it," he said, turning. "Officer Galloway. Go interview the donkey with your sister, please."

"Which one?" Asher called.

Kellan pulled his hat over his perfect hair and let Keats herd him back to his car. "The stubborn one."

Asher still looked confused, but I laughed.

"Keats, leave it," I called. "Chief Scrooge doesn't need more holes in his cuffs. The joy's already draining out of him too fast."

CHAPTER NINE

M om tried unsuccessfully to cross her legs on the high stool at the counter in Daisy's kitchen. "I will not apologize for defending my family, Daisy. If someone else holds a sword to Ivy's throat, I will do it again without hesitation. I'm sure she'd do the same for me."

I slouched in the chair behind her at the kitchen table. "I'd defend you if someone held a sword to your throat, yes. But this weapon was a conductor's baton, and my life wasn't in peril. I have reason to know what true peril feels like."

"You most certainly do," Mom said. "Someone's always trying to kill you. A mother worries."

She tried to cross her legs the other way and failed again. Each time we had a family meeting it was the same awkward scrabble. Pants would improve her chances of the demure cross but they were few and far between in her wardrobe. Mom's special talent was redesigning secondhand dresses and skirts. Taking pants apart to fit her petite frame would be way more work. Besides, she liked being one of the few women in town who "knew how to dress like a lady," in her words. There was no denying she stood out in a community of homesteaders, and her attire went over well with the men in this region and far beyond. Mom never lacked for a date and her rotation had grown since an unfortunate encounter with a charming conman recently. At first she'd threatened to take herself off the market but then went to the opposite extreme instead. There was safety in numbers, she said. My own philosophy was quality over quantity, but there was no point arguing about that. Not when there was so much else to argue about.

Daisy passed Mom a paper cup of coffee while the rest of us drank from white china mugs. The battle over red waxy lipstick stains had taken a bold new turn. "Mom," Daisy said. "You threatened Felix Milloy. What will it take for you to learn to zip it?"

"Daisy," Mom said. "What will it take for you to learn to treat your guests like... well, guests? You won't last long as co-manager of Runaway Inn if you offer the mayor's relatives paper cups. Picnic season is long over."

"The mayor's relatives are real guests—paying guests—so they're welcome to leave lipstick stains if they like. Besides, Ivy is paying me to polish her china."

"I don't need to pay you for anything," Mom said. "I gave you the ultimate gift: existence. Without me, you wouldn't have this lovely house with stools meant for giants."

"Roger gave her those giants," Violet said, with a placating smile. "That's the ultimate gift, as far as Daisy's concerned."

"My boys are my greatest blessing," Daisy said, eyeing me uneasily. She probably wondered if I'd shared her secret about the younger twins with the rest of the family. I hadn't and never would. Only Jilly knew for sure. And Kellan, of course, but he'd learned about it as police chief, not boyfriend. "If only they'd inherited my love of cleanliness."

The boys had fled when we arrived, as usual. Keats and Percy went with them as a way to gain access to the ferret cage in the younger twins' room. Normally the ferrets were loose anyway, and then the games truly began.

"I'm glad to be putting your hygiene gene to use at the inn," I said, raising my hand in a salute as Asher came in. It was hit and miss whether he'd attend a family meeting when Jilly couldn't come along, but Kellan had probably sent him to spy on us. Or me, more specifically. Luckily Asher was fairly easily decoyed. He would never make a good detective but he was an excellent peacekeeper and negotiator. In neighborly disputes, of which there were many in Clover Grove, he was the charming constable of choice. These skills were extremely valuable in a community where people kept firearms to protect their livestock and could easily turn to them in heated moments. "Any news for us, brother?"

"Nope," he said. "We're just doing our due diligence. You know, as police officers."

Kellan had given Asher some canned messages and he was trying to stick to them. But his bright blue eyes—the only blue ones among various shades of hazel in this room—wouldn't meet mine. He had information all right, and it was my job to pick it out of him.

"Is your team done at the Swenson farm?" I asked. "It's hard to imagine how Vinnie and Felix Milloy had anything in common. Especially when Felix hasn't been home in decades."

"I never met Felix," he said. "Don't know anything about him."

"But you met Vinnie, right? It sounded like he was a frequent flyer in matters of lawbreaking."

"I don't know about that." Asher's broad shoulders shifted uncomfortably under his uniform. He hated lying, or even evading the truth. "Personally, I was only ever called out there about disputes over the property line. And trespassing." He thought for a second. "And the usual livestock issues."

"What livestock issues?" I asked.

Asher's face showed the internal battle over relevance and decided it was safe to share. "Vinnie believed that any animal that wandered onto his land became his property. That didn't go over so well with the original owners."

"Especially when his standard of care was abysmal," I said. "Do you think one of those irate former owners might have done this?"

He shrugged. "Possibly, but there'd be no connection to Felix Milloy."

"Vinnie had plenty of enemies from what I heard."

"Your intel isn't to be trusted," Asher said. "According to the chief."

"The chief has used the same source," I said. "He's quite willing to listen to the Rescue Mafia when it serves him."

Asher took a seat at the table and slumped into the perfect image of discomfort. "I hate being caught between my boss and you guys." He made a circle to include the entire family. "It's been happening a lot lately."

"Only since Ivy came home," Mom said, happy to deflect the blame to me.

"Not true," Asher said. "What about you and Buttercup? I was a laughingstock when you were knocking off stop signs. There was a pool over who'd be the first to die under your wheels."

"A pool! That's the most insulting thing I've ever heard," Mom said.

"Untrue," Poppy said. "You hear more insulting things every day. I make sure of it."

Mom finished her coffee and stared at Poppy over the rim of the paper cup. "You and Ivy share an unsavory sense of humor. It comes from your father. He found himself amusing but others rarely did." She crunched the paper cup with a manicured hand and delivered another shot. "I always wondered if that got him killed."

"Mom!" All five Galloway Girls sang the protest in a shrill soprano.

"It didn't," Asher said. Then he examined his fingernails as if he hadn't just dropped a huge bomb.

There was an electrical charge in the room. If I had any doubt, the fact that Percy's hair suddenly stood on end proved it. Keats came back from ferret hunting to sit by my side. My hand dropped to his ears.

"What do you mean?" Mom said, thrashing wildly just to stay upright.

My brother's face had turned bright red but when he looked up, his eyes had rare sparks of defiance. "I mean his sense of humor hasn't killed him," he said. "Yet."

I stared around to see if I was the only one who'd been left in the dark about our father's current existence or sense of humor. Everyone looked equally confused and uncomfortable. Mom was trying to restore the paper cup to its former wholeness without success. Her hands were trembling.

I wished Jilly had been there to stickhandle the situation. Mind you, Asher probably wouldn't have dropped this bomb if she had.

"What are you talking about, Asher Galloway?" Daisy said. "Do you keep in touch with that—"

Raising my right hand, I cut her off by doing a passable imitation of a conductor. "Ladies. This right here is called a decoy. Asher threw down a slab of meat expecting us to go after it like a pack of starving wolves. Let's disappoint him."

My sisters' mouths opened and Asher achieved his end.

"But he can't just—"

"That's not fair. We deserve to—"

"How are we supposed to—"

"I thought we shared—"

"Everything?" I finished Violet's statement. She was the most gullible Galloway Girl and probably the only one deluded enough to think for a moment we shared everything. As the most cynical sister, I knew we shared far less than most families. The secrets had started long before our father left and it didn't surprise me at all that someone knew of his whereabouts. It only surprised me that Asher, the least duplicitous—or so I thought—had kept it a secret. Maybe there was more to him than I imagined. "We don't share everything. But I'm going to make a radical suggestion here."

"What?" Violet asked. She looked more rattled than Mom but only because Mom was better at hiding it.

"Let's all step around the landmine Asher planted and leave it to dig up at a holiday dinner. Isn't that what regular families do? They make entire movies about it."

"We will not ruin Christmas talking about your father," Mom said, turning. "Asher, you have stabbed me twice in the heart today."

Asher sank even lower in his seat. "Sorry, Mom."

He *was* sorry to upset us, I could see that. But he wasn't sorry to deflect attention from the murder investigations. That had been the chief's order, no doubt. Kellan would likely be surprised and upset to hear about how Asher had done it. If my brother was willing to go that far to throw me off the trail, I would go even farther to figure out what was going on. I'd just use my own channels to do it.

Poppy met my eyes and accepted the challenge. "What I really want to know is... who got the most votes in the pool of people Mom might run down in Buttercup?"

Asher shook his head, flushing even more. "I can't say. I won't."

"I know," Poppy said. "Edna Evans. I bet that was your vote."

"Poppy, Edna is my friend," I said.

"She wasn't when Mom was still driving her killing machine," Poppy said. "I bet Asher put Edna's name forward."

"I did not," he said. "Although I wouldn't have objected if her broom crashed into a wall." He offered me a peacemaking grin. "I know she's saved your life—"

"More than once," I said.

"But you know she used to be a—"

"Witch. I do. It just proves that personal transformation is possible," I said.

"Yeah," Poppy said. "If Edna Evans can turn from zero to hero, anyone can."

Daisy pulled a china mug out of the cupboard, filled it with coffee and slid it across the counter to Mom. "Let's take that as a personal challenge. We can all afford to up our game, can't we, Galloways?"

Mom took a long sip and then forced a smile. "I've already transformed myself and I give most of the credit to my rotation. It's something I heartily recommend for you girls. It wouldn't hurt the chief to have a little competition, Ivy. He's getting complacent."

"That's the best you've got?" Daisy said, making a move to reclaim the mug.

Mom held it out of reach, and then rubbed the rim of the cup with a tissue. "I do think I'm too hasty sometimes. Always for the good of my children." She glanced over at Poppy. "It's sad to see you inherited my worst trait."

"You know what?" Poppy said. "I'm sad about that, too. So I'm going to work on it, using Edna Evans as my role model for personal transformation."

Asher rubbed his forehead and rose from the table. "Aim higher, Pops. I still have nightmares about school vaccination day."

"I'm going to start with an ATV," Poppy said. "And fatigues."

It was good to see everyone smiling again after Asher's bombshell. There would be time to worry about that later. Now I was even more inspired to do my own investigation. If I had to work around Asher and Kellan to save Christmas, then fine. It was just days away but I'd done more with less. Two murders meant twice the clues and half the analysis, I figured.

Keats swished his tail and looked from me to Percy. They headed for the door, tails up.

"Gotta run," I said, brushing past my brother. "Good luck with your due diligence, Ash. Hope you'll work on your deflection game. That was total overkill, and now you got nothing."

He was grinning when I looked over my shoulder. "Maybe. Maybe not. I wouldn't underestimate me, sis."

I *had* underestimated him. One thing I'd been totally sure of in life was my brother's personality. I thought I knew him inside and out. Obviously I'd lost my HR edge since moving home, and over-confidence was a fatal flaw in a sleuth. I'd consider this a valuable wake-up call.

Still, my worldview had shifted suddenly and it was a shock.

Keats whined in sympathy as I bent to put on my boots and I whispered, "It's okay. I'll be okay."

I opened the front door but Percy stayed back. He crouched suddenly and then leapt at Asher's midriff. After clinging for a second, he dropped and bounced out the door.

Judging by Asher's scream, the cat needed another claw trim.

CHAPTER TEN

Hazel Bingham greeted me at the door of her old manor without using a walker or cane. When we'd met a couple of months ago, she'd been unsteady on her feet long after breaking her hip. Then her nephew, Michael, moved to Clover Grove and brought her home from Sunny Acres retirement villa. Since then, she'd made a remarkable recovery.

"You're like that guy in the movie who reverse ages," I said, following her into the dining room, where a gleaming silver tea service engraved with an ornate "B" sat waiting. The old oak table— a gift from her grandfather to her grandmother—gleamed too. Michael had worked hard to restore it to its former glory after a mishap with too many cats. Percy jumped on it now and I shooed him gently, worried he'd autograph it with fresh claw marks.

"Benjamin Button?" Hazel asked, proving her mind was sharp, too. "Michael says the same thing." She let me pull out the chair and smoothed the folds of her blue wool dress before adding, "That dear boy is behind it."

"That dear boy is dating my mother. I hope you know that," I said, as Hazel welcomed the cat onto her lap. "I asked her not to, just so you know."

Hazel laughed, and once again I admired her deep, rich voice. With her elegant dress and stately twist of hair, she looked like an old-time movie star. In fact, she was as close to royalty as we got in Clover Grove as a descendent of one of the classy founding families. It was essentially her idea to revive some of the culture she remembered from the town's glory days, and Jilly and I were doing our best to bring her vision to life. It had gone surprisingly well, so far. Maybe Hazel was right that the homesteaders who'd taken over yearned for an identity—to be grounded in more than backyard chickens and preserves.

"Don't worry about Michael," Hazel said. "He's on the rebound from that—" She choked off the word and frowned as she poured tea into two porcelain cups. "Never mind. Dahlia's a pistol, but she might be just what the doctor ordered to help him get over what happened."

What happened was that Michael's wife had been exposed as a sociopath decades into their marriage. With her out of the picture, he was restoring the Bingham Manor and rebounding with Mom. The fact that Mom's rotation was large and her business at the salon thriving meant that he had to work hard to book time in her schedule. If she broke his heart it would be in slow motion and there would be plenty of time for Hazel to rescue him.

As we caught up on the Clover Grove Culture Revival Project, Hazel opened a familiar red box of gingerbread Christmas trees and displayed them on a festive china plate.

"I see that Secret Santa made it out this way," I said, taking one. "The cookies are from Mandy's, but she claims to know nothing about the good Samaritan because so many businesses buy in bulk. The gesture has stirred up Christmas spirit like nothing else this season."

"Actually, that honor goes to you, my dear," she said. "I heard your wonderful duet in town square."

I had already taken a bite of the cookie, which was a shame

because my gasp pulled crumbs into my windpipe and the subsequent cough distributed them on the table's fine patina. Hazel nudged the teacup toward me and I sipped until I could speak. "You *heard* it? You weren't there."

She lifted a bejeweled hand from Percy's purring flank and waved. "Well, saw it and heard it, to be precise. Someone posted the video online. I assumed you knew because it's very popular. Michael played it over and over. I hear that poor donkey in my sleep now."

My face probably rivaled the cookie box for color. "I'll see if Kellan can have that taken down. For his own pride, if nothing else. That poor man puts up with a lot from my animals."

Hazel laughed again. "I don't think there's anything you can do to jeopardize your standing with Chief Harper. I see the way he looks at you. More important, I see the way he *doesn't* look at you when he's in uniform. He wants to keep up his tough professional front."

That just made me blush harder. Hazel was a staunch supporter of my relationship with Kellan and her opinion meant a lot to me. We'd recognized each other as kindred spirits when she was still at Sunny Acres. Now I considered her a friend and visited regularly. She ranked near the top of Percy's list and slightly below Mom on Keats'. Normally the dog sat gazing at her, but he was nosing around collecting cookie crumbs. I whisked a few more off for him.

"I hate to embarrass Kellan like that, though," I said. "It's bad enough that I'm always running into, you know, problems. Of the murderous kind."

Her lips pressed together, perhaps recalling how her own family had contributed to my murder problem. "At least this time it wasn't on the farm," she said. "And as much as I hate to speak ill of the dead, Vincent Swenson was a nasty bit of trouble. As was his father, and especially his grandfather. Old Frank swindled my father in business once. He was a rumrunner who ruled all of hill country with a little charm and an iron fist. But each generation lost more of the charm and got more heavy-handed." She finally smiled. "At least the Swenson line ends here. Vinnie was connected with a young lady who had the good sense to flee after getting to know him."

"Do you remember her name?" I asked.

She shook her head. "Try Edna. She has a photographic memory of anyone she ever vaccinated."

"Comes in handy now," I said. "But we suffered for it then."

Pushing the plate of gingerbread Christmas trees toward me, she said, "Ask her about the rumors, too. The rural myths about the Swenson farm."

I was already hoisting another cookie to my mouth and let it dangle. "What kind of myths?"

She topped up my teacup, no doubt worried I'd choke and spew more crumbs. "I'm sure the stories are as exaggerated as any others in this town, but people say there's treasure buried on the property. Plenty of it."

"I heard whispers about buried treasure. Do you think there's any truth in them?"

"Possibly, yes. By treasure, of course I mean loot. Ill-gotten gains that date all the way back to Frank Swenson." She sipped her tea and her eyes lost focus. "My father always wondered if the money Frank conned out of him was buried there, and my brother Aaron used to sneak out there as a kid to poke around. Most boys—and plenty of grown men—went through that phase. The added thrill was that the Swensons would sporadically patrol the property with a rifle. Many have dramatic stories to tell of being chased off the land. The Swensons must have had a collection of metal detectors that were left behind."

"But wouldn't Vinnie have used the metal detectors himself to find the loot? The place didn't look like he was rolling in cash."

"If Vinnie found any loot, he'd have squandered it on gambling and other vices." She looked over the rim of her cup. "I would imagine Chief Harper kept an eye on him."

I chewed the cookie carefully, savoring every spicy bite. I was becoming addicted to these Secret Santa specials, and would have to drop by Mandy's Country Store to stock up before she ran out. After swallowing the last crumbs, I asked, "What about Felix Milloy? You must have known him, too."

"Oh yes." She set her cup down so firmly that the saucer was in peril of cracking. "He was an unpleasant boy and an irascible man. The only difference between him and some of the town's other disreputable characters was that Felix had talent. We had a wonderful teacher back in the day who could dig up the treasure in any child and polish it. I think she sensed Felix would go off the rails unless he had focus. She gave him that focus, and by all accounts, he had a successful life."

"But then he came back nearly sixty years later. Why?"

Hazel's right hand, with its many sparkling rings, made a rippling movement. "We're like salmon who swim home to die where we spawned. Sunny Acres is full of people like that. They ran off to find fame and fortune, leaving the community diminished, and then lamented about how it had changed. It's one reason I didn't mix much when I was there. I always wanted to give them a piece of my mind. This town was the heart of hill country until we lost our best and brightest." She pushed her chair back. "I understand wanderlust but have the decency not to complain about what you left behind."

"What possible connection could Felix have had to young Vinnie Swenson? If they were poisoned within days of each other, I doubt that's a coincidence."

She shrugged. "I can't imagine Felix knew young Vinnie well. But he'd most certainly have crossed paths with his father and grandfather. They were neighbors, you know."

"I didn't know. Edna gets uncomfortable talking about Felix. There was animosity."

"The octopus story?" Hazel said. "We were all grateful she put him in his place. It was a public service."

Keats gave a low mumble and I looked down. His blue eye fixed on me and he offered a suggestion.

"No," I told him. "I am not doing that. Come up with a better idea."

He repeated his suggestion. Even Hazel could tell that from his "phrasing," because she clapped her hands and beamed. "Ah, a glimpse into how your magic with that dog works. I don't understand what he said, but it sounded like good advice."

I sighed. "You have no idea how much it will cost my pride, Hazel."

Percy stepped from Hazel's lap onto the oak table and then leapt onto my shoulder. He began grooming my hair with his raspy tongue.

"Percy feels for you," Hazel said. "But he agrees with Keats."

Scooping Percy off with one hand, I lowered him to the floor and then rose from my seat. "Fine. Take their side, Hazel. But if this ends up online, I do *not* want to hear about it."

CHAPTER ELEVEN

In honor of our first official performance, Edna, the new choirmaster, had exchanged her fatigues for a pair of wool slacks and a long double-breasted gray coat accessorized by a hat, scarf and gloves in a mottled blue yarn. My neighbor might be eccentric, but she knew how to dress for an occasion. I had considered doing the same but decided my role as comic relief with Bocelli required me to look like a country bumpkin. It was all the excuse I needed to wear overalls on top of long johns covered by a ratty parka. As a nod to the season, I wore a red knit toque featuring Santa and his reindeer.

Edna loaded the donkey on the trailer and pulled the truck around to wait for us. Rolling down the window, she tapped her watch and yelled, "Chop chop, choirgirls. I can't be late for this. People are standing outside in the cold while you're kibbitzing."

She had probably seen me chasing Keats from one room to another and thought it was a game. The dog found his new jacket—sensible, black and lined with faux lamb's wool—only slightly less reprehensible than the yellow parka. Zipping him into it was almost as exhausting as getting him into the bath. We'd had a terse exchange and were both sulking as we walked to the truck.

"Into the passenger seat," Edna said. "You're obviously in a mood and I don't care to be thrown about while you stall the truck."

I crossed my arms beside the driver's door. "Out. If Kellan catches you driving my truck again, I could be taken off the road like my mother. I don't care to repeat that bit of family history."

She held her ground. "Everything rides on our first performance, Ivy. Conducting means becoming one with the music and I need a calm commute to prepare."

"You've obviously been Googling the how-to of conducting, and that's great. But keep in mind that without me—and more specifically, my caroling donkey—the audience will be disappointed. Bocelli and I have become media darlings, whether I like it or not. And we're not coming unless I'm the one pulling the trailer."

"She's right, Edna," Jilly said. She looked smart in a skirt, heavy wool tights, high boots and a hat and scarf that made her green eyes pop—or would if it weren't already so dark. Overcast winter nights in hill country were like being trapped in a black velvet sack with no means of escape. "It's one threat Kellan would make good on," she continued. "Worse, he'd make Asher do the dirty deed and ruin his Christmas. And therefore, mine. And therefore yours, because I'd be too depressed to cook a big dinner."

Jilly crossed her arms over the strap of Percy's carrier. Inside, the cat lounged comfortably in his little yellow parka.

Edna huffed as she got out of the truck and stomped around to the passenger door. "Have it your way, but make it fast. And Keats, don't even think about sitting on my Sunday best coat."

After a few miles of zen-like peace, during which I stalled once, Jilly dared to ask, "Is there a plan for tonight? I mean, other than running through our caroling lineup?"

"There's a reception afterward," I said. "You, Percy, Keats and I will talk to as many people as we can."

"While I do what, exactly?" Edna said, breaking her silence.

"Make idle small talk. Create a distraction." I tossed her a grin. "These are your people, after all."

"My people? I have nothing at all in common with them."

I laughed as I pulled into the long driveway. The spotlights were on and I recognized the coats and hats of some of our caroling cohort gathered at the doors. "You went to school with some of them and nursed others. You have a history."

She gave an exasperated sigh and gestured to the big sign for Sunny Acres with its cheery sunbeam logo. "This is God's waiting room. And being locked in here is my worst nightmare."

"It's a retirement home and people come by choice," I said. "When I visited Hazel here, people seemed happy enough. But I can see it wouldn't be your thing."

"You bet it isn't." She opened her mouth and tapped a tooth. "That's why I keep a cyanide pill in one of my crowns. When my time comes, I'm heading down to Huckleberry Marsh to ride it out in my bunker." Glancing over her shoulder she said, "I'll take a final order of your beef stew to go, Jillian. The fancy one with the wine and bacon."

"I'd be honored to cook your favorite stew for you anytime," Jilly said. "Over the holidays, if you're nice."

"Nice?" Edna jumped out before I'd even turned off the engine. "You've got the wrong prepper."

She barked orders at the choir in the parking lot. At first I thought none of the villa's residents had shown up to watch but the night manager gestured for us to follow the path into the rear of the building. The courtyard had been lovely in autumn and was magnificent now. They'd brought in potted Christmas shrubs with flaming berries, and a 12-foot fir sparkling with lights in full view of the recreation room on the second floor.

"It looks nicer than town square," Jilly said, taking off her mitten to touch the plants. "They're real."

Letitia Smart, owner of Flora to Fawn Over, joined us. "The

villa's budget was bigger than the council's, believe it or not. I brought in holly, mistletoe and yew for the courtyard, as well as the tree. Inside I built a glorious Christmas display out of red and white poinsettias, and there's a blue spruce as well. It took five trips in my van."

"I hope you don't mind if I steal some ideas for the inn. I'll stock up in your store, of course," Jilly said, taking photos.

"My pleasure," Letitia said. "But I really think you should go out and cut down your own tree this year. There's something so magical about that." She waggled her eyebrows at me. "Very romantic."

"I love that idea," Jilly said, squeezing my arm. "The perfect double date."

Beverly Roxton had been openly eavesdropping and spoke up now. "I wouldn't count on that happening. Seems like your gentlemen constantly have their hands full fighting the crime that's overtaken this town." Her blue eyes met mine and when I held the stare, hers dropped to Keats. Then her lips puckered with either distaste or disapproval. For someone who married a vet and ran his office, she didn't seem like much of an animal-lover. Maybe she kept a clinical detachment to protect herself from heartrending outcomes. "Clover Grove has changed so much since you got back. I feel very sorry for the police."

Ah. So she was one of the critics who felt I'd brought bad luck upon Clover Grove. I couldn't entirely blame her but it stung just the same.

Edna had also been eavesdropping, apparently, because she said, "Beverly, if you still want a solo, I wouldn't dry out your vocal cords giving Ivy a hard time about things she can't control. There are so many fine voices that I'll decide based on who's naughty or nice."

Beverly's pucker smoothed into a firm line and then a fake smile as she turned and walked to the center of the courtyard. Tipping her head back, she waved. That's when I saw the residents lined up against the glass of the second floor recreation room inside. Jilly, Edna and I waved too, and dozens waved back.

"Better get your partner," Edna said, giving me a little shove. "Beverly doesn't stand a chance against Bocelli."

Keats and I went back and opened the trailer. I switched on my phone light, let the dog go in first, and then slid beside the donkey to give him a pep talk. "Hey, Bocelli. Ready to belt out a few?"

The donkey ignored me, keeping his eyes fixed on a point straight ahead. I'd worked hard to connect with him over the past couple of days but he rebuffed all my advances. It was a shame because I could sense his intelligence in a way I didn't with the other three donkeys. Bright animals gave off a special kind of energy.

Keats seemed to agree with my assessment. With the trio of donkey thugs, he was wary and almost scornful, whereas with Bocelli, he was gentle and respectful. They were building a relationship, even if the donkey didn't overtly acknowledge it. Percy liked Bocelli, too, and often sat on the fence of his pasture sharing the sunshine.

I tried scratching the donkey between his ears and he ducked away from my hand. "Fine," I said. "I feel a little used, Bocelli. You only care about me when I'm singing. That hurts a girl's feelings."

Keats rumbled something soothing, letting me know I was his number one.

"Same buddy," I said. "Always. No matter what critters come and go."

"Ivy!" Edna's booming voice startled all of us. "What are you doing in there?"

"We're having a moment, if you don't mind."

"I do mind. I'm trying to run a choir here."

I slipped out of the trailer and let Keats unload the donkey.

"Singing in front of an audience isn't easy for me, Edna. I need to psych up for it."

"You've faced down killers, for heaven's sake. How can a carol or two faze you?"

"One carol," I said.

"Possibly two," she said, unzipping her purse. "We'll let the crowd decide. If I were you, I'd be prepared for an encore."

"One carol. It's in my contract."

She pulled a long, slim brown case out of her bag, almost dumping a can of pepper spray in the process. Flipping the lid, she showed me a conductor's baton.

"It's an antique," she said. "Twenty-two inches, and once owned by a conductor of the Boston Philharmonic Orchestra. Heddy and Kaye Langman charged me a pretty penny for it."

"You're sure it's authentic?"

"I had its provenance verified. I wasn't born yesterday, Ivy." She glanced up at the villa. "As young as I might seem sometimes."

"You're definitely young for your years," I said, following her back to the courtyard with Keats in front and Bocelli behind. "Is the baton coming into the bunker with us?"

"Perhaps. It won't take up much room. Even in an uprising a woman needs a few earthly pleasures." Giving the baton a dramatic swish, she grinned. "It could come in handy to poke out the enemy's eyes."

I led Bocelli into position in the back row of the altos. The donkey was wearing Florence the mare's cast-off coat. It had been far too big, but help came from surprising places.

"Darling, I thought you'd never get here," Mom said. "The donkey looks splendid. It was a pleasure using my seamstress skills for a good cause. The Santa decals are detachable."

"It was kind of you, Mom," I said. "I hope he's in the mood to sing tonight. I wouldn't want to disappoint anyone."

Mom pulled a very long scarf out of her bag and coiled it twice around Bocelli's neck. It was the same pattern as my Santa hat, which couldn't have been a coincidence.

"Adorable," she said. "Now, you look like a vaudeville act."

I yanked off my hat. "I'd rather have staticky hair and cold ears than match my donkey. It reminds me of how you used to dress all five of us girls the same. So embarrassing."

She rolled her eyes. "You girls and your grudges. I need a ledger to keep track of who resents what. How about thinking about it from my perspective? That made it easier to find you in a crowd. There were so many of you and you all looked so similar. That's why Asher was such a relief."

"And he was the one always escaping and getting into trouble."

"Darling, you need to lighten up. We've talked about this. Being too serious will age you early. Look at Daisy."

"Mom, that's terrible. If she's haggard it's because she had too much responsibility raising us."

She shrugged. "I didn't ask your father to leave, but I certainly didn't ask him to come back, either. If he never does, that'll be too soon." Reaching for tissues in her purse, she patted her eyes lightly, to preserve the delicate skin. "I was so terribly upset by what Asher said at the family meeting. What if he stages a surprise reunion for all of us?"

"He'd never do that, Mom," I said. "Never."

"How do you know? I never thought he'd keep a secret like that. He's always been my favorite." She blew her nose. "My favorite son, I mean. Obviously you were my favorite daughter."

"I know he wouldn't for two reasons. First, it's six against one and we can handle him together."

She sniffled, unconvinced. "And the second?"

"Jilly. She'll serve up a stiff dose of reality to him, if she hasn't already. It's his right to keep in touch with his father, but he can't impose that man on the rest of us."

"Imagine what the rumor mill would do," Mom said. "As if we

don't provide enough fodder already. And my rotation would be rocked to its core."

"Men like a little competition," I said. "Or so you told me recently."

"Husbands are different, I'm afraid. There's a code of honor."

"Ex-husband," I said. "Long since."

She chafed her nose in silence. Conspicuous silence.

"Mom... You did divorce him, didn't you? I mean, formally?"

"Darling, we really must pay attention to Edna's baton." Giving a last sniff, she shoved the tissue into her pocket. "I have complete faith in Jilly. Our little chat has made me feel so much better."

I couldn't say the same. My intuition had been prickling since we got here, anyway, and Keats' ruff was up, too. He gave me a sharp look with his eerie blue eye. A warning to stay alert.

As Mom went over and wedged herself firmly between Iris and Violet, I muttered, "As if we didn't have enough to worry about already, buddy. I think I'd rather deal with murderers than family strife."

He mumbled an opposing view. For him, keeping me safe was more challenging than family squabbles, I supposed.

"Okay, well let's get our minds in the game. All we have to do is knock off a few tunes and get inside to talk to people. Some of the villa's residents are bound to have ideas about who might have killed Vinnie and Felix. Old squabbles bring new life in closed communities like this. Christmas came early with plenty of gossip."

Keats gave his happy pant and his tail came up in a swish. We were on the right track, I was sure of that.

"We won't have much time in there," I said. "I count on you to help me triage."

The tail swished again.

"And see if you can make any sense of what's troubling the donkey. I can't read him at all, but maybe you can."

Now he offered a mumble that sounded less confident.

"Well, aren't you two adorable?" I turned to see Beverly Roxton standing a little too close. How much had she heard?

"We are," I agreed. "I know your husband chitchats to his patients as well. He had quite a conversation with Percy before he castrated him. Man to man. I think he felt worse because Percy had been a tomcat for so long in the feral colony. It was like he was losing something." I added quickly, "The cat, I mean."

Beverly gave me a look that said I'd confirmed all she'd heard: "Poor Ivy's still suffering from her brain injury. She used to be one of our greatest exports and now she's so odd."

Sometimes that bothered me, particularly when I felt I'd already contributed a lot to this town and was fast becoming a communitarian. Other times, I felt the distraction served me well. If they were so busy talking about my eccentricities, they couldn't focus on everything else I was doing.

Thankfully, Edna called the choir to order before the conversation could continue. She was standing on a wooden box and we got into formation around her.

"Relax, everyone," she said. "Uncross those arms. Stand up straight. And for pity's sake, smile. You're bringing comfort and joy, not getting a root canal."

Everyone did look a little tense. It was probably a combination of stage fright and worries about Edna's leadership. She wasn't well liked and there was no telling how she'd wield her newfound power. If I was viewed as eccentric, she was viewed as dangerously so, but people had a guarded respect for her, too.

She pulled a pitch pipe out of her pocket and blew a note. We responded with a hum. I couldn't help but grin when I heard a rumble from Keats on one side, and a sound deep in Bocelli's broad chest on my other side.

Edna directed the baton at me. "This isn't a game, Ivy. Even if you are the comic relief."

"Understood," I called back.

"Again," she said, and puffed out another note on the pitch pipe.

The hum was louder but I could sense it more than hear it, because Bocelli vibrated visibly. His mouth began to work, as if he were chewing.

"And... begin," Edna said, counting us in with the swooping baton.

Everyone began on cue with an upbeat God Rest Ye Merry Gentlemen. I waited an entire verse before adding my voice. Instantly, Bocelli threw back his head and brayed. It was louder than ever and downright painful at close range. The rest of the choir migrated away from us but continued to sing.

When the carol ended, Edna pointed at me again. "You two sit the next one out, Ivy. O Holy Night deserves better than that noise."

In my view it was no worse than what Mom was doing to the song. Her head went back so far that her hood fell off and she warbled, yowled and hooted without the slightest embarrassment.

Beverly Roxton kept turning from the front row to give Mom dirty looks. Finally, she stepped out in front and raised her voice in an unauthorized solo. Edna's baton paused in midair as she considered what to do about the breach in choir etiquette. There was no question, however, that Beverly had a lovely voice, and many others stopped singing to listen. Not Mom, of course. She got louder. It turned into a battle of the caroling divas.

When the song ended, Edna pointed to Beverly with the baton and summoned her. I expected a strident lecture, but instead, Edna did the same with Jilly, my sister Iris, and Heddy Langman, of all people. She said something to them I couldn't hear and then turned back to the rest of us.

"Everyone else, stand down."

She led the quartet in a version of Silent Night that sent chills up my spine. No matter how many times I heard it, this carol moved me like no other. Looking up, I saw millions of pinpricks of ice in the dark sky. For a moment I felt small and insignificant—too small to do the job that had been given me. But then warm pressure against my leg said otherwise as Keats leaned into me. I wasn't alone in the vast universe. Far from it. My anchors were many, and now included a rather sizeable performing donkey.

The quartet performed two more carols before Edna brought the rest in again for a grand finale. After that, she signaled for the crowd to part. They formed a large circle around Bocelli, Keats and me. My eyes found Jilly's and she gave me an encouraging smile.

Standing on her box, Edna counted me in for Hark the Herald Angels Sing. Bocelli started out softly but by the end of the first verse, his head was back and he was braying as if his life depended on it. Who knew, maybe it did. He clearly had a message for me, at least, and quite possibly the townspeople. It sounded more like a warning than ever before.

Others didn't hear it that way. The villa's residents thumped on the windows and their applause requested the encore Edna had predicted.

I tried to give the donkey a pat but he took a step away from me. This was serious business for him. So, with the next carol, O Come All Ye Faithful, I didn't hold back. No one could hear me anyway, but my voice mattered to Bocelli. He needed my backup to tell his own story, and I would indeed have faith that I'd understand in time. That approach hadn't steered me wrong since I found Keats as a neglected puppy and decided to rescue him, no questions asked.

The braying got louder and louder—grating, harsh, impassioned. It was different than the first time, and the intensity of it struck me to the core. At the finish, he opened his eyes and stared up at the audience, or perhaps the same daunting sky I'd faced, and let out a long screech that was painful to hear, both literally and figuratively.

Bocelli didn't wait around to receive his applause. He turned, jerked the rope out of my hand, and walked back to the trailer.

Instead of herding him, Keats switched to crowd control, preventing the choir from patting the donkey. Bocelli's heart was heavy and he just wanted to be alone.

As I shut the trailer door behind him, I said, "I'll figure it out, pal. I promise. Just have a little patience."

His heavy sigh said everything but he kicked the trailer wall in a resounding exclamation mark.

I looked at Keats and shook my head. "Another drama queen. Just what we need."

CHAPTER TWELVE

Nearly thirty residents gathered in the music room on the main floor at Sunny Acres. Letitia had outdone herself with the flaming red poinsettias mixed with white, the tall spruce and fresh wreaths everywhere. The smell of pine transported me back to childhood. We only had a real tree one year, when Asher brought it home. I figured he'd probably stolen it from a tree lot. Daisy and Mom must have thought so too, because the following year an artificial tree arrived from a thrift store. Instead of hard needles, it had green plastic fluttery bits that blew around in a way no real fir ever could. Mom spritzed pine air freshener around and used a diffuser with essential oil but it just felt... desperate. I stopped giving Christmas a chance after that.

"If you don't look too closely, you could almost forget where you are," Edna said, shuddering. "I've updated my will, by the way. It's on you to make sure I go down in action."

"Oh Edna, I have no doubt at all you'll end crushed under your own ATV," I reassured her.

"Or get shot saving you," she said.

"A worthy cause," I said. "But my money's still on the zombie uprising."

"Suddenly I want to believe in your foolishness." She sighed. "Carpe diem, Ivy. Let's divide and conquer. I'll talk to my old schoolmates and see what they recall about the Swenson and Milloy families. I'm sure I'll get an earful about the so-called treasure. It's all malarky."

"Try to be subtle," I said. "Draw them out. It's better to circle back another day than raise suspicions with the sledgehammer approach."

"I can be subtle." She smoothed the front of her sweater. It had a pattern of holly that looked like an impressionist painting. "You're the one in overalls flanked by a dog and cat. Why not just roll in on a red tractor yelling yee-haw?"

"You're stalling," I said. "I know it's difficult seeing your cronies here but remember that many don't have the support you do. There's a brigade behind you now."

She took a deep breath and said, "I'm going in."

I'd seen her take on criminals and rampaging livestock with less trepidation, but she didn't look back as she joined the residents who were crowding around the refreshment table.

"Where to?" I asked Keats. Percy was zigzagging through slippers and walkers and wheelchairs doing his own reconnaissance. He ended up circling Beverly Roxton, who was pushing a man I recognized around the room.

"Ivy," she called. "Your cat is going to get run over if he isn't careful."

"He's always careful," I called back. As if to prove it, Percy leapt onto the back of the wheelchair and balanced there for a moment. I was afraid he'd do his pirate parrot act and cause a scene, just for kicks.

Keats and I hurried over and I plucked Percy from the wheelchair and set him down. Moments later, I saw the cat leaving the music room with his tail low and flicking. He was annoyed at either me or the situation. Or maybe just the parka Jilly claimed he liked.

"Beautiful peacock," the old man in the wheelchair said. "Nothing a good shower won't fix."

"Pardon me?" I said. I glanced at Beverly.

"My father-in-law mixes up his words sometimes," she said, flushing to match the poinsettias. "It's, you know..." She made a little circle with her index finger at her temple to signify dementia. I was glad he couldn't see the gesture. Dr. Roxton was a well-known and well-loved veterinarian in his day and had established the practice that his son now ran. The focus had been on livestock then, whereas Beverly's husband, Cliff, specialized in small animals.

I moved around the chair so he could see me. "He is a beautiful peacock, Dr. Roxton. And here's my other beauty."

Keats stared up at the vet, swiveling to give him the full force of his blue eye. Reading this confused man was probably complicated.

"Fireworks," Dr. Roxton said. "Watch out for the bulldozer."

"See?" Beverly said. "Word salad. My husband wanted to keep him at home but I was afraid we'd find the place burned to the ground. Or worse. For someone so confused, he managed to find the keys to the van and go out for a spin. Now that he's here, I can finally sleep at night." Shrugging, she added, "Cliff will forgive me eventually."

"Kite off a cliff," Dr. Roxton said, clapping gnarled hands. "Bullseye."

Beverly shook her head. "How about a sandwich, Pops?"

"Horse blanket Santa," he said. His blue eyes darted up to meet mine for a second. "Tooth serenade."

His expression was earnest and I felt the same frustration I had earlier with Bocelli, wishing I understood his private language.

"Horse blanket Santa..." I mused aloud.

"Don't bother trying to figure it out," Beverly said, starting to roll the chair forward. "I gave up long ago. It's an exercise in futility."

"Wait, wait," I said, following them. "He means the donkey."

The old man's eyes met mine again and I thought I'd guessed right. Then they danced away to the buffet table. "Piglet," he said.

"The singing donkey is fine," I told him. "I'm taking good care of him. His name is Bocelli."

"Fred Astaire on the ceiling fan," Dr. Roxton said.

I looked up but there were no ceiling fans in the room.

"Ivy, you're wasting your time," Beverly said. "I need a cup of tea to soothe my throat. Being a soloist is more stressful than I expected, especially in that wind tonight."

"Big wind," the old man said, and then blew a raspberry.

It was all I could do not to laugh, wondering if the vet was calling his daughter-in-law a windbag. Perhaps Beverly wondered, too, because she gave the wheelchair a sharp little shove that almost knocked over a lady with a walker.

"Rude," I whispered, looking down at Keats. "It's not his fault he has memory loss, and he might understand more than she thinks."

The dog was staring after them, ears forward, tail down. He didn't like Beverly either. It wasn't the best advertisement for their vet practice, but everyone loved Cliff Roxton and he was wonderful with pets. A real chip off the old block, it seemed.

"I would have expected Cliff to marry someone who loves animals," I said, as we moved through the crowd. "Then again, Kellan is no big fan and I have over fifty of them. At least he's kind."

I put my hand on my chest and sighed. Sometimes when I thought about Kellan I got a pang in my heart—as if there wasn't enough room in there to hold my feelings. I'd frozen my emotions for more than a decade and had to thaw them again. Hopefully time would take care of everything.

Keats nudged my hand and I realized I had stopped moving, lost in my thoughts.

"Right, who's next, buddy?" I blinked a few times under the fluorescent lights and then allowed him to herd me to a resident sitting alone at the side of the room. She was nearly as well dressed as Hazel Bingham, but her short frizzy white curls looked like they gave her a fight every day.

"What a lovely performance," Martha Kincaid said, after I introduced myself and Keats. "You and that donkey are wonderful together."

"The choir started out as a culture raising activity but I'm afraid it's turned into a farce because of me," I said.

I offered to get her some food but she shook her head and nodded at the empty seat beside her. Keats gave a swish of the tail to encourage me.

"The world is better for some humor," Martha said. "Clover Grove takes itself far too seriously these days. It wasn't like that when I was a girl. I'm not saying it was perfect. Far from it. But nowadays, there's more interest in what goes wrong than what goes right." She caught my eye and winked. "I probably don't need to tell you that, do I now?"

"No, Martha, you do not. I provide endless material for the rumor mill, which I know from Hazel Bingham functions very well in here."

"Oh my, yes," she said. "I miss Hazel. She was a voice of gentility and reason. But I'm happy she was able to go home." She knotted her hands and sighed. "My children and grandchildren are scattered around the globe I'm afraid, and I wanted to stay close to my roots. So here I am, making the best of it. It's better than being alone."

"You spent your whole life in Clover Grove?" I asked. "Then you must have known our original choirmaster."

"Felix? Of course. And Vinnie, too, in case you're wondering, and I bet you are."

"Am I that transparent?" I laughed. "I must be losing my corporate edge."

"Like everyone else, I've heard about your exploits with this dog." She unknotted her hands and reached for Keats' ears. I held my breath, knowing he usually rebuffed strangers' advances. Tonight, he permitted the pat. "What a handsome boy. It feels like he looks right into your soul with that blue eye. I'd like to know what he sees."

"That's easy: he sees a good person. I can tell from his posture and his tail. You're getting a gold star from a very discriminating dog."

"What a relief. At my stage of life, you start looking at your past record and taking stock."

"Keats says you have nothing to worry about. But he also thinks you might know a little something about Felix and Vinnie that could help me put the matter to rest."

Her forehead creased into fine lines. "I don't know that I have more information than you'd hear from the grapevine. We lived down the road from the Swensons and Milloys. My father managed to stay on good terms with them for a long time. It wasn't always easy, what with the trespassers. People came looking for that so-called treasure and shots were fired. My father turned a blind eye unless the animals were at risk." After a moment, she added, "That's how he finally ran afoul of both Frank Swenson and Nathaniel Milloy, Felix's father. He didn't like the way they treated their livestock. One day Frank's cow and tiny calf wandered onto our property and my dad hid them in an old barn way out in the woods. Eventually Frank found them and things got ugly. The sheriff of the time had to intervene. I was scared, I can tell you. It was like the Wild West in those days. But eventually Frank and Nate got so caught up in their property dispute that they forgot all about my father."

"They were neighbors?"

She nodded, frizzy curls bobbing. "Their battle was so public and so vicious that I always wondered if Frank's so-called treasure was the contested land. If so, he couldn't move it because Nate and Felix guarded the perimeter. Finally my mom got her way and we moved into town. Dad opened a grocery store and boarded his animals elsewhere."

"When did the feud end?"

"Never. At least as far as I know," Martha said. "I think that's what drove Felix out of town. The feuding and bitterness. He had dreams of something more. After that, it seemed like some of the wind went out of Nate's sails. It's hard on a man to lose his son because of his actions."

"I had no idea," I said. "This town has plenty of secrets."

"Here's another one for you." She crooked her finger so that I'd lean in. "My father boarded his animals at Runaway Farm, many owners before your time. I've been on your land often, Ivy. It was well loved. A safe harbor for animals even then."

I smiled at her. "I can feel that at the farm despite all that's happened. Good feelings must have seeped into the soil. Perhaps you'd like to come out and see it again sometime."

"I would love that, if you can spare the time."

"I'll make time," I said, looking around for Keats. He was missing in action and had probably gone to collect Percy. "My best friend is going to turn the inn into a Christmas wonderland."

"You are every bit as sweet as your grandmother. She was a lovely woman and we did a lot of charitable work together. Always laughing at one thing or another."

"Huh." I looked across the room at my mother, who had gathered half a dozen male residents. Her gestures suggested she was imparting the secrets of the straight edge shave. "Mom said her parents were totally boring."

Martha laughed. "Well, Dahlia was born in the worst electrical storm this county has ever known. Many of us wondered if your poor grandmother got a little zap during labor."

I laughed out loud as Mom made slashing motions at her throat and the old men leaned away. "That sounds about right," I said. "Thanks for solving at least one mystery for me, Martha."

CHAPTER THIRTEEN

E arly the next morning, I took my second cup of coffee into the family room to enjoy a few quiet minutes "surveying my domain." That's how Jilly described my habit of standing beside the ceramic town Mabel Halliday, from Miniature Mutts, had made. It had been on display in her store and included a replica of my farm when some of my new friends bought the whole town for me. Mabel kept adding to it when she could, and gradually the various neighborhoods and even the outskirts were filling out. Each little building was snow-capped and easily recognizable, from the various sweet churches to the post office and civic buildings. Mine had been the only farm but now half a dozen sat around the perimeter. Several had popped up when I wasn't paying attention. That would be Daisy's doing. She wouldn't leave unopened boxes lying around and she'd also know exactly where to place everything.

"I don't know what to do next," I told Keats. "If you've got big ideas, don't hold back."

He mumbled a question to me. Sometimes we just had to poke around until he smelled, heard, saw or sensed something. I didn't know what triggered his discoveries but a drive often helped.

"Okay, we'll go into town after breakfast," I said. "Maybe stop at

Mandy's and see what she knows. All we need is a few crumbs, right? Like a gingerbread trail."

Keats gave a little yip that approved the plan.

Another member of my dream team had other ideas. Percy jumped directly into the ceramic display, somehow managing to avoid knocking anything over. At Thanksgiving he'd trampled a little man in the town square that just happened to be holding an open book on which Mabel had painted a golden treble clef. Jilly and I both thought the incident represented Felix Milloy's unfortunate demise. Another man had also been trampled, but the Swenson farm didn't exist in my ceramic world at the time.

It did now.

While I was running around, a rundown gray barn had found its way into the ceramic town. It might have been any farm, but the weathervane on the roof featured tiny painted pigs, just like Vinnie's. I studied the properties on either side. One had a red brick farmhouse with a blue door and a tiny gold knocker.

Percy picked his way through town to the outskirts and raised a paw.

"Don't you dare," I said. "This is a treasure map, Percy."

The cat stared at me with big green eyes, blinked twice, and then scraped invisible litter over the Swenson farm. Then he gently nudged the red farmhouse with the blue door.

"The Milloy homestead, I presume?"

Percy looked at me and blinked again.

"All right then. That's what we'll do. It's as good a guess as any."

"Does he answer back?" The voice in the doorway startled me. It was Bronwen, the obnoxious teen who'd released the emu. She didn't look so obnoxious now in her pink flannel pajamas. Daisy had taken her under her wing, to the obvious relief of her parents. Bronwen mostly chose to stay behind when the rest of her family toured the towns in hill country, so I guessed she appreciated having more structure, too.

"In a way," I said. "You need to know how to speak cat, and I'm still learning. Sometimes I can't tell whether he's a genius or a fool. Maybe both."

"And the dog?" Bronwen asked.

"Sheer genius." I smiled. "He doesn't even play like a regular dog. There's always work to be done. Sheepdogs need puzzles to solve."

"My mom won't let me have any pets," she said. "Allergies. Or so she says."

I nodded. "My mom said the same thing when I was young. Now I'm grown up and can have all the animals I want. You can too, someday."

She stared at me with big dark eyes that would be striking when she grew into them. "Your mom doesn't sneeze when she's here."

"True. Good observation." I gave her a wry smile. "She must have outgrown her allergies. No one lasts long on a farm with them."

"Well, my mom doesn't sneeze here, either." Her eyes dropped to Keats again and she asked, "Do all parents lie?"

I downed the last of my coffee and thought about my answer. "This is just my opinion, Bronwen, but I think *everyone* lies at some point or another. I worked in human resources for a big company. It was a bit of a shock at first to see how easily people skirted the truth. Later I realized how subjective the truth can be."

"Then who do you trust?" she asked.

Setting my cup down beyond the outskirts of my ceramic town, I crossed my arms. "You start by trusting yourself to know the good people. I can already tell you're observant. So you watch how people behave over time and that helps you develop good judgment."

The smirk she'd arrived at the farm with was gone. "That'll take *years*. How do I get through high school?"

I laughed and then caught myself. This was serious for her. "That's a tough one, no question. Honestly, if I were you..."

The big eyes were intent. "Yes?"

I looked over her shoulder to make sure we were alone. "I'd keep working on your parents for a pet. A non-shedding goldendoodle would be just the thing. If you have a dog, you won't care as much about other people. Trust me on that."

She shook her head. "They'll never say yes."

"Never say never. I'm going to make a bold suggestion. You could try earning it."

"Earning it! How?"

I grinned at her. "Only you know what's important to your folks. Is it good grades? Volunteering in your community? Cleaning the house? I can't give you the answer, but if you observe them closely, you'll find the sweet spot. Then you work the angles. And when you win, which I know you will, I've got the right dog breeder in mind to find your perfect match."

"Huh." She crossed her arms and nearly smiled. "You're kind of scary, but I like you."

"Ditto," I said, picking up my cup. "Let me know how things go."

Percy launched himself off the sideboard in Bronwen's general direction and she dodged with a little scream. "Hey!"

"You could have seen that one coming if you'd been paying attention," I said, heading into the kitchen. "So I repeat lesson one: Observe. And then observe some more."

I WAS HALFWAY down the lane in the truck with Keats and Percy in the passenger seat when I heard the roar.

"Seriously?" I said, looking in the rearview mirror. "Can't a gal sneak away once in a while?"

Pulling over, I let the ATV catch up and rolled down the window. "Morning, Edna. What's up?"

"Where are you three going?" she said, peering in at the pets.

"Just taking a drive. Doing our thing."

"Doing your *sleuthing* thing?" she said.

"Getting some fresh air and maybe a fresh perspective."

"Fresh air. What a great idea. I'm coming with you."

Before I could argue she pulled in front of me and parked the ATV in the bushes. I thought about driving off but worried she'd hoist herself into the bed of the truck or worse, hang onto the bumper and get dragged behind. Instead, I shrugged at Keats as Edna shooed the boys into the back seat.

"Where to today?" she said, rubbing her camouflage gloves together. "I smell adventure."

"I smell pine sap," I said.

"Just chopped down a tree in the bush and brought it home. My first Christmas tree in decades. Last night's performance got me feeling festive."

I laughed. "Well, that's a turnaround. You didn't arrive at Sunny Acres in a good mood."

"But I got to leave, you see. I'm alive and free and I'm going to enjoy every minute of it." She rolled down the window and pulled off her camo hat so that the wind could blow through her perm. "Even if it means following whatever nebulous lead these two threw in your path."

"Nebulous leads are our speciality," I said, turning onto the highway. "We're heading over to the old Milloy homestead."

"The Milloy place? Bad idea, Ivy. Bad idea."

"Percy and Keats said otherwise."

"Percy and Keats don't know Gertie Rhodes, the current owner, like I do. If you think I'm crazy —"

"I do."

"Well, Gertie's certifiable. Since her husband passed, she's shot three people."

I tried to gear up and stalled the truck instead. "Shot three people? Why isn't she in jail?"

"Because she didn't hit them. She grazed a couple of boots and claimed it was an accident."

"Oh my," I said, turning the key in the ignition. "Good thing I have you with me. Sounds like you and Gertie are kindred spirits."

"Gertie and I have nothing in common," Edna said. "I'm insulted in advance."

She sank into a disgusted silence that was almost as good as being alone, except that then I could chat freely to the boys. I was about to drive into town when the camouflage hand gestures began and she guided me wordlessly through back streets I'd never noticed before. At one point, she directed me into a farmer's field and down into a shallow creek. I got so nervous I stalled again. "Why am I in the water, Edna?" I said. "Are the roads not good enough for you?"

"I'm cutting fifteen minutes off our drive. Time is money, Ivy." She tapped her big watch that was probably meant for a man's wrist. "Now we need to subtract the minutes you sat here fretting about a foot of water. It's not like spring runoff. I'd never take a chance with you on that."

Sighing, I started the truck and gunned it up the bank. "Here I was hoping for a peaceful outing."

"Peaceful isn't in Gertie's vocabulary," Edna said. "The sooner it's over the better." After jabbing her finger at the entrance to a side road, she added, "I did think the creek would have frozen over by now. It's been so mild."

Our definition of mild certainly differed, but I focused on her haphazard jabbing. It was highly unlikely I'd find my way home via this route. If Gertie shot Edna, I'd have to use GPS.

"You're wearing steel toed boots, right?" I asked.

"Of course. I even had the presence of mind to wear my bulletproof vest this morning." She tapped my shoulder to get me to go left. "Maybe I'm turning psychic like you."

"I'm not psychic," I said. "If I were, solving these murders would go a lot faster."

"Woo-woo then. Communing with your pets is not exactly normal."

I gave her a look. "You commune with your cats, too. In case you need a reminder, Jilly filmed Asher carrying you through Huckleberry Swamp yelling at me to chat to your cats."

"She did not."

"Oh, she did. Some nights we just queue it up and watch it over and over, marveling over how times have changed."

She gave a few short sniffs through her nose, collecting herself. "I do the same with the video of you braying with that donkey. It's got about a billion hits already. Someone filmed last night, too."

"What? That's not fair to the Sunny Acres residents. What about their privacy?"

"One of the residents shot the video and uploaded it," she said. "Don't underestimate seniors, Ivy."

"I never underestimate seniors, Edna. You've saved my life twice now."

"That's very true." She sounded mollified. "However, I'm not your typical senior."

"Also true." I turned at her signal into a long lane that was probably very pretty in summer with its arching boughs that met overhead. Now, the branches looked skeletal under the gray sky—arms that tried to hold us in a bony embrace. Keats whimpered behind me and even Edna gave a little shudder.

"Some say this place is haunted," Edna said. "I never believed that but it sat empty for years after Felix's father passed. Gertie and Saul finally snagged it for a pittance."

"I'd say they lucked out," I said, as the skeletal branches released us into the parking area. The original farmhouse was exactly as it looked in my ceramic village, with red brick, a blue door and a gold knocker.

We didn't get a chance to try the knocker, because an old woman with a very long gray braid draped over the shoulder of her brown poncho came out onto the porch and aimed a rifle at us.

"Same old Gertie," Edna muttered.

"Get out of the truck," the woman yelled. "Hands where I can see them."

Did they really say that outside of movies? "Hi there," I called, opening the door and jumping down with my hands up. "I'm Ivy Galloway, and this is—"

"I know who you are and I know what you do," Gertie said. "Miss Do-Gooder. Miss Doggie Do-Right. Miss stick your snout where it doesn't belong."

"She's put a few killers behind bars, Gertie," Edna said as she jumped out and walked around the front of the truck. Her hands hung loose at her sides.

"You're just as nosy and reckless as this young fool, Edna. Give me two good reasons I shouldn't shoot off the soles of your boots right now."

"I only need one reason," Edna said. "I'd shoot you first, Gertie. You know I'm an excellent marksman and my reflexes are better than ever. I train every day."

"She does," I said. "I hear the beer cans pinging during target practice."

"Soda cans," Edna corrected. "Bet you're happy I stay sharp, Ivy, because I can ping off old Rapunzel here."

"Edna! We come in peace, remember?"

"I never agreed to that," Edna said. "I came for fresh air, but I'm afraid it still stinks out here."

Gertie tossed her long braid over her shoulder and it stretched to the back of her knees. Her legs and feet were bare under the poncho and I found myself hoping she was wearing *something*. Otherwise she was going to get quite a chill bickering with Edna.

"If you don't tell me why you're here in thirty seconds, I'm going to shoot out your truck windows, Doggie Do-Right," Gertie said.

"Fiddlesticks," Edna said. "Gertie, you're a vicious piece of work but I know for a fact you'd never shoot an animal. Ivy has two pets inside that truck."

The rifle's muzzle dropped a few inches. "Move over so I can shoot you both without hurting the dog."

"The window's open and my dog will defend me," I said. "You know that since you've been following my illustrious career."

"Is that how you want to go down, Gertie?" Edna said. "Wearing a poncho and nothing more? What a way to undermine your legacy."

The gun dropped to her side. "You've got a point, Edna. I need to think about my reputation." She let out a hearty laugh and beckoned with the rifle. "Let the pets out and come inside for a cup of tea."

Edna laughed, too, and I wondered if the whole thing was a skit they'd rehearsed in advance. When Gertie turned however, Edna bugged her eyes at me and whispered, "Crazy."

"What was that?" Gertie called.

"More tea, I said," Edna called. "I can never get enough."

I wanted to leave Percy and Keats in the truck but they'd already made their own decision and jumped through the open passenger window. They bounded up the stairs ahead of us and the white tuft of Keats' tail gave his resounding approval of Crazy Gertie. My breath had been coming in jagged puffs but evened out now. That was the problem with winter. The steam was a giveaway.

We followed Gertie and the animals inside. I'd expected a rough shack, but the place was lovely. The upholstery on the furniture was tasteful, the rugs understated and the oak accent tables elegant.

Gertie smirked at me. "Never judge a woman by her poncho, Ivy."

"Or her braid," Edna added. "You could trip over that thing if you're not careful. That's another way not to go, if you ask me."

"I didn't ask you. I stopped asking you anything when you cackled like a maniac that day in Doc Grainer's office. I'd never seen someone take such delight in a routine vaccination. I said to my Saul, Edna's crazy. Like you said about me just now."

"And neither of us is wrong," Edna said, laughing. "Isn't it grand?"

I looked down at Keats to double-check his assessment. His ears, ruff and tail said all systems go. I trusted him, but I still didn't like being trapped in here with Gertie one bit.

Edna and I sat at the kitchen table beside sliding glass doors. On a shelf to one side sat binoculars and night vision goggles. I couldn't help grinning. Edna used the exact same equipment to spy on me.

"What's so funny?" Gertie asked, setting her rifle on the counter as the kettle heated up.

"Edna has binoculars and night vision goggles at her place, too," I said.

"I never said she was stupid," Gertie said. "Just crazy. And also sadistic."

Edna chuckled. "Says the woman who shoots off boots."

"I have a right to protect my land from trespassers," Gertie said. "Unfortunately, that's a full-time job. I never would have allowed Saul to talk me into buying this place had I known it would be crawling with treasure hunters all the time."

"Still?" Edna said. "Old myths die hard."

"After Felix Milloy came home they showed up in droves. I suppose everyone figured he planned to claim the booty himself and people got desperate. I mean, coming here in broad daylight when I'm a known hazard?"

She cackled in much the same way Edna probably had in the doctor's office.

"Did you see Felix on the property?" I asked, as Gertie carried a teapot to the table.

"Oh yes. Him I didn't want to shoot, since it's his childhood home and all. I know how sentimental people get about that. So I called your boyfriend instead. Felix heard the sirens and left before the cops got here. He knew the back roads, like most of us lifers."

"Who else?" I asked. "I'm trying to help Kellan—"

"The chief doesn't need your help, Doggie Do-Right," she said, pouring tea into mugs and offering cream and sugar. "He was keeping the town safe enough until you came back."

"You had trespassers long before my time. Like Vinnie Swenson, I bet."

"Vincent was a regular," she said. "I left him alone, too, because he was crazier than we are." She flicked her index finger between Edna and herself. "We're just eccentric, but he was evil. I don't say that lightly." She pulled her braid around again and it dropped heavily like one of the big pythons I'd met in the dead dogcatcher's basement.

"Evil?" I asked, sipping my tea. "How so?"

"He was cruel to his animals. Starved them. Maybe worse." She sighed. "Like Edna said, I have a soft spot for animals. Used to break my heart to hear that donkey wailing. That's one place I'm glad you interfered, Ivy. I heard the roundup was impressive, Edna. Kudos."

Edna smiled and raised her mug of tea. "Cheers, Gertie. To the bad old days."

"To the bad old broads," Gertie said, clinking her mug against Edna's.

After they had their moment, I asked, "Who else have you seen poking around lately?"

"The Langman sisters, of course," Gertie said. "Treasure hunters like none other. Their dad had a tiff with Frank Swenson, like a lot of men of that era." She sipped her tea and added, "There was another woman. Looked like Beverly Roxton, which kind of surprised me. Plus a younger woman with a blonde ponytail who was stupid enough to wear heels. She's down one stiletto now." She added more sugar to her tea and cackled. "One man in a balaclava comes at night. Can't place him. And then there's the usual collection of boys who are probably better off running from me than playing computer games." She rubbed her eyes with her free hand. "That's all been in the past two weeks, since Felix came home."

"You've kept the police in the loop?" I asked.

"More or less. Normally I prefer to handle things myself but I tire more easily these days." She sipped her tea. "Don't let that get around, please."

"You need to be careful, Gertie," I said. "I hope the police are patrolling."

"This will settle down soon enough," she said. "Felix's homecoming made skeletons rise from the graveyard and start shaking moneybags."

"I hope someone just finds the Swenson treasure so all this can stop," I said.

"Me too, as long as I get a cut of what's on my land. The longer it goes, the more reckless they get." Gertie picked up her braid and examined it. "Guess I'd better set up some beer cans and practice."

"I'll join you one sunny afternoon," Edna said. "You can tape my face on the cans."

"I'd like that very much," Gertie said. "Bring Ivy and the chief along and I'll let them choose the fir of their Christmas dreams."

"Lovely," Edna said. "I should have waited for mine because you have some gorgeous blue spruce back there." She caught herself. "Or so I've heard."

"Edna, you sly fox, I know full well you've been by a few times over the years with a metal detector. I let it slide because I knew you'd split the booty with me if you found it."

"You can have it all," Edna said. "I just like the thrill of the hunt."

"Then get out there and finish the job, for pity's sake."

"After our target practice," Edna said. "And please let me snip that braid off for you. Be sensible, Gertie. Someone could strangle you with that thing. Is that how you want to go? It's time to think about that, old girl."

"Oh, I have," Gertie said. "I want to die rolling after a zombie on my ATV."

"Me too!" Edna said.

The two octogenarians cackled in unison and gave each other a high five.

I looked down at Keats and shrugged. Growing old in Clover Grove wasn't what it used to be.

Now it was a lot more fun.

CHAPTER FOURTEEN

"I don't want to," Mom said, pouting, as I took her coat off a hanger in Bloomers, her salon, and handed it to her. "They're always so mean."

"That's why I need you," I said. "I'm no match for them but you always come out on top."

"Flattery will get you nowhere," she said, reluctantly sliding her arms into the sleeves.

"But that Dr. Zhivago coat will," I said, nodding to Iris and steering Mom to the door. "You're the envy of the entire choir."

"That's because of my voice not my coat," Mom said. "No matter what you girls say, I believe I can sing."

"Keep on believing. There's no harm in that."

Mom's stiletto boots clicked along the pavement, slowly at first, but the spirit of adventure soon quickened her pace. "Maybe I should try out for one of those TV singing competitions."

"Why not? If they recruit nearby, I'll drive you in Buttercup."

She looked up at me, hazel eyes narrowing. "What's going on? You're never this nice to me."

"That's not true," I said. "I'm always nice to you... when I need something."

"That's not true, darling. You're usually just as mean to me while you're using me for my many skills."

I smiled. "You're right, and it's not fair. I should always be nice when exploiting your skills."

"It's okay. The fact that you're acknowledging my skills now is enough, really."

"Aside from your singing, you're a talented woman," I said. "You deserve more credit."

"Everyone underestimates me." She pulled up her hood and straightened her shoulders. "I decided long ago not to let naysayers hold me back. Including my own children." She gave me a sly grin. "But it's lovely to surprise people occasionally."

I had to work hard to keep up with her without jostling Percy too much in his travel bag. Jilly had made carrying him look like a breeze but with Keats' leash in my other hand, I couldn't keep pushing the strap back up. There was a frustrated yowl from the bag. For a cat, Percy was a good sport, but I was reaching his limits.

"Could you slow down?" I said.

She sped up. "It's not my fault you travel with a menagerie. And it's cold out."

Mom had always walked like there were springs under her feet. It made her seem taller when she was scarcely five feet. We rushed past the stores on Main Street with their festive displays and I tried to take in the blur of lights and color. People had gone all out this year, in a blatant—and fruitless—effort to compete with Dorset Hills, the Christmas capital of the state. Still, it was nice to see the community spirit growing, and perhaps our tadpole of a town would turn into a princess one day.

"Just because it's nearly Christmas, I'll tell you that I was super impressed by how you handled our escapade at the yoga studio a while ago," I said. "Jilly couldn't have done any better. You outran Keats and Percy, even."

"I try to stay fit, darling. Aging isn't what it used to be, you know. Even in Clover Grove. I hope those homesteaders realize in time. So many seem content to let themselves go." She gave my battered parka, overalls and boots a significant look. "Present company included."

"I don't have time for the niceties. Between the guests, the farm work and choir, it's go-go-go."

"Go-go-go to seed," Mom said. "Chief Harper deserves more."

"I make an effort for the chief when I see him," I said. "He's busier than ever, with a double homicide. The mayor is pressuring him to get it sorted before Christmas."

"Understandable, but the man deserves to have a life." She gave me another sly grin. "To have a wife, perhaps."

"Mom. I really would prefer you stop putting the cart before the horse. Kellan and I are nowhere near anything like that." I sped up and got ahead of her. "I don't know why you're so invested in the idea of marriage. You were just complaining about how it didn't end well for you."

"It certainly didn't." She slowed just a touch. "I've been reflecting on how that impacted all of you."

"You mean scarred all of us," I said. "Except Asher."

"Asher, too," she said. "You were away during his wild years. He broke a lot of hearts and didn't seem to realize or care. Refused to listen to me, of course, but Daisy couldn't get through to him either. I am so grateful Jilly came along."

I nodded. "The right woman will make the golden boy shine even more."

She caught up with me and then passed me. Keats sped up, too. He was enjoying this new game, whatever it was.

"I often wish I could get a do-over," Mom said, over her shoulder. "Not with your father, but with how I handled his leaving."

I caught up with her again. "It was hard, I can't deny it. But I know getting left with six mouths to feed and no support was even harder."

"I tried not to sit around and wallow."

"You never did that." I laughed. "You were in constant motion. A moving target."

"I suppose I still am." She gave a little laugh, too. "That's the beauty of rotation, darling. I'll never get my heart broken again."

"I understand," I said, and the moment the words came out of my frozen lips, I did understand. My heart filled with compassion for the woman who'd always annoyed me. "And now you need to understand that I'll take things at my own pace with Kellan."

She blew out a gusty sigh. "Fine, but don't dawdle too long. He's a good man, darling. The best this town has to offer. My biggest worry is that you'll let him slip through your fingers because of my mistakes."

"Don't let my love life be your biggest worry," I said, trying to lighten the mood. "There's so much more to concern you in this town."

"I suppose. But it keeps me up at night thinking that you, Iris and Violet may never marry. Poppy is beyond help, I'm afraid."

"Mom, don't you dare give up on Poppy."

"I ruined her. She was a feisty, smart-mouthed rebel as a teen. Like that girl who's staying with you. The one who set the emu loose."

"Bronwen," I said.

"I was at the inn this morning and she followed me around staring at me. It was unnerving."

I couldn't help grinning. Bronwen had taken my advice to heart. "Poppy will be fine. She hasn't dyed her hair blue in a while and she's toned down her outfits."

"Thank goodness. I've offered many times to stitch some nice dresses together for her, but she doesn't appreciate my style."

"Yet many are jealous," I said, stopping outside The Langman Legacy, the antiques store owned by Heddy and Kaye. Their white van, with the grandfather clock painted on the side, was parked at the curb. "Watch for a little dig about your style from the sisters."

"So very frumpy, both of them," Mom said, tossing back her hood and fluffing her hair. "Am I spectacular?"

"What's better than spectacular?" I asked.

"Nothing, darling. That's as good as it gets."

She gave the door a sharp push and strutted inside.

"Not again," Kaye Langman called from behind the old oak counter that had been in the shop since her father's time. "Do I have to put a sign on the door with six Galloway women and a cross through it?"

Her sister Heddy gave a bitter laugh. I actually didn't blame them for disliking me. I had suspected them of murder twice before, and they knew it. I'd been wrong in the end, but that didn't mean they were innocent this time. Keats' ears, ruff and tail always gave the sisters a failing grade in the character department and it would only be a matter of time before we figured out what they'd done to warrant it. They both lost all sense when there was an elusive collectible in the vicinity.

"Darlings," Mom trilled. "Don't be like that. Anyone else might consider that a threat."

"Consider it a threat," Heddy said. "We'll say it's a joke. And it is funny. Ivy's the tallest and you're the shortest. You practically fit inside each other like Russian nesting dolls."

The same thought had crossed my mind but it annoyed me that they noticed it, too.

"What a lovely idea," Mom said, and I could tell she meant it. "We need a logo. Maybe your arty friend could do it, Ivy. The one with the"—she made a gesture with her hand—"the strange frock."

"Caftan," I said. "Teri Mason. I'm sure she could do a Galloway logo that the Langmans could deface. But we couldn't leave Asher out and I don't know what the police would say about graffiti like that."

"There they go, throwing their police connections around," Heddy said to Kaye. "Again."

"Darlings, we've gotten off on the wrong foot, today," Mom said. "I know everyone's still touchy about what happened with—" She faltered for real this time.

"The ballroom dancing situation," I said. "So many people were caught up in that unfortunate situation."

"Have you hung up your sequins for good, Dahlia?" Heddy asked, smirking. "Few could wear netting like you. You always make quite a fashion statement."

I gave Mom a significant look.

"Why, thank you, Heddy, darling. I'm thinking of holding seminars for the fashion-challenged as part of the Culture Revival Project. You two would be most welcome."

I unzipped the cat carrier and Percy slipped out. The Langmans were cat people and powerless to resist his charms. When he jumped on the counter, Heddy reached out to stroke his marmalade fluff and then drew her hand back as quickly. She wanted to continue her show of strength when we'd seen her at her weakest. The dance instructor had driven a wedge through the sisters, and their bickering had been heard up and down Main Street.

"Let's put that whole ballroom dancing experience behind us," I said. "I'm just glad I could help."

"Well, we did appreciate seeing the end of that chapter in Clover Grove's life," Kaye said. "We recovered most of our money, luckily."

She glared at Heddy, who glared back.

"Our father's antique safe was destroyed, though," Heddy said.

"Ancient history," Mom said. "Ivy and I were chatting on the way over about letting old slights go. We had a wonderful moment on Main Street, didn't we, darling?"

"We did," I said. "It's the magic of Christmas. You ladies have felt it at choir practice, I'm sure. Heddy, you have a lovely voice."

Mom's smile faded as she said, "Yes indeed. Lovely."

"I wish I could say the same for you, Dahlia," Heddy said. "Honestly, you're as bad as that donkey."

"Nothing's as bad as that donkey," Kaye said. "Ivy's turning the town into a laughingstock."

Keats' ruff rose a little more and his ears flattened. "It's okay, buddy," I said. "We're just doing as the mayor asked."

"I don't know what Meryl was thinking," Kaye grumbled.

"I suppose she's trying to bring good cheer," Mom said. "Everyone's so rattled right now. Two men have died and the killer is at large. Aren't you worried?"

"This will pass," Heddy said. "I'm sure the chief will get to the bottom of it. What motive has he found, Ivy?"

I shrugged. "He doesn't tell me much, I'm afraid. I'm left to speculate, and from what I've heard it may have something to do with an old dispute over ill-gotten gains."

Heddy and Kaye recoiled slightly. If I hadn't been observing closely I'd have missed it.

"Old disputes are a dime a dozen around here," Kaye said. "So many family feuds."

"This one would make a good movie, wouldn't it?" Mom asked. "Who would play your father?"

Kaye flushed bright red. "Do not speak ill of our father. He was a great, great man. One of the most notable historians and antiquarians in our state."

"All I heard is that your dad and Frank Swenson had a falling out over something valuable," I said. "That Frank swindled him, in fact."

Kaye looked too furious to respond, but Heddy nodded. "Our father paid Frank well for collectibles and he didn't deliver."

"Interesting," I said. "I also heard Frank buried the treasure on his property and people have been hunting for it ever since."

"That's a myth, I'm afraid," Heddy said. "I'm sure he sold those coins at a loss and—"

"Heddy!" Kaye's voice sounded strangled. "Leave the past in the past."

Percy had climbed to the top shelf where the Langmans stored their most valuable collectibles. Every night they locked them away. Every morning, they dusted or polished them lovingly and set them back out. Today, Percy gave a casual flick of his fluffy paw and sent a coin spinning into the air. There was a gasp and the sisters clawed madly to catch the coin as it fell. It hit the floor and rolled under an oak armoire.

They both started to come around the counter and I held up my hand. "Relax, ladies, I'll get it for you." I knelt and reached under the armoire till I found the coin and pulled it out. Turning it over, I let Keats sniff it and his blue eye told me this was an object of interest.

"Give it to me," Kaye said.

"Of course. Doesn't look like much to me," I said.

"Then you lack the eye for collectibles," she said. "Just as your mother lacks the eye for style."

She stomped back to Heddy, who held out a velvet bag. Kaye dropped the coin into it and Heddy slipped the bag into the cash drawer before closing it with a bang and twisting the key.

"I assume you've been looking for more of those?" I asked. "Out at the Swenson and Milloy properties?"

"What are you talking about?" Heddy asked, polishing the glass overlay on the counter rather vigorously.

"Just rumors," I said.

"You two are so distinctive," Mom said, smiling. "Unlike the Russian nesting dolls of our family. All just a chip off this old block." She tittered and struck a pose. "Not so very old, though, are we?"

"Never too old to treasure hunt," I said. "It fires everyone's imagination."

Kaye leaned on the counter and stared at me. "Ivy, you're the one with too much imagination and too little common sense. Here's a chance to turn that around."

"Turn around!" I said. It was a beat too late. Percy leapt off the shelf behind them, brushing Kaye's bristly hair and bouncing lightly off Heddy's rag. They both screamed.

"Darlings, don't strain your voices," Mom said. "We have choir tonight. Of course, I'd be thrilled to step in for the quartet if you're under the weather, Heddy."

"I'm sure Heddy will be in fine voice," I said, scooping up the cat.

"Yes, of course," Heddy said, too stunned to deliver a smart remark.

"Take good care of that cat," Kaye said. "He's gorgeous but a little too bold for his own good."

"Most of the time he's as good as gold," I said. "Something about this place brings out his mischievous side."

"Goodbye, darlings," Mom called as she sailed out the door. "You're both absolute treasures."

CHAPTER FIFTEEN

The new cat carrier came in handy that afternoon when I took one of the barn cats into the veterinarian's office for a suspected case of ear mites. The agrarian vet, Senna York, visited the farm at least twice a week, but there was more on my mind than itchy ears.

Dr. Roxton walked out to the waiting room with the cat and offered his cheerful smile. "Not a mite in sight, Ivy, but I trimmed his nails to make the trip worth your while."

"I'm always happy to see you," I said. "As long as I leave with healthy pets."

"And I'm happy to see someone who treats her barn cats like housecats," he said. "That's rarely the case, unfortunately."

"They're family," I said. "I want them to move inside but they refuse. Maybe Percy told them they're unwelcome." I looked down at Keats, whose tail swished for the vet. "The dog rolled out the red carpet."

"Keats, my boy, you're a prince," the vet said, and the white tuft shifted to high gear.

There was a loud sigh behind the counter. Dr. Roxton looked over my shoulder and said, "What's wrong, dear?"

I turned in time to catch Beverly Roxton's eye roll. "I find this talking to animals business a bit much. You should see how she carries on with the donkey."

"Bocelli," I told Dr. Roxton. "He's a good boy. A little too placid compared to my others."

"You had Senna York check him out?"

It spoke volumes that the two vets were respected colleagues, not rivals. They consulted often if they had a fur-patient in common. In Clover Grove, there was plenty of business to go around with homesteaders building their menageries almost as fast as I did. Dr. Roxton preferred to leave the livestock to Senna anyway.

"Senna says Bocelli's depressed," I said.

"Donkeys are smarter than anyone gives them credit for," he said. "He must have had a bond with—"

His wife cleared her throat conspicuously and glanced into the waiting room, where a teenager waited with a guinea pig in a cage.

"—his former owner," Dr. Roxton continued, unfazed. "Animals need time to adjust, even when their original home was—"

"Cliff," Beverly said. "The waiting room has ears. Furry ones, waiting for treatment."

He laughed. "True enough, dear. But I wanted Ivy to know how much I enjoyed the videos of her performance."

This time Beverly gave a huff that made the barn cat shift in the carrier. "I suppose it would be fun in a humor sketch, but this is our Christmas choir. It's irreverent. And ridiculous."

"It is ridiculous," I said. "You know the mayor put me on the hook, Beverly. It was a direct order."

"Well, I think it's hilarious and I love that you're so good to that poor donkey," Dr. Roxton said. "He obviously has a story to tell."

"Cliff, don't encourage her."

Her husband shrugged. "I've treated many a donkey and that's what they do when they're troubled."

"Sing?" I asked, smiling.

"They make noise, and plenty of it. It's hard on the ears, I grant you that, but donkeys deserve a voice, too."

"I agree with you, Dr. Roxton. I'd love to figure out what story he's telling. Then maybe he could settle in and enjoy the good life at Runaway Farm."

He patted my arm. "Just observe him constantly and he'll give you the signs. At least, that's how it works for me."

"Maybe he's just an attention seeker," Beverly said. "Some are never satisfied with being in the back row. They've got to shove themselves into the spotlight."

The topic had apparently shifted from the donkey to me. "I've never understood that," I said. "I far prefer flying under the radar but it's tough to do with a donkey on a rope."

"And a dog and a cat that you chatter with as if they can actually understand you."

"They can," I said. "I don't know about the donkey but the cat and dog understand me."

"The donkey can too, trust me," Dr. Roxton said. "You just need time to learn his language."

"That's exactly what I told him."

We both laughed and it just riled Beverly more. She got out of her seat and put her hands on her hips. "Clifford, that's enough."

"Dear, I'm allowed to share my opinions," he said, calmly. "And I happen to agree with Ivy. You might think differently after a good night's sleep."

"She's the reason I can't get a good night's sleep," Beverly muttered.

I raised my eyebrows. "The donkey act has you that upset? Maybe the mayor will let me off the hook if people are losing sleep over it."

"That's not what I'm talking about and you know it."

Now her husband was the one giving a pointed look at the

waiting room. The teen didn't even pretend not to eavesdrop. "Dear, let's drop it."

"You started it," she muttered.

I set the cat carrier on the counter and looked at her. "All I did was coordinate a choir at the mayor's command. You seem to enjoy it and you even got a solo."

"There's never been a moment's peace for any of us since you moved back to Clover Grove. We're all wondering who'll turn up next."

"Dear." Dr. Roxton's mild voice got a little louder. "You can't blame Ivy for that."

"I can and I do. Now there are creepers and lurkers. We've even found footprints in the yard. It's almost enough to make me want to get a dog."

Her husband's face brightened. "Yes! Let's."

"I said *almost*. If someone actually breaks in, we'll talk about it."

I put in a vote for Cliff. "Why wait till it's too late? I've never felt safer than after I got Keats."

Her glance would kill a houseplant. "You're hardly one to discuss safety. Always throwing yourself in harm's way and provoking murderers."

"Beverly, enough. You're not yourself."

She *was* herself, I was quite sure of that. He'd obviously deluded himself in order to live with her.

"Cliff," she said, softening her tone. "Nothing like this ever happened before Ivy came home."

"That's not true," he said. "My dad told me stories that would curl your hair."

She took one hand off her hip to wave it. "Oh, your dad. Can't trust a word he says."

"It wasn't always that way," Cliff said. Finally he grimaced. I could see she'd taken it too far, but she'd missed the line.

"Your father was very well respected," I said. "I've heard great things about him."

"Thank you." His kind eyes lit up. "I wanted to keep him at home with caregivers but it made Beverly too anxious."

"It would make anyone anxious," she said. "Plus it was draining our own retirement savings. Your father never could handle his money."

"Because he was always donating to rescue." Dr. Roxton beckoned the teen and directed her into an examination room. "I should visit more but Beverly says I upset him. I always feel so awful when I leave. It's like trapping a wild animal in a cage."

"If it helps, he seemed happy at Sunny Acres when I was there," I said. "Smiling and very pleasant."

"Thank you, Ivy," he said, walking into the examination room. "It's good to hear an outsider's perspective."

"An outsider is right," Beverly muttered after the door closed. "People who leave should stay gone. Like Felix Milloy."

Keats put his paws against the counter to get a closer look at Beverly and his ears went back. His tail stopped fluttering and stiffened. A warning to watch her words, perhaps.

I pulled out my old corporate smile. It was rusty but still ready for action. "Are you saying Felix *deserved* what happened? Just for coming back?"

"No. Not just for coming back." Her defiance was impressive. "Everyone knows he was up to no good."

"They do? How come I didn't hear about it?"

"Because you can't hear anything over that donkey's braying. The story is that he came back to collect on an old debt. Frank Swenson owed Felix's father money."

"I heard Frank owed lots of people money."

"Maybe, but only Felix knew where to find it. But then someone killed both Vinnie and Felix to get it."

"Interesting," I said. Did they find the money? Or did I miss the end of the story in the braying, too?"

She withered me again. "You think you're so funny. And you're not."

"My mom says exactly the same thing." I added a little twist to my smile.

"Do not compare me to Dahlia Galloway. Noted eccentric."

"Mom is definitely a character," I said. "Keeps us guessing."

Beverly sat down at her desk with a little thud. "She'll end up like Cliff's dad one day. Mark my words."

My HR shields continued to hold, which was impressive after all that had happened lately. As much as I'd hated my corporate life I'd gained some truly valuable skills.

I waited a couple of beats and then hit her with the surprise question. "Did you have any luck finding the treasure?"

Her faced flushed and she bent over the desk to hide it. "What are you talking about?"

"I heard you were out at the old Milloy place thrashing in the bush with all the teenage treasure hunters. If you found it, you could bring your father-in-law home."

She took a long, slow breath and when her eyes rose to meet mine, they were calm. "Wouldn't that be wonderful? But all I was doing was looking for the perfect Christmas tree, Ivy. Still haven't found that, unfortunately."

"Don't get yourself shot over it, Beverly," I said, slinging the strap of the cat carrier over my shoulder again. "No tree's worth that much. And we can't afford to lose a soprano."

Dr. Roxton came back out. "Dear, I need some—" He stopped. "What's wrong?"

"Nothing at all," Beverly said. "Ivy was just leaving."

"I do have one question for Dr. Roxton..."

"No more questions," Beverly said.

"Fire," he said.

"Can my donkey walk and sing at the same time? Because tonight we're going door to door."

He laughed full out and it was nice to hear. "I have a feeling that nothing will stop that donkey until he's done with his story."

"Only then will we have the heavenly peace we deserve," his wife said, gesturing to the door.

Keats stood up on his hind legs and gave her a lingering stare with his blue eye. When she shuddered, his mouth dropped open in a happy pant. Then he led me out with the tuft of his white tail waving gaily.

"I love a dog with a sense of humor," Dr. Roxton called after me.

"Me too," I said. "This one keeps me in stitches."

CHAPTER SIXTEEN

I had invited the Stout family to come caroling that evening but was relieved when they already had plans in Dorset Hills. What's more, I was grateful that Dog Town continued to be such a draw that they only came back for occasional meals. Bronwen typically stayed behind with Daisy, however, and the two were developing a bond. My sister had longed for a daughter but after the second set of twin terrorists, she'd understandably closed down for baby business. Hopefully she'd have a granddaughter one day. In the meantime, Bronwen was a good training ground.

The night was crystal clear and bitterly cold. There'd been very little snow since the tree lighting ceremony and I was fine with that. When push came to shovel, I preferred working on my manure pile to shaping snow drifts. At least there was an end goal with fertilizer.

Jilly and I swung by Edna's place in the truck and she waited outside the passenger door for her throne to be made available. Keats went through the seats grumbling and Jilly grumbled even louder as she got out, shivering.

"Buck up, Jillian," Edna said, climbing into the truck. She was wearing a rabbit fur wrap over her wool coat, and a matching hat. The scent of mothballs filled the truck instantly. "It gets mighty cold out here in hill country and you won't last if you let a breeze get you down."

"I see you've brought out your pelts," I said, as she settled in. "Did you snare those rabbits yourself, like Asher said?"

"Don't be silly," she said. "I raised them in a pen and then—"

"Never mind," I said, quickly. "Some things we don't need to know."

"Then don't ask."

Jilly poked through the headrest and turned Edna's collar. "Barkley's Emporium. The retired furrier."

"He didn't retire. He was forced out by tree hugging homesteaders," Edna said. "Most don't survive their first winter here, you know. The 'For Sale' signs go up with the spring thaw and then the next wave of fools moves in. If they embraced fur they'd find things more tolerable."

"Good in a winter bunker," I said. "No room for tree huggers there."

"Exactly." She stroked her wrap. "Plus, fur looks elegant and I wanted to make things special tonight. It's our first professional caroling outing."

"Professional? Is someone paying?" Jilly asked.

"Professional in the sense that we are taking ourselves seriously and making the rounds in town," Edna said.

I laughed. "How seriously can I take myself when I'll be leading a donkey who drowns me out?"

She switched on the overhead light and scrutinized me. "Ah. Makeup. Either Kellan's coming or you're getting ready for the phone cameras. I can hardly blame you for wanting your fifteen minutes of fame, I suppose. For some it's not enough to put killers away."

"I wish Kellan *were* coming," I said. "He'd keep the cameras down. But since he isn't, you can't blame me for wanting to look my best for the prying eyes of the online world."

Edna snorted. "I happen to know that's not your best. You're the most attractive of a good-looking clan." She glanced over her shoulder. "Aside from Asher, who got dropped by a very generous stork. And still he managed to bat out of his league."

Jilly laughed. "Well, thanks. I think. Ivy is stunning when she puts in a little effort. But all she ever puts in is a little effort."

"I like to surprise people. Fly under the radar and then BAM, it's Cinderella time." I shifted to take a quick look in the back. "What's wrong, buddy?"

"He's fine," Jilly said. "Just sitting here."

"Exactly. He's just sitting there. He's not trying to drive. He's not trying to unseat Edna. And he's not talking to me. Hence he is not fine."

Keats moaned softly and put one white paw on my shoulder.

"What's bothering him?" Jilly asked, squeezing Percy's carrying bag until he let out an indignant squawk.

"Not sure," I said. "Something's bothering him. He has a bad feeling. Or maybe he just doesn't want to get anywhere near Edna's rabbits."

"Good," she said. "We're in agreement. But I hope everything goes off without a hitch tonight. It's only two days till our grand performance."

"And yet we're nowhere close to figuring out who killed Felix or Vinnie," I said.

"I don't think you've been showing your usual hustle," Edna said. "Is that because it didn't happen on the farm?"

"I've been hustling," I said. "You don't know everything."

"Well, I know you and Dahlia got Heddy Langman in such a twist she called in sick for choir. There's no malingering on my watch, however. If she doesn't come out tonight, she doesn't get to sing for the mayor, either."

"She didn't seem any more upset than usual when we were questioning her," I said. "It's old news by now."

"Maybe she's actually guilty this time," Jilly said.

"I always assume so and then I'm disappointed," I said. "I guess that sounds weird. I never *want* someone to be guilty, I just want the rest of us—and our animals—to be safe."

Keats mumbled something comforting and it was a relief to hear his commentary.

"Maybe Keats is worried you took Beverly's rant too seriously today," Jilly said.

"Ivy knows better than to take cranks seriously," Edna said. "Look at the practice she had with me."

"My early visits with you were excellent training," I said. "I dreaded and welcomed them at the same time." I started to pat her pelts and pulled my hand back. "No offense."

"None taken. I was a different woman then. We both were." Keats put his paw on Edna's shoulder and mumbled something else. "Exactly. We're warriors now. All of us."

"If I'd ever imagined myself as a warrior—and I didn't—I wouldn't have pictured the donkey." I slowed the truck and started looking for a huge parking spot. "Fate seems to enjoy having a laugh at my expense."

"We all do," Edna said. "Isn't that right, Keats?"

He gave a noncommittal grunt, clearly not in the mood for humor.

"At least he's talking again," Jilly said.

"And better yet, Edna is having a chat with him," I started backing the trailer into a spot and fishtailed, as usual. "I knew she'd break down eventually."

"I was going to offer to park for you," Edna said, smoothing her coat. "Now maybe I won't."

Flipping on the hazard lights, I said, "I surrender to your greater skills, Edna."

"Well, since you put it that way..." She was out of the vehicle and charging around the front in a second.

"Be careful tonight, Ivy," Jilly said, before I got out of the truck. "If Keats is worried, I'm worried."

"I will, I promise." I turned in my seat. "It's just caroling. What could possibly go wrong?"

We both burst out laughing and Keats relaxed enough to happy-pant along with us. It only lasted a moment before the driver's door opened and Edna hauled me out of the truck.

"This is no time for merriment, you two."

I managed to land on my feet despite her rough handling. "I would think caroling was the perfect time for merriment."

Keats jumped out after me, and Jilly came around the back with Percy in his bag.

"That just proves you know as little about show choirs as driving a truck," she said, climbing in with a flourish of fur.

"A show choir? Seriously?"

"In case you hadn't noticed, we're really quite good," she said. "And here I thought I knew this town inside and out. Never too old to be surprised."

I watched as she turned the wheel this way and that until everything slipped neatly into the parking spot. There was only room for a breath between the trailer and the curb, yet plenty of space to unload the donkey.

As we walked to the square, Jilly and I somehow managed to link arms despite juggling the cat, dog and donkey. It seemed like the right way to start an old-fashioned caroling outing. There were more lights on the Main Street stores than I had ever seen, and it was the same down every side street. Unlike Dorset Hills, where Council mandated clear lights only, Clover Grove was a riot of color. I liked it that way. Mind you, we only had clear lights at Runaway Farm due to Jilly's preference for simple and tasteful. Left to my own devices, the lights would be purple, pink and blue. Showy.

The square was full of carollers chatting and laughing in small groups. Everyone fell quiet as we joined them. All eyes turned to Bocelli, the unwitting and unwelcome star. There were more than a few scowls, which told me that Beverly and Heddy had been stirring things up over *my* stirring things up. I looked down at Keats and his ears, ruff and tail were all in neutral position. There was no immediate threat here.

Edna got straight to business by hopping onto a bench and waving for attention.

"You know the playlist and I hope you memorized all the verses," she said. "I don't want anyone to slip on ice while reading lyrics. Consider yourself warned that we will step over you and carry on. Including the donkey."

Everyone laughed. They thought she was joking. She may in fact have been joking. You never knew with Edna. What I did know is that people never used to laugh on her cue. This choir had gone a long way in a short time to launder her reputation. There was so much discord in town that beautiful harmonies were very welcome. If only we could hang together so well all the time.

We settled quickly after another shout from Edna. With a dramatic sweep of her arm, she led us out of the square singing Deck the Halls. Jilly and Percy were at the front with Beverly and the rest of the sopranos, the altos followed, and our two bass gentlemen brought up the rear, followed, of course, by Keats, Bocelli and me. Since I was on strict orders not to open my mouth until my big moment, I had the pleasure of listening to the voices and taking in the sights. Tilting my head back, I saw the sky had filled with clouds that started spitting flakes of snow. Someone must have placed an order for the perfect night for caroling.

Edna had mapped out a route that would take us up and down the prettiest streets with the most prominent citizens in the town's core.

"Everything okay, buddy?" I whispered, as we trailed after the choir.

He looked up at me with his eerie blue eye and his tail dropped. If he mumbled an answer I couldn't hear it. But it was enough of warning that I looked around to make sure no one was following us.

I was shocked to find quite a large crowd following us. With the music and the clacking of hooves, I hadn't noticed. As we carried on, more and more people ran out of their homes to join us. Many sang along, which brought down the quality of sound but raised the good feeling. I shook my head and smiled over all that had changed since last year, when Jilly and I played rock 'n' roll Christmas tunes and congratulated ourselves over avoiding all that was saccharine about the holiday.

"We were missing the point, Keats," I murmured. "Community is the point. Raising your voices together is the point." Mom's horrendous bellow rose over the rest and I snorted. "Family is the point, for better or worse."

Keats' tail rose a little but it was clear something was still bothering him.

We walked up a long curved driveway and stopped in front of the double front doors of a grand house. The doors opened and Mayor Martingale came out with her husband.

After leading a stellar version of Joy to the World, Edna called out, "Ivy! It's showtime."

I glanced at Bocelli. "You ready for your close-up, my friend?"

Sure enough, hands started rising in both the choir and the crowd behind us.

Bocelli and I were set to perform our usual, but on a whim I started singing the *other* version of Joy to the World—the one by Three Dog Night. When I belted out "Jeremiah was a bullfrog," Bocelli threw back his head, gnashed his teeth and then let out a bawl that startled even me.

Every face in the choir looked horrified except Jilly's. She was grinning from ear to ear. Mom raised a red leather glove and snapped to silence me. But the crowd behind us had a different opinion. When I reached the chorus, they joined in, singing "Joy to the fishes in the deep blue sea, joy to you and me."

That raised the bar for Bocelli and he screeched and groaned along. It was hard to know if he was happy or sad or a little of both. But he was donkey-full of emotion that had to come out.

When we were done, the applause was louder than the song. I laughed and patted the donkey's horse blanket.

The mayor was laughing, too. She said something to her husband and he went inside as the quartet stepped out to perform O Holy Night and then Silent Night.

After that, Edna let everyone take a break. The mayor and her husband moved through the choir offering gingerbread from red boxes we'd all come to know from the Secret Santa. No one took a cookie except Edna. Most people were probably worried about drying out their throats. When the mayor offered the box to me, however, I happily selected a gingerbread tree. I never got tired of Mandy's cookies. These were a little fancier than the others, befitting the town's leader. They were sandwiched back to back with a layer of thick, gooey filling in between.

Meryl raised hers to mine and said, "Cheers."

My mouth opened and I was about to take a bite when a black and white missile launched from the pavement and knocked the cookie right out of my hand. The mayor and her husband gasped. Keats had never done something so blatantly rude in polite company before. He was not a mooch, let alone a thief, even of cookies this good.

When I looked down, however, he wasn't eating the cookie. It was lying in the light film of snow. Percy darted out between many boots and began covering the cookie with his paw as if it were something noxious in his litter box. I was just beginning to digest what was happening when Bocelli raised his left front hoof.

"Percy, move," I said.

The donkey brought his hoof down hard on the cookie, crushing it completely.

Everything became clear to me in an instant, and I yelled, "Edna, Meryl! Drop the cookies!"

I couldn't see if Edna did but Mayor Martingale certainly listened, and when her cookie hit the snow, Bocelli walked over and dealt that one a death blow as well. Percy moved back in to cover the crushed cookies with snow and invisible litter.

Pulling out my phone, I called Kellan.

CHAPTER SEVENTEEN

"**P**oison!" Mom had said the word half a dozen times since she arrived during breakfast, and with each repetition I reminded her calmly that we couldn't know that for sure until the toxicology reports came back.

I had no doubt it was true, however. My animals were faster than any lab. In time, Kellan would confirm that Edna, the mayor and I nearly bit the big one. Those gingerbread crumbs were laced together with something intended to do serious harm. Presumably the mayor and her husband were the intended targets of the toxic treats. The sick Secret Santa wouldn't have expected her to share them with a crowd of carollers. Or perhaps the poisoner didn't care. Maybe this was a statement about Christmas in Clover Grove. I could see that tying choirmaster Felix to the motive, but not Vinnie Swenson.

My guests, the mayor's family, were very quiet. They let Mom do the heavy lifting with the panic and she was happy to seize the baton. I did notice that she'd taken time to put on her favorite red knit dress and match her accessories accordingly. When she was truly rattled she looked it, so some of this was just drama. Jilly looked across the table at me and raised her eyebrows to show she knew that, too. Mom's act didn't bother Keats, however. He followed her up and down with Percy as she clicked across the hardwood from dining to family room and back.

Finally Mom slowed and snapped her fingers. "I need coffee, darling. I'm parched."

"Of course you are," I said, pouring her a cup from one of the thermoses. "It's all that hyperventilating."

"Not to mention the singing last night. It's very drying, particularly in cold weather." She went to her purse and pulled out a compact. "I worry about my complexion with these outdoor performances."

"Maybe there won't be any more," I said. "Kellan might call off the final show, depending on what he finds."

"He can't!" Mom and Jilly said together so loudly Bronwen jumped.

"If he thinks people aren't safe, he'll need to," I said.

"That was an isolated event," Mom said. "Someone obviously wanted Meryl—"

"Mom! Get a grip on yourself. My guests are traumatized enough. The mayor is Bill's sister."

"It's all right," Bill said. "Meryl speaks very highly of the chief of police and I'm sure he'll get to the bottom of this situation shortly."

Mom started pacing again. "Kellan could probably use some help, Ivy. How about less barn work and more leg work? I am available if you need backup."

"I always need extra hands in the barn," I said, grinning. "That's why I hired Poppy part-time. She's down there now with Charlie, if you'd care to join them."

Bronwen looked down at Mom's favorite faux crocodile pumps and smirked.

Mom saw the look and smirked back. "You'd be surprised what I can accomplish in heels, young lady. Tell her, Ivy."

As if I'd tell a 13-year-old about trespassing at a crime scene with Mom. For some reason, the kid looked up to me. It didn't happen that often and I wasn't going to ruin it.

"My mom is very good in heels," I said. "Jilly too. They're like movie star spies."

"I'd rather wear boots," Bronwen said, sticking out a Doc Marten lace-up.

"Oh, me too, obviously," I said. "But there's much to be said for heels. People start looking at your footwear and stop noticing what you're doing."

Bronwen grinned and tapped her temple. "Got it."

"There's still time for you to learn how to work a nice pair of stilettos," I said. "I'm past that now, and even in boots, I take some terrible pratfalls."

"So true," Jilly said. "I tried to sell her on heels in college and she wouldn't hear of it."

"One of my biggest regrets," I said, grinning at Bronwen. "I was very stubborn back then."

"I can attest to that," Mom chimed in. "Oh, how I tried to convince her of the power of heels. Of all my girls, only Violet shines in stilettos."

Daisy stood in the kitchen doorway and shrugged. "The rest of us developed other skills. We've done okay for ourselves."

"Of course, Daisy, darling. Don't be so touchy. There's not a better housekeeper on the planet. You didn't get that from me."

"I did, though," Daisy said, grinning. "Because you wouldn't do it, I had to learn."

Bronwen's mother and older sister listened to us banter with apparent fascination. Their family probably didn't bicker this way. It may not have been the finest example to set, but Bronwen needed to find a way to communicate with her family somehow before the rift grew too wide. Even smart aleck banter served a purpose. We Galloways clashed all the time but we understood each other. Every family had—or should have—its own secret language. A way to get things out while doing the least damage. Bottled up feelings tended to backfire dangerously, as I had good reason to know.

Keats went to the front window and stood up on his hind legs.

"Kellan's here," I said.

"How can you tell?" Bronwen asked.

"Observe," I said. "What do you notice about the dog?"

"His ears are up and forward. His tail is wagging."

I nodded. "It's all in the wag. See how fast it's going? That says 'fun.' Keats loves herding Kellan."

"Like a sheep?" she asked.

"Or a goat, or a cow or even a pig," I said. "Keats loves herding almost anything, but nothing more than Kellan."

"Does Kellan like it?" she asked.

I looked at Jilly and we both laughed.

"He does not," Mom said, before we could answer. "It's a disrespectful way to treat the chief of police."

Keats looked back at her and his mouth dropped open in a happy-pant.

"Did he just roll his eye?" Bronwen asked. "The blue one?"

"Bronwen," her mother said. "It's just a dog."

"Oh, he's not an average dog, Mrs. Stout," I said. "This border collie keeps me safe and helps so much with my anxiety."

Mom started to speak and I cut her off. "Mom, how about some more coffee?"

Bronwen took the hint and started to work on her Mom. "I'd feel safer if we had a dog. Especially after what just happened to Aunt Meryl."

"We don't know what happened to your aunt yet," Bill said. "Let's not worry unless the chief says it was poison."

"It was poison," I said, as Kellan stepped into the house.

"How do you know?" Bronwen asked. "He hasn't said anything."

"Look at his eyebrows," I said. "Drawn and low. Shoulders hunched. No smile."

Now Kellan added a scowl. "Why is everyone studying my posture?"

"Now look at the dog's," I added. "I've mentioned he likes to play with Kellan but what is he doing?"

"Circling him. Panting. Like he's worried."

"Exactly! Impressive," I said.

Kellan shook his head. "Sorry to interrupt this lesson in reconnaissance but I've just come from Mayor Martingale's house and she'd really appreciate some company right now."

Bill jumped to his feet. "Of course. I take it the cookies were spiked with something."

"All I can say is that we've issued a recall on Secret Santa cookies. We have officers and volunteers going door to door through the town."

Daisy went into the kitchen and came back carrying two boxes in her rubber-gloved hands. Everyone flinched as she walked toward Kellan except Jilly, Bronwen and me.

"It's okay, they aren't toxic," I said.

"And you know that *how?*" Kellan said.

Bronwen raised her hand. "Because Keats wouldn't let Ivy get near them. And Percy would treat them like—"

"Bronwen." Mrs. Stout's tone was crisp. "Go get ready. We need to be with your aunt."

"I want to go with Ivy," Bronwen said. "And Jilly and Keats and Percy."

This time I took the other side. "Your family needs you today, kiddo. Besides, Keats, Percy and I are going out with the chief for a bit."

"Ivy," Mom said, "your family needs you today."

"Dahlia," Jilly said, "I need you today. And Ivy needs Kellan."

Mom's lips pursed in a red pout. "But—"

Jilly did as good a job as Keats in cutting the herd and directing all of us where we needed to go. As Daisy took over driving the Stout family upstairs to get ready, Jilly brought my parka and boots from the back door.

"I'm trusting you with this, Ivy. It's not easy for me," she said.

"I know. But I have Kellan with me. It'll be fine."

"This is really, really important. I cannot overstate that," Jilly said, slipping the yellow parka on Percy.

I trapped Keats in a corner and wrestled him into his coat while he flopped around like a slick seal. "I have support," I reminded Jilly. "I have my cell phone. I promise it's going to be fine."

Kellan took off his black hat and ran his fingers through his hair. "I'm getting nervous here, ladies. I don't like surprises. What exactly are we tackling today, Ivy? Do I need to call for backup?"

I shook my head, grinning. "I suppose I should have clarified that it's *boyfriend* Kellan I need on this important mission. Not Chief Harper."

His smile appeared for the first time that day. "Well, that's different. Although it's not exactly the best time for a date." He squeezed my arm through the parka. "I mean, I always enjoy a date, but there are cookies to worry about."

"This is where the grapevine comes in handy," I said. "I bet there are red boxes sitting outside waiting all over town. How about we collect some killer gingerbread when we've completed this important mission?"

"Deal," he said. "I can actually enjoy myself knowing that."

"Don't lose sight of the goal, though," Jilly called after us as we walked down the front stairs. The cat and dog were racing toward the police SUV. "This is a critical mission."

We were on the highway before Kellan asked, "How long are you going to keep me in the dark?"

"Just trust me," I said. "You're going to enjoy this. It's super romantic."

Kellan sometimes complained that I was less romantic than him and he wasn't wrong. Although he took his job very seriously, he was more skilled at shutting it off to focus on what we were doing. That was tough for me. I was always worrying about the animals, the inn or my family. There was never a time I *didn't* have something to worry about and it was hard to relax and be in the moment. I liked to think I was improving but there was a way to go yet.

"I'm all for romance, you know that," he said. "But a double homicide with the threat of more is stealing some of my buoyancy."

"I know. Me, too. But I have to keep up the front for everyone else." I glanced at his handsome profile as he drove through town. It was nice just to have someone else drive for a change. With Buttercup out of commission from the cold, plus the responsibility of pulling the donkey in the trailer, I was under even more pressure to manage the truck. I'd been doing pretty well, but it was just one more thing to stress over. "Can you tell me about the poison now?"

His lips formed a thin line but then he said, "Yew."

My face furrowed. "Me what? Me nosy?

"You nosy, for sure," he said, grinning. "Yew is also the toxin."

It took me a second to put the puzzle pieces together. "The bush with the pretty red berries?"

He nodded. "The bark and the seeds are the problem. Someone ground them up and added them to the filling in the cookies. It only takes a little to cause fatal heart arrythmias. The lab has confirmed that as the cause of death for Vinnie Swenson and Felix Milloy."

"I've seen plenty of yew in Clover Grove," I said. "It's nearly as popular as holly and mistletoe. Even with the risk to livestock and pets. And children, of course."

"I doubt many people realize how dangerous they all are. They don't have our early expertise." He glanced over at me and smiled. We'd learned a fair bit about plants during the many hours we spent in the privacy of Clover Grove Gardens during high school. One of us may have studied botany in college had our breakup not ruined us for plants. I still had bitter flashbacks when I smelled cut flowers but Kellan was steadily desensitizing me by bringing fresh bouquets.

"Isn't it funny how the plants most associated with Christmas are all toxic?" I asked. "Even poinsettias and fir trees."

"That is odd and just plain wrong," he said, following my hand signals as we left town and kept going. "Do you mind telling me where we're going now?"

"Still a surprise," I said, hoping I could navigate to our destination on regular streets, rather than the maze of trails. "In the meantime, I presume poor Mandy McCain is shut down for business again."

"Yeah, and at her busiest time of year. I'm sure we'll find she had nothing to do with this, but we need to search her kitchens at the store and at home."

"Everyone's been buying her gingerbread cookies in bulk," I said, pointing left down a dirt road. "Especially since the tree lighting ceremony in town square. It was like the cookie symbolized the revival of Christmas in Clover Grove."

"Ironic, again." He turned down the road and then frowned. "We're getting too close to the Swenson farm for my liking, Ivy. I'm sure you have some key messages prepared about why we're here."

"Of course I do. No HR rep worth her salt would come into a situation like this unprepared." Pointing to the lane to the old Milloy place, I said, "We're taking Gertie Rhodes up on a very kind offer."

He slowed before turning into her lane. "I've never heard a kind offer come out of Gertie's mouth, Ivy. In fact, she's toxicity in human form."

"She liked Keats and Percy, so she's not all bad."

"And you discovered this when you were secretly interrogating her?" he asked, moving toward the house at a glacial pace. "Gertie's erratic to say the least. I've fined her several times for shooting at people and confiscated her firearms. They replenish like magic."

"She aims to miss," I said. "People come onto her land at night sometimes and she's scared."

"That's the only reason she's not behind bars. I can't believe you're defending her." He pulled up in front of Gertie's house and turned to give me the full force of his intense stare. "Care to explain?"

"She's like Edna," I said. "All crusty on the outside and sweet on the inside."

"We've just established that sweets can carry terrible poison. You'd better chew very carefully."

I squeezed the hand that was still on the wheel. "It's all good, Kellan. Like I said, Keats and Percy gave her a passing grade."

Keats mumbled his agreement from the back seat, and Percy landed lightly on the headrest and then took his parrot pose on Kellan's right shoulder. Now I couldn't see his face, but his sigh told me he was far from convinced.

"You'll pardon me if I allow her prior record to outweigh the musings of your pets," he said, getting out of the SUV.

Gertie Rhodes was already on the porch, her rifle quickly disappearing into the folds of her poncho.

"Not fair," she called. "I can't shoot a man with a cat on his shoulder."

"Otherwise you would, Mrs. Rhodes?" he said.

"Of course not, Chief. You know how much I respect you."

Kellan actually laughed. "Well, we come in peace today." He tried to look at me and got a face full of Percy's parka. "I don't know why we're here, but Ivy will enlighten me shortly."

"Hi, Gertie," I called. "We've come to take you up on your offer to find the perfect Christmas tree. You have no idea how much rides on this. My best friend is counting on us."

She gave a cackle and I could tell by Kellan's shift in posture that the sound startled him.

"Knock yourselves out," she said. Stepping back, she reached inside the front door and pulled out an ax that just happened to be handy. Setting it down, she kicked it to the top of the stairs. I was happy she was wearing flannel pajamas today.

Realizing Kellan couldn't bend without dumping Percy, I went over to collect the ax. Keats frolicked ahead of me up the stairs and whined until Gertie gave him a pat.

Turning, I said, "See?"

"Yeah," Gertie echoed. "See, Chief? If Ivy's brilliant dog likes me I can't be all bad."

"Is that a rifle in your poncho, Mrs. Rhodes?" he said. "Just curious."

She put the rifle inside and put her hands on her hips. "There. Satisfied? Now go and have fun, and then come inside for hot cocoa when you're done."

CHAPTER EIGHTEEN

Kellan turned right around to stare at me as Keats escorted us under the lattice arch that led from Gertie's yard out into the acres of bush that ran between her house and Vinnie Swenson's.

"How exactly did you pull that off?" he asked. "Gertie is probably the most feared woman in town and now she's inviting you in for cocoa."

"Told you. Crusty on the outside and sweet as cocoa on the inside."

"Not buying it," he said. "The dog couldn't pull all that off in one visit."

"Don't underestimate the power of marmalade fluff on a cat lover like Gertie," I said, signaling the cat to jump down. "Use your paws, Percy. Kellan will need both hands for chopping."

The cat jumped down and I handed Kellan the ax. He took it and then invited me to loop my arm through his. Here on the outskirts, a few inches of snow had accumulated on the ground and the branches of the many and varied fir trees. Edna had been right about Gertie's forest of options.

"But seriously," he said. "Will this sweet cocoa be spiked with something noxious? Will I need to pay for it in pride like I do with your rescuer friends?"

"Gertie's not the scumbag Secret Santa if that's what you're thinking," I said. "For one thing, Keats likes her, as you saw. For another, she only has an ATV and couldn't cover as much territory as the killer apparently has in their mission to terrorize people."

"She still has a van registered under her name," he said. "It's probably in the barn."

"I just don't see her leaving the property long enough to do that." I examined and rejected a few trees. "Gertie's a cockroach, like Edna. I mean that in the most flattering way. They're survivors and soul sisters. I bet there's a bunker out here stocked for the zombie apocalypse."

"Edna and Gertie actually like each other?"

"It's not friendship in the traditional sense, considering each threatened to kill the other. More like an armed neutrality. A mutual respect." I looked around at all the trees wondering how we were going to choose just one. "That said, it took a bit of HR fancy footwork to keep their hackles down."

He let his hand slide down to mine and raised my mitten. Planting a kiss on it, he smiled. "You amaze me. You scare the daylights out of me, but you also amaze me."

A flush radiated instantly from head to toe. It was better than the little heat packs I kept in my pocket for days when I didn't have a handsome man to keep me warm.

"That might be the sweetest thing you've ever said to me." I squeezed his police issue glove with my mitten. "You amaze me, too."

He leapt away as if he'd been scorched. "Ow!"

"What...?" I looked down. "Keats, stop that right now." The dog had circled to grab Kellan by the pant leg and probably used a little too much fang. "You just ruined a beautiful moment."

The dog gave me a happy pant. He was glad to have us together, that much was clear. A gleam in his blue eye told me a tree wasn't the only thing on his mind, however.

"He didn't ruin the moment, only my pants," Kellan said, peering down. "It's been a couple of weeks since I had to get the dry cleaners to darn my uniform. I'll give them something extra for Christmas."

"Cash only. All baked goods will be viewed as suspect now."

"Indeed. Good thing I never fancied gingerbread."

"I loved Mandy's," I said. "I've eaten dozens already. Everywhere we went someone was offering the cookies and I was happy to partake. I guess I got lucky... till last night."

"Last night you got even luckier." He took my hand again. "That was a close call."

"Why on earth would anyone want to poison Meryl Martingale?" I asked. "She's the most popular mayor we've ever had. Got in by a landslide."

His brow furrowed under his black police hat. Few could look as good as he did in fleecy ear flaps. I appreciated anything that made him seem more accessible because he seemed to get handsomer by the day and it was a little daunting sometimes. Maybe I *should* up my style game a little.

"I could come up with a few reasons," he said. "Politically motivated. What I can't figure out is how they would link to what happened with Vinnie and Felix. Nothing connects."

"You've checked out Heddy and Kaye?" I asked.

"Alibis. Again. Those two keep busy and make sure people see them." He smirked. "I know you're disappointed."

I made a face at him. "I don't actually want them to go to jail. Just move somewhere else."

"Dorset Hills," he suggested. "Let Cori Hogan deal with them."

"What about Beverly Roxton?" I asked. "She's been seen out here in the bush, too. Treasure hunting, no doubt. She said she's worried about money so she has motive."

"Wouldn't connect to the mayor, though," Kellan said. "But I'll look into it." He peered over his shoulder. "Gertie had run-ins with all of the victims, Meryl included. She's motivated, too. By lunacy."

"Gertie's not as crazy as she seems. She's tired and frustrated, that's all. This land is all she has and it's something she shared with her husband."

"I bet you ten bucks she won't have an alibi."

"That's a bet I'm not taking," I said, swinging his hand. "This will all piece itself together eventually."

"Not before Christmas, I'm afraid. What a shame when it was shaping up to be special."

"It's terrible timing," I said. "Not that there's ever a good time for murder."

"Christmas can still be special," he said, leaning over to kiss my cheek. "Maybe more so. You truly value those you love in unsettled times. At least, I do."

Clutching his hand, I let out a long, slow breath. I hadn't even realized how much tension I was carrying around. We were proving his very point.

"Let's focus on Christmas for a bit and forget everything else," I said.

"You got it. What are Jilly's specifications for this tree?"

I pulled out my phone to double-check her text. "It needs to be nine feet tall, blue spruce and, you know, perfect."

"That's it?" he said, giving the ax a gentle swing.

"Cones are optional but definitely preferred," I said. "They open in the heat and crackle, apparently. I wouldn't know from experience as we didn't get real trees after— Well, you know. We had the ugliest artificial tree imaginable. Plastic ornaments, too, although that was on me. One of the stray cats I brought home tipped the tree and smashed the glass ones. At least Mom waited till Boxing Day to make the cat disappear. All the rescues I brought home vanished amid plenty of fake sneezing."

Sliding his arm around my shoulders, Kellan pulled me close. "I guess that explains the abundance of rescues now," he said. "I'm making it my special mission to rehab Christmas for you. Although my holidays weren't great either, I admit. That's why I always volunteered to work through Christmas. Crime never takes a day off."

I reached up and took his glove, warning Keats with a glance to leave us be. "Holidays remind everyone of what they *don't* have," I said. "They push people over the edge if they're on the brink. I saw that a lot in HR, too."

"You get it," he said. "That's why we're so good together."

I gave him a smile that was happy and sad all at once. We'd both seen human nature at its worst and fought hard to balance that with gratitude for the best. Even as teens we'd understood these complexities and challenges. I knew how I got that way. One day, perhaps he'd tell me how he had. There were plenty of things I tried to pry out of him, but not that.

"This Christmas *will* be special," I said. "Whether or not the crime is solved. And whether or not there are cones to crackle."

"The cones we can probably guarantee," he said, looking around. "Keats. How about it? We need a great big blue spruce with cones on it. Can you handle that order?"

I laughed. "You're working outside his purview. He's better with crime."

"Don't underestimate your own dog," Kellan said. "I think he can do it."

Keats and Percy picked their way through the snow, tails high like flags. As we followed, the only sound was the snapping of twigs under our boots. It was tranquil and beautiful—a scene from a greeting card.

Suddenly Keats went into a point. I sucked in a breath, bracing for the worst. "What is it?" I called.

Kellan released me and walked ahead. "Aha!" His big hat

tipped up and then down. "Nine feet, give or take an inch, blue spruce, plenty of cones."

I clapped my mittens together like a child. "It's perfect! But is it perfect enough?" I pulled out my phone again. "Let's get it certified by Jilly before the ax falls."

She replied with a row of hearts and I gave Kellan the go-ahead to start chopping.

Keats and Percy moved well away from the flying wood chips but I was mesmerized. Watching my guy chop down a big tree for me did something rather perilous to my heart. Not perilous like yew, but enough to unnerve the former grim reaper of HR. I didn't like feeling vulnerable yet every thud of the ax chipped away at my resistance. When the spruce finally toppled, Kellan straightened and I ran over to hug him. He laughed and swung me around.

The hug went on for a while. Much longer than Keats and Percy would normally allow. Where were the disruptors of romance?

Pushing Kellan away gently, I turned. "Keats? Percy? Come!"

The silence and stillness became ominous now. Panic soared up from my abdomen and pushed the joy right out of my heart.

"It's okay," Kellan said, leading me forward. "They've left tracks and can't have gone far."

It was only a few minutes before Percy came out of the brush, stopping periodically to shake the snow from his paws. I expected him to demand a ride, but he turned and led us back the way he came.

"Keats," I called. "Come! I don't like this game."

Finally we emerged in a clearing to find the dog frozen in a point, one white paw raised over equally white snow.

"We've already got our tree, pal," Kellan said. "We can only take one."

"It's not that," I said. "His ruff's up and his ears are down."

Kellan spun around. "I don't see anyone."

"Whoever it was is long gone," I said. "The snow's been trampled, but the prints aren't fresh."

We walked over and Keats dropped his paw and started rooting around with his nose. Eventually he resumed his point and I knelt beside him.

There on the snow lay a coin just like the one Percy had flipped off the shelf in The Langman Legacy.

CHAPTER NINETEEN

Gertie set a mug of steaming instant cocoa in front of each of us at her kitchen table. "My side or Vinnie's side?" she asked.

"This one's yours," I said, pushing the coin in the plastic bag toward her.

Kellan pulled it back. "It's mine until the case is closed."

"*This one?*" Gertie said, picking up on my hint. "Are there more?"

I nodded. "Keats found several sites. Two have already been pillaged, I'm afraid. The digging is fresh. Someone must have used a jackhammer to break up the earth."

"Probably when I was in town," Gertie said. "Or I'd have heard it." She gestured to her tools by the window. "Or seen it."

"The sites were in dense bush." I pointed to scratches on my face from branches and thorns. "Far denser than it was in Frank Swenson's day, I'm sure."

"But the dog found them?" She turned to look at Keats, who was sitting beside the hot air vent with the cat. Both had clumps of burrs in their tails, but only Percy was trying to remove them. Keats left that kind of work to me.

"That's right," I said. "Five sites in total."

"Unconfirmed," Kellan corrected. "My team is on the way and you'll know soon enough."

"I believe the dog," Gertie said. "I'm sure the cat helped, too. He's a clever one."

"He did and he is," I said. "We'll work with the police to see if there are any more. Then maybe this can be the end of it. Maybe you can feel safe again."

She shook her head. "The animals might find everything but no one else will believe that's all there is. They'll keep coming and keep coming. I'm surprised the gingerbread I got wasn't tainted."

That surprised me, too, to be honest. Surely anyone hunting for treasure would have wanted Gertie out of the picture, too.

"Have you considered moving into town?" Kellan asked. "Winters are long and harsh here."

"You don't need to tell me that, Chief. I've lived through eighty-three of them. But Saul loved this place and I plan to be carted out of here in a pine box." She got up, cackling. "My own pine, thank you very much. Do you hear that, Ivy?"

"Duly noted," I said. "Although you can afford better than pine now."

"Pine's good enough for me." She opened a cupboard and pulled out a small, rectangular tin. "I've got all I need, except peace. The problem with people today is they want too much."

"That's not just a modern problem," Kellan said, as Gertie twisted a can opener. "This loot is very old. Greed planted it in your bush and strife kept it there. Vinnie and Felix are the most current victims, but there may well be others. I've got a stack of cold cases and we probably only know about half of Frank Swenson's battles."

The stench of fish filled the kitchen and overpowered the smell of cocoa. Gertie used a fork to distribute sardines between two saucers. Keats and Percy looked at her hopefully and she nodded. "For you two heroes. Better than hot chocolate."

They left the heating vent and licked the plates clean.

Kellan signaled me to go and I finished my drink in a few gulps that flamed on the way down. "Gertie, would you like to join us at the inn tonight for our own tree lighting? It's going to look gorgeous."

She stepped backward, away from the offer. I should have known better than to approach a wild animal so suddenly. Excitement and cheer made me lose my finesse.

"I need to be here," she said. "Once the word gets out—and you know it will—more people will start rooting around."

"I'll have officers patrol around the clock," Kellan said. "Until we get to the bottom of everything."

"Chief, with all due respect," Gertie said, running her hand down her long braid over and over, "this started long before you and it will probably go on long after me. We're just seeing the latest bubbles pop up from the Swenson cesspool."

Now she looked a decade older than when we arrived and I felt for her. It had been a long fight and no wonder she'd become eccentric. Isolation, fear and sadness did that to anyone. I had experienced it myself during my stint at Flordale Corporation, especially when I traveled for months at a time and didn't have Jilly to keep me sane. Ten years of that was enough to leave a permanent imprint on my soul. It also left me with compassion for others who didn't find the dog they needed to lead them out of misery and into happiness.

"Have you thought about getting a dog, Gertie?" I asked.

"No dogs," she said. "Cats are harder to kidnap or heaven forbid, pick off."

"Oh, Gertie." My heart hurt for her, because the tears that welled up in her eyes suggested something like that had happened in the past.

"Out you go, both of you," she said. "I'm sure Edna Evans told you never to pity an old woman."

"She most certainly has," I said. "Especially one who's become suddenly rich."

"I wish I could celebrate but money brings more trouble." On the porch, she offered a grim smile. "My record's about to get a little fatter, Chief. More boots to shoot."

He shook his head. "Don't do that, Mrs. Rhodes. Let's work together to find another solution."

"You do things your way, I'll do mine," she said. As we went down the stairs, she called after us, "Lovely tree. Too bad your dog's leaving his mark on it."

"Keats, don't you dare!" I ran down the last few steps and caught him before the floodgates opened.

"See, that's exactly how it works around here," Gertie said. "Something great happens and someone has to pee on it."

Kellan and I both laughed as he tossed the tree onto the roof of the police SUV and used bungee cords to strap it down.

"I'll see you again in about an hour, Mrs. Rhodes," he called.

"You could make it in half that if you used the back routes, Chief," she said.

"They may not find me before Christmas if I tried. You have to start young with the off-road business."

She tossed her braid back and then flapped her arms and clucked like a chicken.

I went back to the foot of the stairs. "My offer stands for tonight. And for Christmas dinner, too. The more the merrier."

Stepping inside the house she called, "Whatever you do, don't eat the gingerbread."

I turned and found Keats poking around in Gertie's front garden. Up came the white paw in another point. His blue eye fixed on the shrubbery under the front window. I expected a squirrel to appear.

Instead, I saw the cheery berries of the deadly yew bush.

CHAPTER TWENTY

Martha Kincaid wasn't quite ready when I arrived at Sunny Acres to pick her up for our tree lighting at Runaway Inn. I was looking forward to showing her how the farm had transformed since she saw it as a child, when her father boarded his livestock there. Also, she would get a chance to meet with Hazel Bingham again.

The concierge sent Keats and me to wait in the recreation room on the second floor to enjoy Letitia Smart's gorgeous decorations inside and out. The courtyard below was even prettier now that snow had settled over the trees and bushes.

"Good job today, buddy," I said, as we strolled from window to window. "Treasure hunting is an extremely valuable skill set. Maybe we'll strike it rich and not have to worry about marketing the inn so much."

Keats mumbled something as he trotted ahead of me. It sounded like he was telling me not to count my chickens before they hatched. Or that he had bigger fish to fry. There was an animal metaphor in there somewhere.

"A girl can dream," I said. "I bet there's more treasure to be found in Clover Grove. But if you're telling me to take joy in the simple things, I hear you. Tonight's going to be amazing. Jilly rallied dozens of people to come to the inn to see our first tree light up. The tree you chose."

He glanced back with his cool blue eye and the intensity of it startled me. Usually he enjoyed a compliment, not to mention some quality time alone with me. We hadn't had many solo outings together lately. Percy and Jilly were normally with us, and Edna horned in whenever she could. It was getting harder to have a private chat with my dog, and I missed them. They grounded me, while at the same time unleashed my imagination.

He mumbled something else—an impatient request to speed things up. Being away from the inn and his livestock when people arrived bothered him. Perhaps that was why Percy elected to stay back. I'd assumed he just wanted to claim Hazel's attention and lap. She'd come early with Michael, and they'd picked up my mother along the way.

"I hope Mom doesn't make things awkward tonight." Keats gave me the blue eye again. "Well, of course she will, that goes without saying. But with both Charlie and Michael there—two key members of her rotation—it opens new avenues for embarrassment."

Keats repeated what he'd mumbled earlier and I decided the metaphor was "bigger fish to fry."

"Really? I thought we might take a night off."

He mumbled something shorter and then his mouth dropped open to pant ha-ha-ha.

"No rest for the wicked? Right. Thanks, pal."

I laughed too, and there was another laugh behind me—a jarring, unpleasant snicker.

Turning, I saw Beverly Roxton pushing her father-in-law into the room. They were both wearing parkas and he had a quilt over his legs.

They rolled toward us and Keats' ruff and tail rose, while his ears flattened. Beverly probably had some verbal ammunition loaded and ready to fire.

"You scare me, Ivy," she said. "Just strolling around chatting to your dog like a madwoman. I wouldn't be shocked to learn you're the Secret Santa delivering toxic cookies all over town."

Keats' tail had puffed to its fullest. It seemed strange that Beverly, who saw stressed animals every day, wouldn't notice the threat. Keats wouldn't hesitate to take her down a peg if her shots turned physical. But words couldn't hurt me and he knew that. Or not much, anyway. Corporate training had built a thick shield and the Beverlys of the world couldn't leave a lasting mark.

"It's okay, buddy," I said, mainly to call her attention to the dog. "Beverly doesn't mean it. She'd never openly accuse me of murdering people in front of witnesses."

She gave an exaggerated twirl. "I don't see any witnesses."

"That's unkind," I said. "You have no idea what Dr. Roxton still understands, even if he can't say it."

My eyes dropped to her father-in-law. Dr. Roxton was looking at Keats but then his eyes drifted to the window. "Silver and gold," he said. "Snow white and red."

"I know insanity when I see it," Beverly said. "And you're on the same spectrum. What were you nattering on about when I came in? Buried treasure?"

The rumor mill was a little slower than usual today. It must be running on holiday hours.

"Keats found a stash at the old Milloy place today," I said. "I was congratulating him."

That silenced Beverly for a moment or two. "Who gets to claim it? Not Gertie Rhodes, I hope."

I shrugged. "Not my business. That's in Chief Harper's hands."

"Better out than in," Dr. Roxton said. "Tootie fruitie."

"Pops, please," Beverly said. "Better in than out with your stupid remarks." She started rolling away. "I'd love to stay and hear more about the treasure, but our ride's waiting. Cliff wanted to take his dad out for a nice dinner since I can't deal with the fuss of bringing him home for Christmas."

"Enjoy it, Dr. Roxton," I called after them. "Hope Santa is good to you."

"There's a lump of coal with your name on it," Beverly called back. "For bringing nonstop terror into this community."

"Naughty and nice," Dr. Roxton called. "Sugar cane fairy."

I followed Keats to the windows on the far side of the room that overlooked the parking lot. After a few minutes, Beverly pushed the wheelchair out the side door and over to a van with the villa's logo. I hadn't realized I could have arranged a ride for Martha and it was something to keep in mind for the future. It would be nice to bring her to the inn more often.

The vehicle's lights came on and it pulled away from the door, eventually disappearing into the darkness. Keats' various war flags came down one by one until he was just your average border collie again. He showed me his warm brown eye for the first time all evening, and it was full of compassion.

"Don't worry about me, buddy," I said. "Sticks and stones and all that. It's poor old Dr. Roxton who deserves our sympathy. She treats him with contempt and I'm sure he feels it on some level. I think I'll talk to the staff about it. Discreetly."

Keats swung his muzzle to show his blue eye, but before he could reply, another, more joyful voice rang out from the doorway.

"This old belle is ready for the ball."

Laughing, I walked back to meet Martha Kinkaid. "Your coach and drivers are at your service."

I LIKED BEING LATE for my own party. Despite all the events we'd had, I wasn't really comfortable being the host or center of attention. More and more Jilly was stepping into that role, where she truly shone.

Tonight she shone literally in a silver dress that caught the light. Mom stood behind her all in red as usual, but seasonally appropriate. Daisy was the real surprise. My domestic goddess sister had dolled up in a coppery dress that made her hazel eyes look topaz. She'd even blown out her hair and the silver strands glistened. In my view, she was always the prettiest Galloway Girl. Helping to manage the inn was giving her a reason to step out from behind her rubber gloves and cleansers.

I'd put on a dress, too. It was black and a little clingy for my tastes but super comfortable. Jilly had picked it out and brought it home for me. There was no reason for me to get claustrophobic in a store when she actually liked shopping. All I had to do was be more appreciative of her efforts than Keats, and that was easy.

Kellan slipped in as I was hanging up Martha's coat. Dropping a kiss on my cheek, he gave Keats a warning glance and then offered Martha his arm before taking off his own coat.

"Oh my," she said, taking it with a smile. "There's a handsome prince at the ball, too. I hope you don't mind, Ivy."

"My prince is your prince," I said. "He'll find you a seat beside Hazel with a good view of the tree."

Percy came to greet us, parading back and forth as I exchanged my boots for heels. It was as if we'd been gone for days. The cat stood on his hind legs to bump the dog under the chin. Keats put his paw on Percy's shoulder, pushed him down and licked his head several times.

"What's going on, you two?" I asked them. "Is Santa watching?"

"Santa's always watching," Bronwen said, joining me. "He's a trained observer. How else would he know who deserves toys?"

"Good point," I said. "And you look great. I like the pairing of the dress with the heavy boots."

She sighed. "It's called compromise. Mom wanted me to look nice, and I wanted her to be nice."

"Part of the puppy persuasion project, I presume?" I said, hanging up my own coat.

"Exactly. But I don't have much faith so the boots stayed."

"Patience. Anything worthwhile takes time."

Kellan came back to the front entry. He was in civvies, and the shoulders of his black wool coat were thoroughly covered in orange fur. I could have sworn that wasn't the case when he came in just minutes ago.

"I got ambushed," he grumbled, brushing at the coat before handing it to me. "Percy landed like a whirling dervish and spun off just as fast. He nearly knocked me into Mrs. Kinkaid's lap."

Bronwen sputtered a laugh and then covered her mouth. "Sorry."

"Don't be," he said, smiling. "I'm off duty. Cops laugh, too."

My brother came over to add proof to that with his own hilarity. "Chief, I thought you were going to take the tree down as well as the lady. Jilly would have raked you over the coals."

"And there are coals to be raked," Kellan said. "You're tending the fire tonight, officer. I'm off duty."

"I'm off duty, too," Asher argued.

"And I outrank you even off duty." Kellan's white teeth gleamed. "Because I'm dating the owner."

"I got the best in that deal," Asher said. "Better chef than farmer."

"Don't disrespect my lady," Kellan said.

Kellan gave him a shove that made Bronwen laugh full out this time. I laughed, too. It was good to see these two men who worked so hard let their hair down, especially when the current case was still wide open.

"Your so-called lady is obsessed with manure," Asher said.

"True," I said. "But never underestimate the power of good fertilizer, brother."

Kellan glanced around. "If you were capable of being objective, officer, you'd see that your little sister is the most beautiful woman in the room."

A flush started tingling in my pinched toes and then coursed upward. I kissed Kellan's cheek before winking at Bronwen. "Remember what I said about heels. Even if I fall over later, I've won, right?"

She grinned at me. "As long as it's not into the fire when Asher's poking the coals."

Asher favored Bronwen with the full power of his golden boy smile. "I like this kid. She's got attitude."

"Me too," Kellan said. "It'll take her far in life."

Mrs. Stout moved out of the crowd and came toward us. "Thank you, gentlemen, but don't give my daughter a swelled head."

Bronwen shrank like an inflatable reindeer whose air pump died. Her grin vanished, too. It wasn't hard to see where the girl's insecurities came from and I had similar memories that rose sometimes like the ghosts of Christmas past. This was such a critical age for a girl. I knew that instinctively—not from being a mom or even an aunt to a girl, but simply from going through it myself.

"Bronwen is very clever," I said. "It's been fun having her here at Runaway Farm. All of you, in fact."

"She set your emu loose," her mother said. "How fun was that?"

"It was fun for me," Edna said, joining us. "An early Christmas present. Don't crush this girl's spirit, Reyna, or there won't be room for you in my bunker."

I covered my mouth and Bronwen did, too. "Edna, Mrs. Stout is an honored guest," I said after a moment. "At the risk of sounding like my mom, she may not appreciate your prepper humor."

"Or even understand it," Mrs. Stout said. "You're speaking a secret language."

"I speak many rare languages," I said. "That's the secret to good livestock and pet management."

"Have you figured out the donkey yet?" Bronwen asked.

I shook my head sadly. "Poor Bocelli. His message about the toxic cookies was certainly clear but the rest is just... noise. I spend as much time with him as I can, but I'm on the run all day."

Kellan dropped his hand on my shoulder. "You could give up sleuthing to focus on your animals. You know, leave the dirty work to the professionals."

I didn't need to offer a comeback because he was punished swiftly with a nip that made him jump and give a little yelp. Once again Bronwen hid a grin and this time her mom did, too.

Edna didn't bother to hide hers. "You were never cheeky like that as a boy, Kellan. When I used to vaccinate you—"

"Never mind, Miss Evans," he said. "I've still got my badge on me and the only disrespect I will tolerate is from the dog."

Percy catapulted suddenly onto his shoulder and Kellan yelped again.

"And the cat," Bronwen said, as everyone but Kellan laughed.

There was a knock on the door and I opened it to find Meryl Martingale taking up more room than a woman technically could. It was a gift shared by movie stars, politicians and my own mother.

"How nice that you have time to stand around laughing when my life is at stake, Chief Harper. Who knows what the killer will try next, since the cookies failed?"

"Meryl, relax," her husband said, nudging her through the door and coming inside.

It was the wrong move. It was nearly always the wrong move for a husband to tell his wife to relax, I figured.

"I will not relax. I've been targeted by a killer. I have to be on the alert constantly."

"You're right to be wary," Kellan said, losing his smile as he became the chief again. "But you couldn't be safer than you are here right now."

"I agree," Meryl said. "Get my bag, Larry. I'm staying at the inn till the chief does his job."

Jilly materialized and squeezed my arm. "We're happy to have you, Mayor. The more the merrier."

"It won't be merry until that Secret Santa is behind bars," the mayor said. "And it had better be by Christmas, Chief, or I wouldn't count on having your badge in the new year."

Kellan blinked a few times, his expression as smooth as a mannequin's. Asher's bright smile switched off quite suddenly, however. In the end, neither man had to respond to the threat. Keats gently prodded Bronwen's leg and she looked up at her aunt, not even bothering to hide her disgust.

"Why so rude, Auntie M? It's a Christmas party. Lighten up."

"Bronwen," Mrs. Stout said. "Respect, please."

"Well, Aunt Meryl should show respect for the police, too," Bronwen said. "Besides, everyone deserves a good time." She turned to Daisy, who'd appeared on my other side. "Can someone get Auntie M some of that mulled wine? Then I'll show her the most beautiful tree ever. Isn't it about time to go live with the lights?"

The mayor shrugged off her coat and handed it to me. I wasn't the only one gaping as she allowed the teen, aided by Keats, to herd her into the family room.

Edna looked after them in open admiration. "Someone get that girl an ATV."

CHAPTER TWENTY-ONE

"Christmas Eve already," Jilly said from the back seat of the truck as we drove toward Dorset Hills. "It's all going by so fast and I wanted to savor every moment."

Edna gave a sigh from the passenger seat. "It *has* gone by too fast. I needed at least another week to bring that choir to competitive status. Last night's penultimate show was an unmitigated disaster."

"What do you mean, 'disaster'?" Jilly said. "It was a huge hit. Town square has never been so crowded. People came from all over hill country. Even from Dorset Hills, the Christmas epicenter."

Edna turned slowly to stare at Jilly, while Keats balanced precariously in her lap. "They did not come to see my choir, Jillian, did they now?"

Jilly laughed. "No, they came to see Ivy and Bocelli."

"Bocelli and Ivy," I corrected. "The donkey gets top billing now."

"The applause was thunderous," Jilly said. "Especially when Keats jumped right onto the donkey's back and howled along with him. You must make him do that again tonight, Ivy."

"I didn't make him do anything. He decided of his own accord to add to the donkey's lament. It didn't make the message any clearer, unfortunately."

"Then I would suggest avoiding the move tonight," Edna said. "Put the dog on a leash."

Keats turned as slowly as Edna had a moment ago and gave her a dour look.

"You got told," I said. "I let Keats make decisions that might help or hinder my work, and just try to keep him safe."

"Well, I'd like to keep the ears of hill country safe," Edna said. "After that move, and all the catcalls and hooting, the choir couldn't carry a tune in a bucket, let alone remember the words. It was like a kindergarten pageant."

"Excuse me," Jilly said. "I did just fine."

"You did," Edna admitted. "I guess your professional experience helps you focus under pressure. In fact, you, Heddy and Beverly were the only ones who could continue at all. The rest were as bad as Dahlia, who was worse than the donkey."

"Tonight will be better," I said. "The crowd will be smaller because people will stay closer to home on Christmas Eve. Especially with snow in the forecast."

"I don't know about that," Edna said. "Your act is growing like a weed, and the donkey just gets louder and louder."

"Plus his sequences are more elaborate," I said. "At first it was like improv but now it's the same few phrases over and over. I wish I understood."

Jilly reached through the seats and patted my shoulder. "You're trying too hard. You know how these things work. Go for a long walk with Keats later and chill out."

Keats gave an enthusiastic rumble. "We could use a little break from the crowds," I said. "The last few nights have pushed this introvert's limits."

"Pressure from the mayor doesn't help," Jilly said. "First she gave Kellan a hard time and now she's looking to you to bring glory to Clover Grove."

The mayor had managed to put aside her woes after seeing the crowd of visitors in town square. Visions of sugar plums and tourism dollars danced in her head.

"Overly ambitious," said Edna, who'd just been talking about choir competitions.

"She said you put us on the map, Ivy," Jilly said.

"And then she added, 'Keep us there.'" I shook my head. "As if I can control a singing donkey. I refuse to become the town's permanent mascot."

"It could be fun," Jilly teased. "Performances on every major occasion, even the county fair. Guest appearances through hill country..."

I shuddered. "I'd rather tackle killers. I'm only doing this to help Bocelli get his word out, whatever that is." I turned off the highway and onto the bypass to Dorset Hills. "When he's done, I'm done."

Keats mumbled something rather complicated and Jilly asked, "What did he say?"

"He's frustrated. In his view, the donkey's message is loud and clear but my ears are closed. Something like that." I glanced at him, "Sorry for letting you down, buddy. I guess I'm tone deaf to donkey dialogue."

"Don't be so hard on yourself," Jilly said. "And Keats, don't be so hard on Ivy."

The dog shot a little blue eye in Jilly's direction and retorted with a mumble.

"I agree with him," Edna said. "Ivy *should* be harder on herself and get all this sorted out. The donkey is the key to the murders, I'm sure of it."

"Kellan's working through his suspect list," I said. "The Langmans have been cleared. Beverly Roxton is still a potential. There are a few other treasure hunters from Gertie's property he won't share with me. Plus Gertie herself. On top of all that, there are half a dozen old enemies of Vinnie's who haven't been cleared."

"No one ever saw the Secret Santa?" Jilly asked. "That's hard to believe when the cookies found their way into mailboxes all over town."

"They arrived by night, apparently. After the gingerbread recall, there was no other poison found. The targets were handpicked."

"I still don't understand what the mayor has in common with Vinnie and Felix," Jilly said.

"Me either," I said.

Keats grumbled something that sounded like, "you should" and I turned to stare at him. "If you think we're slacking, you could give me more of a clue. Normally you're a little more forthcoming." Percy yowled in his carrier and I said, "Don't you start. And no, I am *not* blinded by Christmas."

Jilly laughed. "Well, this meeting might enlighten us. I hope so, because we've got plenty going on without traipsing over to Dog Town on Christmas Eve."

"I'm not convinced," I said. "Cori was laughing so hard over my performance with Bocelli that she could barely get the words out."

"Only her trademark gloves kept her from breaking her fingers clapping," Jilly said.

Keats gave a happy ha-ha-ha as we drove through Dorset Hills to the address Cori Hogan had texted us. He was always glad to see the tiny but mighty dog trainer, and today his fanning tail picked up such speed that Edna sneezed and said, "Oh, for pity's sake, she's just a dog trainer, Keats. Has she ever saved Ivy? No. But I have, and I deserve better than a feather duster up the nose."

"The Rescue Mafia has helped me with valuable intel on previous cases," I said. "And they most certainly helped save you when you were targeted by a killer. So dust away, Keats. Cori Hogan rocks."

My heart sank, however, as we got out of the truck and walked to the front door of an old house. Cori's mockery was tough on the ego and mine had taken a good beating lately, thanks to Bocelli.

Evie Springdale opened the front door before we knocked. The pretty redhead had quickly become my favorite Mafia member because of her relentless optimism and creativity. She had worked in politics for as long as I had in HR and she was skilled at issues management. I always had issues to manage. I probably always would. The first murder of the dogcatcher on my land would never go away, let alone the others. No one would forget that and it was a huge hurdle in gaining a following for the inn. I looked forward to our strategy session, but today wasn't the day.

Evie led us into the kitchen at the back of the house. "I want to introduce you to Clarence Dayton. He's a good friend of the Mafia, and an esteemed member of Dorset Hills' founding family."

Clarence, with his grizzled beard and spectacles, probably had a few years on Edna. "Evie, we've talked about the big buildup," he said. "People are always disappointed." He gestured to several battered wooden chairs set up around the equally battered oak table. "It's a pleasure to meet you, ladies. I've heard about all of you, of course. Especially the furry heroes."

Keats and Percy circled his chair, competing for his attention. His magnetic appeal was even greater than Cori's, although both animals gave her a courtesy swish as they passed. Evie, Bridget Linsmore and Remi Malone they mostly ignored, while Leo, Remi's beloved therapy beagle, got a hard pass. Clarence had some kind of pull over both my pets.

"I heard you weren't a dog person," I said, as Percy jumped into Clarence's lap and head-butted him under the chin. "Keats says otherwise."

"I'm not a Dog *Town* person," he corrected. "The dog-themed branding is ridiculous. I remember more sensible times."

"Me too," Edna said. "Dorset Hills has become a victim of its own success."

"I couldn't agree more but we're in the minority," he said. "People were just smarter in our day, weren't they, Edna?" There was a rumble of protest around the table and he grinned before adding, "Present company excepted."

Cori clapped her black wool gloves with their orange middle fingers. "Can you two reminisce after we get to business?"

"No," Clarence said, pouring tea into a variety of mismatched teacups and saucers. "These women are my guests, Cori. Have some manners."

Very few people told Cori Hogan to stand down and got away with it. She glowered at him while trying to pick up a fragile teacup between her gloved finger and thumb.

"That's not going to end well, Cori," I said, smirking.

"It isn't my first teacup rodeo, Ivy," she countered. "Let's talk about your donkey rodeo, instead."

"Everyone saw it but Clarence. What more needs to be said?"

Clarence chuckled. "Oh, I saw it. Evie kindly did a highlights reel. A stunning performance. Bravo." He started to clap and then stopped. "Send my sympathies to the donkey, though. His heart is broken."

I leaned forward. "That's what I think. But how can he still be grieving over Vinnie Swenson, the man who neglected him?"

"Animals and humans grieve abusers all the time when they don't know anything better." Clarence took a sip of his tea and pondered. "But I don't think it's that." He turned to Cori. "Are you sure you rounded up every single animal at Vinnie's? Is there one this donkey is missing?"

"We checked the footage over and over," she said. "All fuzzy heads accounted for, except for the donkey, who'd been MIA for months. We had a spy cam inside and outside the barn. And before you ask, Ivy, yes I shared the footage with Chief Hotstuff."

"Before showing me?" I was surprised and a little hurt.

"I told you everything I know," Cori said. "But Kellan had some intel we needed so I had to pay up."

Clarence waved one hand. "Leave that till later, ladies. I'm telling you, that donkey is grieving for another animal. I've heard it before. You missed one."

The spark went out of both Cori and me fast. "There's no way," she said. "Clem would have known."

"Keats, too," I said. "He wouldn't have let us end the search."

"Oh no," Remi said. "If an animal was left behind it probably couldn't survive this cold weather."

"That's where Vinnie's neglect may have actually paid off," Cori said. "The animals had thick coats and were used to living off scraps." She pushed back her chair. "We'd better get going. I assume you brought the donkey?"

I shook my head. "He had a stressful performance last night."

"Well, go back and get him, and I'll circle home for Clem." Her gloved fingers flew. "Gear up well because this could be a long, cold search."

Everyone stood except Clarence, who continued to sip his tea. "If the critter has survived this long—and the donkey's increasing urgency suggests he has—he'll last another few hours while we discuss why I called you here."

Jilly and I sat back down but Edna crossed her arms. "What could be more important than a rescue, Clarence?"

"Murder?" he said. "Or maybe not."

"Mr. Dayton, do you know something about what happened to Vinnie Swenson and Felix Milloy?"

He shook his head. "Not really. But I knew Frank Swenson and Nate Milloy. They were nasty heartless men. As founding families in Clover Grove, they often had cause to meet with my grandfather. I was just a child, of course, but I listened to how they browbeat Granddad and ridiculed him for being an advocate for animals."

Evie sat down again, too. "Clarence's grandfather was the

town's first official rescuer. He adopted retired or abused circus animals."

Tears filled Clarence's eyes. "He treated those animals like people and I loved them, too. One day the township came and seized them all. I still hear the elephant's screech in my nightmares, and have no idea where they all ended up. Granddad searched for years."

Percy scrambled out of Clarence's lap and up onto his shoulder, rubbing his fluffy orange head against the old man's cheek. Keats, on the other hand, came back to me and rested his muzzle in my lap as my own eyes filled.

"I'm so sorry, Clarence," I said. "Did Frank and Nate have something to do with what happened?"

"Granddad said both men made a fuss about the dangers of keeping wild animals. Frank had most politicians of the day in his back pocket. Worse, he threatened to take matters into his own hands and do some big game hunting if the township didn't act. That threat tied Granddad's hands. He surrendered the animals and hoped for the best."

Tears rolled down his cheeks and into the saucer. The grief was as fresh today as when it happened nearly 80 years ago.

Jilly and I both cried with him, but the Mafia—even sensitive Remi—maintained their composure. Rescue work had toughened them up but I wasn't there yet. Might never get there.

Evie put her hand on the old man's arm. "Ivy, Clarence thinks you need to dig a little deeper into the motives for these murders."

"You're barking up the wrong tree," he said. "The loot was nothing new. It's been buried there for decades and treasure hunters have come and gone, as I'm sure Gertie Rhodes told you. People only cared about the money. What's different about this time?"

"Someone freed the animals," I said, pulling out my phone. "And one of them is still on the lam."

CHAPTER TWENTY-TWO

W e regrouped just over an hour later in the hills above Vinnie's house where we'd searched before.

Keats and Clem greeted each other quickly, like old colleagues, and then pranced around, eager to get to work.

"Kellan confirmed there was no sign of a house pet," I said. "Nothing at all."

"A feral cat, maybe?" Cori said. "Nothing bigger could have gotten under our radar."

"I wouldn't know about that as I never saw the footage," I said.

"Chief Hot Stuff reviewed it," Cori said, avoiding my eyes.

"Kellan wouldn't have paid much attention to cat tracks," I said. "But I might have."

"Fine, I should have showed you first," Cori said, following me to the trailer. "But sharing that footage with Kellan got us information that saved many other animals."

Keats pressed against my legs, entreating me to get on with the task at hand. "Okay. I understand. Let's just see what Bocelli, the dogs and Percy have to tell us today."

I unlatched the door and gasped. Bocelli wasn't in the trailer alone. We had a stowaway.

"Wow, that was a bumpy ride," Bronwen said, jumping out. There was a sheepish, yet defiant look on her face. "You stalled so many times I nearly got whiplash." She patted Bocelli's blanketed side. "Held onto the donkey for dear life."

"Bronwen, that was so dangerous," I said. "You could have been trampled back there."

"Your mom's going to throw a fit," Jilly added.

"Only if she finds out. She's too busy shopping to notice I'm gone."

"Daisy isn't," I said, pulling out my phone. Sure enough, there was already a worried text from my sister.

"Everything's fine," Bronwen said, as Keats brought the donkey out of the trailer. "Bocelli would never trample me. We're friends. I visit him when you're running around." She stroked him between the eyes. "See?"

"Trampling isn't always intentional," I said. "Sweet animals bang me up all the time."

"How about I drive her home while you guys get started?" Jilly said.

Bronwen crossed her arms. "I'm not going."

I studied her face and realized this wasn't about acting out. The kid was looking for a purpose. She wanted to belong. We couldn't work miracles in just a few days, but we could show her something she'd never see in the city. I turned to the others. "What do you think?"

"Let her come," Cori said. "The stowaway earned it."

"Kid's got guts," Edna said. "I'll help keep an eye on her." She turned to Bronwen. "Are you scared of me, young lady?"

"Yeah," Bronwen said. "Kinda."

"Good. Because then you'll listen to me. Remember, I have a full range of vaccinations in my kit that I won't hesitate to administer. For your own safety."

Bronwen blanched. "Okay, Miss Evans."

"Onward," Edna said. "We have important work today."

I texted Daisy that we had things under control while Cori broke everyone into teams and issued directions. Edna, Bronwen and I started out with the donkey, Keats and Percy. I'd encouraged the cat to go with Jilly, and he refused. So the five of us trudged over snowy trails, waiting for a sign from one of the pets.

"Maybe you should sing," Bronwen said. "Bocelli will join you and the lost animal might come out."

"Good thinking," I said, and she looked proud. Cold, but proud. The next time she stowed away she'd remember to dress for it.

Hark the Herald Angels Sing normally got the best response from the donkey and today was no different. His braying was both strident and soulful and by the time the song ended, Bronwen was wiping tears away with her mitten.

"Someone broke his heart," she said, "But whatever he lost, I don't think it's here. At least, not anymore."

I caught her meaning. "It's not a hopeless case," I said, pointing at the dog. "Keats doesn't believe it, so I don't believe it."

"Does he think something's out here?" Bronwen asked, hugging herself and shivering.

"You tell me. What do you observe in the animals?"

She studied the dog, the cat and then the donkey before shaking her head. "Keats is just enjoying the walk. I guess he'd be on alert if he smelled or heard something."

I nodded. "Percy, too. They're happy to get out but they're not driven by a mission. And Bocelli is just as flat as usual."

"Let's turn around," Edna said. "Maybe one of the other groups will find this escapee."

Everyone else came up empty, too, and Cori put gloved hands on her hips. "Something's not adding up. And I don't like it when things don't add up."

"Me either," I said. "Let's regroup later online and swap ideas. I need to get Bronwen home before she goes into deep freeze."

"Agreed," Edna said. "I need time to freshen up before our performance. This is the big one and I want to look my best."

Cori gave us a cheery wave with a flash of orange as she turned to go. "See you there."

"You're not coming again?" I said, shaking my head. "Don't you have anything better to do on Christmas Eve than watch me make a fool of myself?"

"No." The chorus was unanimous.

"We're all coming, silly," Remi said. "We support our friends in tough times."

A warm feeling filled my heart and then fired a welcome burst of heat to my extremities. My eyes started to water from the stinging wind. There was no way this grim reaper had become so soft she'd cry over new friends doing something nice.

Bronwen let Jilly and me sling our arms around her and turn her into the filling of a friend sandwich as we walked back to the truck.

Small Christmas miracles were starting to pile up.

MOM SAID I'd never regret wearing a nice dress and heels for an occasion, but on Christmas Eve in town square I learned the hard way that she was wrong. The wind was howling, snow was blowing and I longed for my long johns and fleece-lined overalls. Mom herself was caroling merrily in a nice dress and heels but she had trained for such feats for decades. Jilly looked content in her skirt, tights and high boots, but she was a veteran, too. The bigger surprise, perhaps, was Edna. Given her fondness for fatigues, it was hard to believe she'd chosen to wear a green velvet dress and patent leather boots along with her pelts, on this blustery night. Her commitment to the choir was evidently strong enough to push the specter of the apocalypse out of her mind for one night.

The festive spirit I'd felt earlier melted away in the frigid wind. It looked like Christmas, with the snow and the pretty lights and smiling faces. It sounded like Christmas, with the beautiful blended harmonies of the carols. It smelled like Christmas, with the hot apple cider Mandy was flogging without much success to the townspeople. It even tasted like Christmas, since I was one of the few brave enough to take a piece of Mandy's boozy fruitcake.

But it didn't *feel* like Christmas.

I couldn't stop thinking about the cold and lonely creature that may also have been set free at Vinnie Swenson's. With real snow coming hard, how would we ever find it?

I was cold and lonely, too, even though I was surrounded by people. A weight pressed down on my heart and I wondered how I was going to get through the big day with a smile on my face for the guests. I thought I'd put fakery behind me but now it was with me again—my shadow under the streetlamps in the cold snow.

"You're not alone," I muttered, as Jilly, Mom and my sisters sang their hearts out around me. "It only feels that way."

My old demons were telling me I'd failed. I'd failed the mayor. I'd failed the murder victims. I'd failed Kellan, Jilly, Edna and myself. Worst of all, I'd failed Bocelli, the grieving donkey, and possibly his lost friend.

Then warm fur pressed into my shins and I remembered. Keats. My best buddy and alter ego. I looked down and his warm brown eye stared up, trying to fill me with the light of his love. He moaned to console me. I couldn't hear it over Mom's so-called singing, but I *felt* it and it comforted me like nothing else could. I hadn't failed Keats.

Claws sank into the back of my best wool coat as Percy scaled me from behind. He perched on my shoulder, purring as he bumped his head on my Santa toque. I couldn't hear the familiar roar, but I felt it, too. I hadn't failed Percy, either.

The donkey's groan I did hear, as he rested his head on my other shoulder. It seemed wrong to make him sing tonight when his heart was so heavy, but maybe this time I'd actually understand him. The way Keats and Percy were acting made me think I hadn't totally failed Bocelli. Not yet. They were comforting me, yes, but Percy was applying plenty of claw as he kneaded my shoulder to keep me alert. Keats turned his blue eye to signal there was still more to see. Bocelli snuffled in my ear to tell me he still had something to say if I was willing to listen.

By the time the rest of the choir fell silent and all eyes turned to us, my shoulders were straight. I lifted Percy off my shoulder and let him settle into the crook of my arm. I touched Keats' ears with my free hand, and then nudged Bocelli. "We're up, my friend."

Edna counted us in to O Come All Ye Faithful. I sang hard and Bocelli wailed and screeched at my side.

The audience clapped and roared and begged us to do another tune. Looking up at the sky, I let snowflakes drop onto my face as I sang O Night Divine. It was an ambitious choice, but less so knowing no one could really hear me. In fact, it was freeing to stretch myself to this beautiful song without risking laughter. People were already laughing anyway. The soaring melody inspired Bocelli, too, and he unleashed some intricate spiraling squeals, all in the same cadence. Somewhere in there was the hint of a whinny.

For some reason, the sound triggered my sluggish mind to make new connections. The timing certainly wasn't great for running off to pursue a lead, but I'd learned to listen to these whispers from my subconscious.

When the last note died away, I pulled on the donkey's rope. "Want to take a drive?"

His mouth worked again and he let out a burp that I took as a "yes."

I TURNED RIGHT INSTEAD of left on Main Street and drove out the other side of Clover Grove.

"Where are we going?" Jilly asked. There was a note of alarm in her voice.

"Dog Town," I said. "We need to make a quick pit stop."

"Dog Town! Ivy, that's not a quick pit stop, especially in a blizzard. We have people waiting for us at the inn."

"Honestly, it won't take a minute," I said. "Other than the commute, of course."

"I've always loved driving in snow," Edna said. "I took advanced handling courses, remember."

"I can handle the truck fine now," I said. "Mostly."

"You just think so because I've stopped commenting," Edna said. "I finally realized distracting you wasn't in my best interest. Not if I wanted to live to see the apocalypse, which I do. But can I ask you something?"

"You cannot drive my truck, if that is what you're asking."

"On the contrary, I want to see how this goes," she said. "My question is more of a plea to keep us out of the ditch because I wore my best dress."

"I'm sure your go-kit is in the back of the truck."

"Well, of course. But I'm a little old to be changing out of velvet in a blizzard." She pressed her nose against the passenger window. "Not that I haven't done it before."

Jilly laughed in the back seat. "Keats and Percy are on board with this mission, so I'll stand down. Just do what you need to do."

"Thank you, my friend."

Neither one questioned me as I focused on getting us to the city core alive. My moment of self-doubt had passed and I was glad to be backed by my besties. How strange to think Edna Evans now qualified for that elite role. It was one of the strangest things in a very strange year.

I pulled the trailer up to the curb outside a pretty little house decorated with the tasteful white lights sanctioned by Dorset Hills' city council. We all climbed out and went up the front stairs. There was music and laughter inside, and I hesitated before knocking.

"Still time to back out," Jilly said. "Especially if you're going to accuse someone of murder and make it a Christmas Eve they'll remember."

"It's nothing like that." Then I shrugged. "Unless it is."

I had to bang the knocker hard till someone finally heard it. The door opened and a blonde woman about our age opened the door. She was wearing a red sequinned sweater, more makeup than she needed, and fluffy slippers. Her right foot was wrapped in a tensor bandage.

"Merry Christmas," she said, smiling. "Are you carollers?"

"Yes," I said. "Yes we are."

Keats looked the woman up and down warily, taking his time before making a decision.

Edna looked the woman up and down, too. "Bailey Miller, is that you? I never forget an arm I've vaccinated."

Bailey's festive smile disappeared. "Miss Evans? What are you doing here, tonight of all nights? I'm up to date on my shots, I promise you."

"It's not that, Bailey," I said. "We just came for a quick chat about—"

The rest of my words were drowned out by the loud screech that came from the trailer, followed by a series of thuds.

"What's that noise?" Bailey asked, peering around us.

"It's a donkey," I said. "A donkey that once belonged to Vincent Swenson. I rescued him after... after what happened."

"After Vinnie was murdered," Bailey said, crossing her arms. "There's no need to pussyfoot around. He got into some bad business and I guess someone finally caught up with him."

"But you were dating him, weren't you?" I asked. When Bocelli was singing earlier, I'd remembered Edna mentioning that Vinnie once had a girlfriend and Gertie saying she'd shot the stiletto off a blonde woman. A quick online search had brought us here. She was a missing link, I was sure of it. And Bocelli sounded sure of it, too.

"Years ago," she said. "When I was too young and stupid to know better. He was older, and he treated me well in the beginning. But when I finally learned what he was up to, I left. The cops have already talked to me, so I don't know why you're bothering me on Christmas Eve."

"It's about the donkey," I said.

"Fred," she said. "What about him?"

"He's distressed. After Vinnie died, someone let all the animals loose and we rounded them up. But he's still distressed, so we were wondering if one is missing." I gave her an entreating smile. "I thought you might know more."

She pulled the door nearly closed behind her. "I felt bad about the animals, truly, but Vinnie only agreed to leave me alone if I kept my mouth shut about everything. I wanted to start a new life, so I moved here."

"But he kept in touch, didn't he?" I said. There was no reason for her to worry about being overheard if he hadn't.

She stepped onto the porch and pulled the door the rest of the way closed. "I can't talk about this. Can you just go?"

Jilly stepped forward. "I know what it's like to have old boyfriends hang on too long. They just keep showing up and showing up. I was too scared to call the police about one of them for fear of what he might do. Or what my new boyfriend might do."

Bailey scuffed at the snow with her slipper. "Vinnie just would not quit. He was always buying me presents. I gave them all back except Clippers." She sighed. "That's how he got me. Jewelry meant nothing but Clippers I loved."

"So you gave Vinnie a second chance?" Jilly asked.

"Yeah, about six months ago. It didn't take long to see it was the same old Vinnie, and this time when I left he had leverage. He broke in here and stole Clippers. I guess he thought I'd give in, but I didn't."

"So then what happened?" I asked.

"I stole him back," she said, simply. "I didn't intend to, but I heard Vinnie was out of town and went over. When I got there, Clippers was just standing behind the house alone. I grabbed him and ran."

"You didn't see what had happened to Vinnie?"

She shook her head hard. "I figured it was my one chance to rescue Clippers. My plan was to get him a good home where Vinnie would never find him. When I learned what had happened, though, I kept him."

I believed her. What's more, Keats believed her. As for Percy, he'd slipped inside before she got the door closed, so his verdict hadn't arrived.

"Could we meet Clippers?" I asked.

"Look, my new boyfriend's here. And my family. Can you come back another time?"

"Well, my cat's gone inside, actually, so you might as well bring Clippers out, too. I only want to see if this is what Bocelli—or Fred —is so fussed about."

I already knew the answer because the donkey was hammering the trailer hard with one hoof and then both. I'd have no choice now but to buy the dented trailer from my brother's friend.

"They were good buddies," Bailey said. "A former friend of Vinnie's told me Clippers was hidden out in the bush so I wouldn't find him. He had to leave Fred with him, too, or Clippers wouldn't shut up."

I remembered Martha Kinkaid mentioning an old barn in the woods. It was old in *her* day and must be a wreck by now. "He left Clippers and Fred in the bush for months?"

"Supposedly, yeah. In a shed or something. I went out looking a few times, but that crazy old lady next door shot at me." She held out her right slipper. "Wrecked a good shoe and sprained my ankle."

"Gertie hasn't lost her chops," Edna muttered. "Impressive."

I raised a hand to signal her to stay quiet. "Someone must have set Fred and Clippers loose too, the day Vinnie died," I said. "And then they got separated."

Edna ignored my gesture. "Well, I for one am interested in meeting this Clippers. Such a fuss over a dog."

Bailey's eyebrows went up. "Clippers isn't a dog."

"A cat, then," Edna said. "Bring him out, young lady."

Sighing, Bailey opened the door and called, "Clippers!"

Percy arrived first, tail up, as if he'd solved everyone's problems. Silence fell in the trailer at the curb, which allowed us to hear an odd clippity-clop sound over the tiles inside. A head appeared in the crack of the door. Clippers turned out to be the smallest horse I'd ever seen—just three feet tall. Sniffing, he threw back his head and let out a high, shrill whinny.

The cacophony from the trailer confirmed that while we were searching the snowy hills, the object of Bocelli's affection had been living the good life in Dog Town.

"Bailey," I said. "These two are best friends. Bocelli has been terribly depressed over losing Clippers."

"Bocelli? Oh, now it all makes sense! I saw you on TV tonight."

"TV?" It came out a little loud and Jilly tugged my arm to get me to stay focused.

Percy slipped through the door and Clippers tried to follow. He was making such a racket that a burly balding man came to the door, too.

"What's going on?" he asked, draping a protective arm over Bailey's shoulders.

"Hi there," I said, with my best HR smile. "We're here to reunite Clippers with uh, Fred, the donkey. His old best friend.

Fred's been inconsolable after losing his buddy, and it looks like Clippers feels the same way."

"There's no room at this inn for a donkey," the man said, snickering over his joke.

Keats' ears went back, suggesting Bailey's taste in men hadn't improved that much. It was a shame, really, because I sensed she was a nice enough woman.

"I'm sorry about what you've gone through with Fred," she said. "But I can't have a donkey in downtown Dorset Hills."

"It's against the bylaws," Edna said. "Just as a miniature horse is."

"Clippers would be better off on a farm," I said. "*My* farm."

Bailey shook her head. "I'm not giving him up. Please go."

Her boyfriend came toward us. "Beat it."

Edna opened her purse just enough to reveal the pepper spray and a hypodermic or two. The guy noticed and quickly backed into the house, pulling Bailey with him. The door slammed in our faces.

"This isn't over," I said, as we walked to the truck. "Do you hear me, Bocelli? Or Fred. Not over."

On that, I was right. Just as we were about to pull away from the curb, someone yanked the front passenger door open. Keats bolted into the back seat, and Edna practically disappeared under a miniature horse that was very much still a horse, even pint-sized.

"He's young but he's housetrained," Bailey said, as she closed the door. "Merry Christmas."

We drove down the road as Bocelli and Clippers started a jubilant call and answer.

"This might be a touching moment in different circumstances," Edna said, trying to ease the horse into the footwell. "Unfortunately, it looks like we're being tailed."

CHAPTER TWENTY-THREE

"Tailed! Why would someone be tailing us?"

Edna stopped wrestling with the horse long enough to stare at me. "Calm down. Would Sherlock Holmes sound so shrill?"

"Sherlock Holmes never got tailed during a Christmas Eve blizzard with four animals along for the ride. I need to keep them safe."

"Real detective work is rarely glamorous," Edna said. "And you have something Sherlock never had." She grunted as the horse resisted her efforts. "Namely, me."

"Maybe Kellan sent a plain clothes officer after us in an unmarked car," Jilly said.

"Good thinking." My breath evened out at the thought of a police officer being nearby.

Edna managed to move the passenger seat back until Jilly was too squished to move. The horse's rear hooves slid down into the footwell but his top half was still on Edna's lap.

"Girls, listen to me," she said. "That is not a cop. Even the sloppiest of cops wouldn't be so obvious about it. I was barely paying attention and noticed the vehicle. The only reason I didn't get a look at the driver's face is because of the snow. Therefore, we have the advantage here."

"I'm driving a truck and pulling a donkey in a trailer. Where exactly is my advantage?"

"Like I said, the advantage is me. You can't keep a cool head because your maternal instincts are spiking your estrogen. Aside from dealing with this stupid horse, I actually relish the opportunity to outwit this fool. Seriously, who would make his move on Christmas Eve in weather like this?"

"A deranged killer, that's who," I said. "Someone crazy enough to follow us here. Someone who may be worried Bailey told us more than she did."

"We don't need to know why right now," Edna said. "We just need to turn the situation around. Our biggest problem is the trailer."

"That problem I can fix," Jilly said. "Remi lives two streets over. I'll text to say we're dropping the trailer there."

"Good thinking, Jillian. Keep up the good work."

"I can't lead a potential killer right to Remi's door," I said. "Plus, what if the person's really after the donkey or the horse?"

"We'll find that out soon enough," Edna said. "After we unload, our tracker will either follow or not. One step at a time."

"Cori and Bridget are going to join Remi," Jilly said. "We'll be leaving the animals in good hands."

Edna squirmed to find a better position under the dreadfully awkward animal. "Just drive along calmly as if you hadn't a care in the world," she said. "Whatever you do, don't lose the tail. When it's safe to confront, this may be our best option for solving the case."

I sought the one opinion that truly mattered in situations like this. "Keats? I can't take my eyes off the road to look at you. What do you think?"

He mumbled something complicated that ended in a question mark.

"What did he say?" Edna asked.

"He said do it. And also asked me not to leave him behind."

As I backed carefully into the driveway, Remi and her husband, Tiller, came out of the house acting downright jolly, just as Jilly had advised. Tiller quickly unhitched the trailer, while Remi took the miniature horse from Edna. Despite the circumstances, she grinned with childlike delight over Clippers.

"Don't get any big ideas, Remi," Tiller said. "No breaking bylaws when you're regularly breaking all kinds of other laws."

"Love to stay and chat but we have laws to break, too," Edna said, walking around the truck to the driver's side. "You can see the headlights down the road."

"What are you doing?" I asked, wishing I hadn't left the truck running.

"Only one of us is trained to handle these conditions and it isn't you," she said, climbing in. "And I bet it isn't the loser behind us. So join me or stay back if you want to play it safe."

"That's my truck."

"Ivy, get on the ride or get off. I'm fine either way but I'm taking the dog. He's a better co-pilot than either of you."

"Keats goes nowhere without me," I said, heading around to the passenger side. "Jilly, do you want to stay behind with Percy?"

"Please." She got into the back seat. "As if I'd ever knowingly leave my best friend at risk from a nutjob."

"We don't know for sure this tail is a nutjob," I said.

"Yeah we do," Jilly said. "But I meant Edna."

Edna gave a wild cackle as she put the truck in gear and rolled down the driveway. "Watch and learn, ladies. Watch. And. Learn."

She turned away from the tail and proceeded slowly, giving the driver a chance to catch up. Rounding a corner, she picked up speed to the next four-way stop. Her eyes darted to the rearview mirror again and again.

"Care to share your strategy?" I asked, clutching Keats.

"Hold tight," she said, entering the intersection. Slowing slightly, she did a tight U-turn. Then she charged back the way we'd come. The tail vehicle did the same, turning on a dime, and now we were chasing our tracker.

"Looks like a big SUV," I said. "Good traction."

"More like a van," Edna said. "At least, let's hope so, because they're much harder to handle in whiteout conditions."

"Oh my gosh, Edna," Jilly said. "No accidents, please. I want to live to see Christmas."

"If this is the killer and we can take him out, you might live to see the new year," Edna said. "My only regret is not changing out of my dress earlier. If we need to pursue on foot, I'll be at a disadvantage. But fear not, girls, my crossbow is in the back."

"A crossbow won't help in the bush in the dark," I said.

"You'd be surprised." She accelerated even more. "But that's not my only weapon. It's good to have choices."

"We can't keep up in the truck," I said, as we left Dorset Hills proper and merged onto the highway to Clover Grove. "I can barely see the taillights now. The chains are slowing us down."

"Don't count us out. I may not be able to outpace this guy, but I can outthink him."

"Him? What makes you think it's a man?"

Her jaw clenched and she leaned closer to the windshield, which was constantly blurring with snow. "Because no woman in Clover Grove can outdrive me, that's why."

"That's a big assumption," I said.

"I was the only woman in any of my stunt driving courses. Ladies fail to see the fun in things like this. I honestly believe it's the curse of estrogen. Yours is on the low side, Ivy, which makes you good in a crisis."

"Are you saying I'm high in testosterone?"

"Don't get testy about testosterone," Edna said. "It's a compliment."

Jilly's hand came through the seats and patted my shoulder.

"You're plenty feminine. A few minutes ago she said you were too maternal. Seems like you can't win with Edna."

"I'm trying to focus. Do your girl bonding around the tree later." Edna pressed the pedal a little harder, and as terrifying as it was, it really did feel like she had full command of the truck. "Darn darn darn," she added. "And also... yay."

"Yay?" I leaned closer to the windshield. "Did he hit the ditch?"

Edna shook her head and geared down. "Took the turnoff to the back route."

"The trails? Edna, no! We won't even be able to see them with the snow."

She allowed herself one scornful glance at me. "Tracks, Ivy. He'll probably be the only one out there, especially tonight. We'll trip him up in no time."

"I'm queasy already," Jilly said, and Percy let out a yowl of agreement.

I braced myself on the dash with one hand and clutched Keats with the other as Edna slowed for the turn. He mumbled something a few times over.

"What's he on about?" Edna asked.

"I really hate to repeat it, but he's saying 'faster.' We do have a chance here, Edna. Just please be careful."

The speedometer said she was technically going slower but it felt like breakneck speed as she raced along short straightaways, turned sharply and bumped through a farmer's field. The other vehicle managed to stay well ahead of us, with short loops into brush probably intended to block our larger vehicle. Edna wasn't easily foiled and deliberately avoided that trap. Eventually, however, she let out a frustrated sigh.

"Dagnabit, our tracker knows the back routes as well as I do. Only a few people on the right side of the grass do, and one of them is Gertie Rhodes. She's a dang good driver, too." She swung down a long lane that would normally be pitch black, but the snow helped show the boundaries on either side. "Maybe I was wrong."

"Why would Gertie have been tailing us?" Jilly asked. "She's getting the loot and people will stop trespassing eventually."

"Maybe she really did kill Vinnie and Felix," I said. "And she's afraid we're getting too close to the truth."

"Gertie works in mysterious ways," Edna said. "I admire that in her, but not when I'm tailing her on terrain she knows even better than me."

"You can do this," I said. "Go faster, Edna."

She took a deep breath and said, "You got it. But this next stretch is a dinner grabber."

"Dinner grabber?" I asked.

"She means I'm going to heave," Jilly said. She cracked open the window to bring in some fresh air and we all sucked in a big breath at once. We'd probably used up a lot of oxygen with our nervous panting.

"This is our last ditch chance," Edna said. "And I do mean ditch."

She pulled a sharp right, rolled into a shallow ditch and out the other side. I gave a little scream as she sped directly at a fence but it melted away to expose a breach she obviously knew about. In the farmer's field beyond, she geared up and charged. From the pinpoints of light ahead, I could see we were running parallel to the other vehicle.

"You're gaining on her," I said. "Or him."

"When the field ends, I'll be able to circle around and corner her," Edna said. "I'll slash her tires and then beat that woman with my handbag for putting the pets through this." She kept the pedal down and after a second added, "Then I'll hug her for giving me an adrenaline high that'll take years off me. I'm probably only seventy years young now."

Keats mumbled something, louder now.

"Focus, Edna. There's a wall of forest ahead so the turn's here."

"Got it." She slowed and turned back to the main trail. "Okay... where is she?"

We all peered around and Edna did a tight donut that caused a gagging sound behind us.

A way off in a field we saw the lights. The vehicle turned abruptly, raced a few yards, and then plunged into what looked like impenetrable bush.

"It *is* a van," Edna said, spinning the wheel to follow. "And it's heading toward Gertie's house. Let's beat her there and I'll apply my handbag without further ado."

I pulled out my phone. "Let's leave that to Kellan. We've done all we can, and I still have sixty animals to bed down."

"Sixty-one," Jilly said. "I assume Clippers is bunking with Bocelli?"

Despite my disappointment over not catching the other driver, I brightened. "I can't wait to see their reunion. Let's hurry."

"Sure, let's hurry," Edna said, mocking me. "I'm the one who needs to navigate this crazy maze in whiteout conditions."

"There's a whisky with your name on it when we get home," I said.

"Make it a grapefruit martini and you're on." She perked up like a wilted flower as she followed the van's tracks back to the highway.

CHAPTER TWENTY-FOUR

I could never sleep on Christmas Eve as a child and tonight was no different. Well, it was different in that the cause of my excitement was a terrifying car chase rather than Santa's impending arrival. Either way, I'd still be wide awake when the clock ticked past midnight.

Everyone else was still gathered around the tree downstairs but I couldn't feign Christmas cheer or hide my disappointment over failing to catch our man. On top of that, sending Kellan out to interview Gertie meant I didn't have him with me by the Christmas tree.

Eventually I pleaded a headache and retreated to my room where I put on my long johns and fleece-lined overalls, climbed under the covers and tried to warm up. I kept the phone close by in hopes that Kellan would call to say he'd nabbed Gertie.

The other reason I couldn't sleep was that four eyes—two green, one blue, and a brown one I couldn't see in the darkness—stared at me from the foot of the bed. Percy and Keats didn't even bother to lie down and get comfortable. They sat there like statues. Waiting. If they were waiting, I had no choice but to wait with them. Hopefully when Kellan called, we could all get a few hours sleep.

A ping came just after 11. Instead of calling, Kellan texted to let me know Gertie was off the hook. She was safe at home, there were no tracks, and her van was cool. He'd woken her up with his visit and she'd torn a strip off him, but now he was heading back to the station to clear up a few things. He'd be here in time for breakfast, he said.

"Kellan came up empty," I told the boys, sighing. "It's selfish, I know, but I really wanted to spend Christmas Eve with him. It feels more magical than the day itself."

If I expected sympathy, I got none. The eyes seemed to glow a little brighter—pure magic that didn't rely on Christmas spirit. The staring was the opposite of soothing. Galvanizing, even.

"What's with you two? Haven't you had enough thrills for one night?"

I closed my eyes and it seemed like their gaze penetrated my lids. Turning on my side, I deliberately pictured the sweet reunion between Bocelli and Clippers. I'd left them reclining together in a stall. Tomorrow I'd give the donkey a choice between his old name and his new one. I knew he'd have an opinion.

Finally I sat up. "*What?* You can't just sit there staring all night without telling me what you want. I'm listening."

Keats jumped off the bed and pranced around the room. Meanwhile, Percy climbed on my legs and flexed his claws, managing to deliver 10 startling jabs through several layers.

"Ow! I'm going to snip those claws, mister," I said. "But first, I have something else to do. Apparently."

My heavy weather gear was strewn on my chair and I zipped on my parka and grabbed my Santa toque and mittens. Last I coiled the Santa scarf around my neck. When I was done, I wished I'd started with the pets, because it was tough to bend over swaddled up like that. Despite everything, Keats put up a fight against the coat.

"Thanks for keeping things normal," I whispered, cornering him. It was becoming so routine I didn't even need the light. Percy, on the other hand, practically put on his own jacket, with fluff exploding comically all around it. "You're my easy child. Aside from the claws."

The music and chatter gave me plenty of cover to sneak down the back stairs, slip my feet into boots and get out the door. The snow lit up the way to the barn, but my tracks from earlier were filling in quickly.

I was about halfway there when a clamor began. It was a combination of braying and neighing so high pitched that Florence, the old mare, must be rolling her eyes. She wouldn't consider Clippers a real horse, I was sure of that.

"So much for 'not a creature was stirring,'" I muttered as I clomped faster through the deep snow. If I didn't calm them, others would eventually notice and Poppy or Jilly would come down to see what was going on.

Keats and Percy raced ahead of me to the truck. The trailer was still hitched and backed up to the wide side door of the barn. Their message was clear: we were going for a ride. Bocelli and Clippers chimed in with a message of their own: they were coming along. And if they didn't get their way, I wouldn't get away without notice.

"Seriously?" I said, shining my phone light into their stall. Both continued their racket at a reduced volume. "You really need to come?"

Bocelli's grating screech delivered a defiant yes. Clippers sounded a little less confident, though enthusiastic.

"Ridiculous," I said, opening the stall and leading the donkey to the trailer. "Your little friend needs to ride in the back seat. I have no idea how to manage a mini horse, Bocelli."

I tried Clippers on the seat itself but it was clear he'd lose his balance. We were both relieved when he was propped in the footwell. Meanwhile Keats and Percy shared the passenger seat, both looking the happier for prime positioning.

"Lead on, fellows," I said. "I'm guessing you've figured out something very important and are waiting for me to clue in."

Keeping the lights off, I drove down the lane, grateful for the heavy snow that muffled the sound of chains on gravel, and even more grateful for the chains themselves. The road crews might be light because of the holiday. In fact, I hoped they were, because otherwise someone would probably recognize the yellow trailer and report me to Kellan.

Keats let me drive past Mandy's darkened store and on into town without issuing orders. "All is calm, all is bright," I said, after a quick troll down Main Street.

That's when the white paw finally offered direction and I turned right. We rolled down a side street until we reached the Clover Grove Veterinary Office and then a general clamor began. Clippers whinnied and Bocelli answered with a resounding thud as he kicked the trailer.

All the lights were out, as I'd expected, since Cliff and Beverly lived in the Roxtons' original farmhouse outside of town. But Keats rumbled for me to pull in and I listened. Tire tracks went around the side of the building to the private staff-only parking lot. I worried about getting stuck back there without space to turn the trailer, but Keats urged me on with a little yip.

"Okay, but I don't like this."

In the parking lot behind the building sat a white van.

"Oh my gosh," I said. "It *was* Beverly! I would never have given her credit for being able to drive like that. She just went way up in my estimation, even if she is a killer."

I turned the truck around before turning my lights out.

"You'd better give the van a sniff, Keats," I said. "As much as I hate to even contemplate this, I suppose it could have been Cliff."

Keats gave no indication of imminent danger, so I opened the door and the cat and dog both jumped out.

They walked around the truck and then Percy jumped on the hood, lifting one foot after another in the accumulating snow. That's when I realized this van couldn't possibly have been the one leading us on a reckless chase through the fields. While someone had taken it out within hours, the snow on the hood and the roof were quite deep and would most certainly have blown off during the pursuit, as it had my truck.

I touched the hood and found it cool. Surely some remnant of heat would remain after a car chase. Kellan had used that to prove Gertie was innocent.

"Huh," I said, heading back to the truck, and pushing up my toque. "Good idea, boys, but a false lead, I'm afraid."

Keats and Percy jumped in but their eyes pinned me again, forcing me to think, and think some more. It wasn't easy when I was so tired. All the adrenaline that had coursed through me during Edna's drive was ebbing away, leaving me drained. Now I felt like I could drop right off here at the wheel. In fact, for a second it did feel as if I drifted but a sharp poke in the cheek with a wet muzzle put an end to that.

"Right, right. Still with you," I said. "How embarrassing to be found here in the morning."

Keats grumbled to give him more credit than that, and I said, "Not your fault, buddy. I'm exhausted, but let's keep going."

I took the side streets, even though Main was cleared. Better to slink around as people focused on their trees and made merry.

"Who else has a white van?" I mused. "Nearly every business in town that delivers. Ah! That's it."

I drove along the street behind Flora to Fawn Over. Letitia Smart certainly had access to yew bushes, although I couldn't imagine why she'd want Vinnie or Felix dead. She lived in the apartment over the store, so if the truck was warm, I'd have to find a creative excuse to chat, when my creativity had gone up the chimney.

My worry was unnecessary. The flower store van had a deep dome of snow on top.

"One down," I said. "What about the Langmans? They've got a white delivery van, too."

Keats gave a noncommittal mumble that forced me to pursue that lead, too. I wondered if he was just enjoying the ride.

A quick turn around their block showed the Langman van in pretty much the same condition as Letitia's. Everyone had gone straight home after choir practice but us, it seemed.

"There's something I'm missing," I said, slowing for the last four-way stop in town. "It's tickling the edge of my awareness. Keats, a little help, please."

He rested a paw on my hand and I just sat there, my wipers beating a steady rhythm.

"There was another one. Another van. Somewhere." My mind backtracked to the day we'd found the donkey. Our first stop had been Carmina Prescott's house. "Got it!" I said. "Carmina Prescott. Right?"

Keats made a blatting sound like a buzzer. Fail.

"Oh, come on..." After Carmina's we'd gone straight to Vinnie Swenson's. "Oh no. Seriously, Keats? I do not want to go out there to see if someone used Vinnie's van tonight."

He clawed at my arm, urging me on.

"That's not it, either? We're out of runway, buddy."

I stared around the empty intersection. Mom had taken out a post here before my brother reclaimed Buttercup. I was trying to remember which one she'd hammered when I glanced up and saw the sign.

And received the sign, in the form of a cacophony of animal sounds. A veritable symphony of confirmation.

"Got it," I said, making a slashing sign at my throat. "Now zip it." I raised my voice. "Bocelli, stop that kicking and get ready for our final verse."

IT WAS NEARLY midnight when I pulled into a larger parking lot and rolled over to the white van in the corner. I drove around the side and saw the logo. During our pursuit earlier, I'd caught a glimpse in our headlights of something bright in the final moment before the van disappeared into the bush. Now I knew it was sunbeams—bright rays that concealed a dark secret.

Rolling down the window, I studied the van. There was a bit of accumulation on the roof and none on the hood. I didn't need to touch it to know it was still warm, because the clicking of the cooling engine gave it away. Even if those signs hadn't been there, Keats confirmed my suspicion with raised hackles and flattened ears. There was another, milder thump in the trailer, and Clippers responded with a nicker. Percy kept his commentary to a big-eyed stare that said, "So now what?"

I drove back around the front of the building and parked.

"Let's take a peek," I said, letting Keats and Percy out of the truck. "Hang tight, the rest of you."

Walking up to the front door of Sunny Acres retirement villa, I pressed my face to the glass. The night watchman was slumped over his desk, sound asleep. I hit the buzzer and he didn't stir. Hit it again, and he twitched a little before resettling.

"That man is sedated, my friends," I said. "But if I keep whacking that buzzer it'll wake the whole place. All I need is one person to let me in."

I went back to the truck, pondering. Keats sat on his haunches, threw back his head and gave a little howl. His mouth formed a perfect "o."

"Yeah? If you say so. Let us sing."

Percy scraped his foot in the snow in the universal litter box sign of disgust, but I figured I could probably depend on the others.

"One carol," I said. "I bet that's all it will take. Let's make it a good one."

I unloaded Bocelli and then, with more difficulty, Clippers. The five of us walked around the building to the courtyard and I let Keats choose our position among the potted plants, all of them toxic.

"Don't touch the yew," I told Clippers, yanking his halter as he sniffed around. "It kills livestock and house pets, too. I'm not sure which one you are, yet."

I straightened my hat and took a few deep breaths. In for five, out for five. It was harder when the air was like cut glass. Finally, I was ready.

"In the key of G, boys," I said. I didn't know what the key of G sounded like and it didn't matter. No matter what key I chose Bocelli would drown me out. At least I hoped so. It seemed like he still had plenty left to say.

I launched into Hark the Herald Angels Sing, the donkey's favorite. Bocelli let out a harsh screech, which made Clippers give a loud squeal. Keats didn't really need to add to the noise but he threw back his head again and chimed in. Percy blinked up at me, arched his back and then released the loudest sound of all—the spooky caterwaul known to feral colonies everywhere.

Looking up, I saw a few bald and gray heads appear at the windows. Then I walked to the side door, fully expecting to be met there.

This time, I wasn't disappointed.

CHAPTER TWENTY-FIVE

"Horse blanket Santa. Night night."

Dr. Roxton Senior was wearing flannel pajamas, a fleecy robe and a Santa toque just like mine. Instead of slippers, he wore heavy boots. I had no doubt his right boot had pounded the gas pedal earlier in the Sunny Acres van as he hurtled over the trails ahead of us. He was one of the few people in town who knew those trails like the back of his hand because of treating livestock out in their pastures.

The only thing remaining was to determine if he had control of his faculties. Keats had swelled like a puff adder and his tail stood out straight. That only proved the veterinarian was a serious threat to my welfare, which could be true whether he had dementia or not.

Slipping my hand into my pocket, I pulled out a tissue and wiped my nose. When I shoved it back, I pressed Kellan's number, hoping he could hear through a thick layer of quilted down.

"Hey, Dr. Roxton," I said. "Fred wanted to sing one last song for you." There was a discordant note of protest at my shoulder. "Ah. Apparently he prefers the name Bocelli. I wondered."

"Dog hoof party," Dr. Roxton said.

"Yes, we found Clippers," I said, guessing at his meaning.

Perhaps dementia wasn't the issue but dysphasia, where people got the words wrong. "What a glorious reunion. I wish you could have seen it. I guess you found where Vinnie had hidden these two out in the abandoned barn and freed them, too. They got split up but it's all good now."

He stared into space and then opened his mouth. I thought he was going to come clean, but instead he released a loud braying sound that was a passable imitation of the donkey. So passable that Bocelli answered back.

"Snooze button," he said. "Make hay."

"Yeah, we're pretty pooped and I'm sure you are, too," I said. "That was one heck of a drive you took earlier. Very impressive. You know the back roads and you know how to handle a van."

"Blow hard," he said.

I figured he meant it as one word because my flattery wasn't subtle at all.

"It was blowing hard," I said, deciding to take him literally. "I couldn't handle those conditions myself so I gave Edna the wheel. I was worried about the dog and cat. They were with me so Edna couldn't go all-in, and trust me, she was mad about letting you get away. I had to put the animals first. Like *you* always do."

His eyes wandered around the parking lot, dancing lightly over the foursome behind me.

"Twenty-three skidoo," he said.

I laughed. "I suppose you enjoyed every second of it, since you're mostly stuck in that chair."

He had a cane under his arm that he clearly didn't need. I knew his room was on the second floor, so he'd made it downstairs in good time for someone supposedly disabled. Others would join us at a slower rate. I might only have a few moments.

"Does Beverly know you can run downstairs like that?" I looked down at his hand. "Or that you have a key to come and go as you like? I assume you dose the watchman with your sleeping pills to make the rounds as Secret Santa."

"Gingerbread house," he said. "Sour puss."

"I would imagine you wished you could poison Beverly, too. Honestly, I don't know why Cliff married her."

"Tick fever," he said, making a popping noise with his mouth. "Kerflooey."

This was much harder than I'd expected. And slower. Either his mind truly was altered, or he was way smarter than me. It was time to see what a little testosterone could do.

"I don't envy you when Beverly finds out what you've done. She already treats you with such contempt. And when she hears Edna Evans can outdrive you, well... I'm sure she'll laugh and laugh."

His thin lips pressed together and his fingers clenched the cane till the knuckles whitened. He didn't say a word but the truth was in his eyes. They only landed on me for a second and the flashing fury made my throat tighten. My lungs froze, too, and my next breath prickled painfully.

He mumbled something I couldn't hear and I might have doubted myself if Keats hadn't growled. Percy coiled between my boots and hissed. And Bocelli pawed the snow. Poor Clippers just whinnied. He was way behind on the story.

"You saved Fred and Clippers," I said. "And all the other livestock that Frank was neglecting. I know about his history, going back to the Dayton circus rescues in Dorset Hills. I know the Milloys abused their animals, too. Felix's homecoming was a way to set things right, and the yew bushes made it easy enough. But you really need to explain to your son before Beverly gets to him. Tell Cliff about all the years you tried to save the animals Frank and Nate, and their sons and grandsons, neglected and abused. You couldn't tell him before in case Vinnie targeted Cliff, too. Now you can. You're the hero, not the villain, Dr. Roxton. But for Cliff to know that, you need to drop the dementia act."

He fired a volley of curses like I'd never heard before, and I was no stranger to salty language.

"Look, you can keep it up if you like. I'll even tell Cliff your side of the story." His eyes landed on me briefly again. This time instead of fury, there was hunger. I pressed my advantage. "As long as you tell me one thing. I understand what happened with Vinnie and Felix. But what did the mayor do?"

There was a long pause and then his mouth worked in the way Bocelli's often did while he brayed. Finally he said, "Nothing."

It was one word, but it made sense.

"Nothing?" I asked.

"She did *nothing*," he said. "And she knew. Like all the mayors before her knew and did nothing. They let the Swensons and Milloys prosper while animals suffered. I was the one who had to tend to those animals. I was the one who had to put them out of their misery when they died of neglect or mistreatment." His shoulders shrugged under the fluffy plaid robe. "So I decided to put people out of *my* misery. And I gave this town a wake-up call."

I nodded. "As a rescuer, I thank you for putting animals first."

"I knew your rescuer friends would make sure they were safe. Livestock are tougher than you'd think."

"Your plan worked," I said, trying to figure out my next step. "I'll make sure Cliff understands."

"I shouldn't have gone after the mayor," he said, clutching the robe around his throat. "Heard you nearly—"

"Bought the farm," I said, smiling. "Luckily the donkey and my own brilliant pets stopped that from happening."

"I was just so... *mad*," he said. "Beverly's been pushing me around for years and crushed what was left of my pride." He waved at the villa. "I wanted to move here because I thought she'd leave me alone. But no. She just kept right on coming to look like a model citizen and kept Cliff away to spare his sensitive feelings."

"Cliff is a wonderful man. He just chose the wrong woman."

"I couldn't think of a way to take her out without risking him," Dr. Roxton said. "I've been waiting for my chance, and now it'll never come."

"I suppose not, but you did rid the world of some nasty business and gave me two new animals I'll treat like gold. You did plenty of good in your time, Dr. Roxton."

He looked over at the donkey and said, "Good luck, Fred, old buddy."

Then he raised his cane and swung at me.

CHAPTER TWENTY-SIX

I ducked and darted away just in time. I liked to think I could have handled a regular old man swinging a cane, but the madness in Dr. Roxton made him unpredictable and completely fearless. He had absolutely nothing to lose.

"Don't, Dr. Roxton," I said, as Keats crouched at my side, ready to launch on my cue. "Because my dog will protect me with his life. You won't hurt him. All this was about helping animals. Don't end by hurting them."

"Then take the hit for him," he said. "Do the right thing for the dog."

He swung again and I dodged out of reach. "The right thing to do for my dog and my fifty other animals is to stick around and care for them. I'll do what I have to do."

"And if I have to take out one animal to get to you, after saving thousands, I'll do what I have to do."

There was a shuffle behind me and then Bocelli moved in front, presenting his side full-on. On top of his broad back sat Percy. Clippers positioned himself under the donkey's belly. And Keats paced in small circles around me, biding his time.

"It isn't just one, Dr. Roxton," I said, over the donkey's back.

"Are you willing to take out four amazing animals to kill me? A rescuer with decades of good work ahead? Are you mad enough to do that?"

He paused for a few seconds, and then instead of lashing out at us, he turned and struck the door. The small group of seniors who stared out at us through the glass leapt backward.

"No," he muttered. "I'm not mad enough to do that."

He turned back and tears spilled out of his eyes and rolled down his face.

"Let's go inside," I said. I tried to walk around the donkey but Bocelli just moved along with me so that I was effectively carried further away from danger.

"I'm not going back in there," Dr. Roxton said. "This is my last chance to—"

He turned again, cane raised, and Bocelli reached and grabbed him by the collar of his robe. The big yellow teeth must have dug in because Dr. Roxton screamed. The donkey lifted the vet clear off his feet but the old man thrashed right out of the robe and hit the ground running.

Wearing only his Santa pajamas, he ran around the corner of the building hampered by deep snow but making good time, considering.

Keats mumbled a question and I shook my head. "Don't go after him. He's mad. Madder than our usual attackers. I can hear the sirens and the police can follow his trail easily enough."

I got the residents to open the door. We all went inside and while it took a bit of maneuvering to get the donkey and the miniature horse through the stairwell, it went quite well overall. Percy jumped back on board Bocelli and took the free ride to the front desk, where the night watchman slept on, oblivious.

Martha Kinkaid was already in the lobby and said, "I don't know whether to laugh or cry."

"Isn't that always the way?" I said, kneeling to hug Keats.

Flashing lights rolled up to the front entrance and someone let Kellan inside. Bocelli blocked him, too, but I stood up and shoved the donkey aside, to let my boyfriend sweep me into his arms.

"Merry Christmas," I said. "All is calm, all is bright. Now."

"Oh, Ivy," he muttered into my hair. "How are you going to top this for New Year's?" He pulled away and smiled. "Don't take that as a challenge. Please."

"I won't," I said. "I feel a little woozy so I called Jilly and Edna to come and get me. Please find Dr. Roxton before he gets to Beverly... or freezes in a snowdrift."

"Can I borrow Keats to help?" he asked.

I looked down at the dog. "Can he?"

Keats accepted the request with a gracious—and slightly overeager—mumble. He wanted to chase that old man and be part of the finale, whereas I just wanted to get home to the fire.

"I'll bring him back soon," Kellan said, taking the leash I pulled out of my pocket. "Safe and sound."

"I trust you," I said. And I did, but it still pulled at my heart-strings to see my dog follow Kellan away. I nearly cried, but when Keats turned at the door, his mouth had dropped open in a happy ha-ha-ha.

Or maybe it was a jolly ho-ho-ho. Regardless, all was right with our topsy-turvy world.

CHAPTER TWENTY-SEVEN

I was flat out on the couch sound asleep with Percy curled up on top of me when a frenzied wet dog landed on my midriff and accidentally-on-purpose knocked the cat to the floor.

"Oh, you're back, you're safe." I tried to hold onto Keats but he squirmed so much that he fell to the floor on top of the cat. Accidentally on purpose.

Percy gave an indignant and entirely justified yowl and went to climb up Kellan. Since Kellan was taking his coat off, that avenue was closed and Percy decided to make a more dramatic statement. Trotting over to the beautiful Christmas tree—Jilly's pride and joy—the cat launched into the boughs and caught the trunk at about chest level. I muffled a scream as the tall tree swayed and glass ornaments clinked dangerously. Some of the prettiest balls came from Jilly's family collection and it would be doubly tragic if the tree fell over.

By the time I jumped off the couch, Kellan had run across the room to grab the tree at the top. The star fell off and I got there just in time to catch it. I set it carefully on the coffee table and then started extricating the cat from the boughs. It was one of my tougher assignments, as Percy dug in hard with his claws and when I pulled, the ornaments clacked and rattled.

"Percy, you let go right now," I said. "If you don't you will *never* come on a mission again."

"Don't say that," Kellan said, fighting to keep the tree upright. "That implies there's another one. Let's assume there won't be."

"It's the only leverage I've got," I said. "Leaving him behind while Keats and I gallivant is what he hates most."

"Use the carrot not the stick," Kellan said. "What can you do for him if he voluntarily complies?"

"I'm too tired to be manipulated by a cat," I said.

"That's how it's going to be with kids, sometimes," Kellan said. "All the time, really. At least from what I see."

I stared up at him and heat swirled around my chest and out to my extremities, which had been nearly impossible to warm earlier. Was he suggesting this was a rehearsal for handling children together one day? Our children?

Suddenly, I had a little more patience. "Percy. Sweetheart. Come down now for a cuddle. I know Keats was rude but it never helps to act out. You can spread some fur over Kellan's uniform while the wet dog sits in my lap. How would that be?"

Percy's head came out of the boughs and he stared at me to see if I was manipulating him. Then he looked at Kellan, who smiled invitingly.

"Stay cool, Ivy," Kellan said. "United front."

The cat burst out of the branches like a fiery volcanic eruption and raced around the room. The dog chased him until the cat leapt onto the sideboard that held the ceramic version of Clover Grove. I could tell at a glance that the town had grown even since yesterday. Mabel Halliday must have dropped off another few buildings.

The cat was perfectly capable of walking a tightrope without slipping. This time he lumbered through town deliberately knocking things over with fluffy orange paws. Then he had the nerve to sit down.

"Oh my gosh, I am going to—"

"Sweet talk him right out of danger," Kellan said.

"He's squatting on a barn," I said. "It can't be comfortable."

"He doesn't want to be comfortable. He's attention seeking. That's what kids and cats do." Kellan looked down at Keats, who fanned his damp tail. "Even brilliant crime-solving dogs sometimes. My best advice is to ignore him right now and he'll come down on his own."

I reluctantly looked away from the cat. "Did Keats find Dr. Roxton?"

"He did. It was a good thing I borrowed him because Dr. Roxton had good field skills. He doubled back and around so many times that we might have lost the trail. But Keats just kept on plowing through the snow, practically laughing at the man's tactics." Kellan went over to throw a log on the fire. "When we caught up he was trying to break into a car and I firmly believe he'd be on his way out of hill country if Keats hadn't yanked down his pajama bottoms, which tripped him. All the fight had gone out of Dr. Roxton by then and he was resigned."

"What are you going to do with him?"

"Not sure, yet," Kellan said, dropping onto the couch and groaning. "Even if he's sane, he's insane, if you know what I mean. He's gone over the edge and he needs to be prevented from harming others, particularly Beverly. At the same time, there was a reason for his madness, and people who care that deeply about animals can do extreme things."

He gave me a pointed look and then grinned.

"If you mean the Rescue Mafia, I couldn't agree more." I perched on the edge of the couch and started to slide down the leather into the comfort of his embrace.

"Wait, watch!" he said.

Percy was prodding a figure toward the edge of the display, with the clear intention of enjoying the crash. I jumped up and ran over just in time to bend and catch the ceramic pig before it hit the hardwood.

"Percy, enough," I said. "You cannot treat ceramic Wilma this way." The orange paw started to move again and the fluffy tail lashed defiantly. Figures and homes were sliding all over. The feline version of King Kong had invaded town. "There are repercussions to such behavior. You will get a time-out in the pantry if you continue." He gave an irritable meow. "I don't care if you're warning me about what's to come. You can't be sure enough of that to break my precious things."

I slid my hand under the cat and lifted him carefully out of my town. As I carried him off, Kellan called, "You can't give him a time-out now. It's Christmas Eve."

"Isn't that permissive parenting?" I asked, although I gave in and set the cat on the floor.

"You started the whole thing by playing favorites. You're setting up the boys for rivalry all their lives."

"So that's how it's going to be, huh?" I said. "I'm the bad cop and you're the good cop?"

"We may bicker about strategies, but when it comes to the crunch, let's go soft on crime."

He beckoned and I took my position in the crook of his arm again. Keats sidled into my lap immediately. Percy sauntered over, used Kellan's uniformed leg as a scratching post, and then leapt into his lap with a flourish.

Once everyone got settled, I said, "The more crime I face, the more nuance I see. It would be easier if things were black and white." I stroked Keats' wet fur. "Like Keats."

"Decisions would be easy if everything was either right or wrong, but it's rarely so simple," Kellan said. "I admit I took some satisfaction in seizing the coins from the Langman sisters. At least what was left of them. They claim they only found one cache, so we'll need to keep digging."

He gave a heavy sigh and I buried my face in his shoulder. "Let's talk about something else."

"I thought crime was your favorite subject."

"Silly. *Animals* are my favorite subject."

He kissed the top of my head. "Did I see a new one tonight? A runty little pony?"

I laughed into his shoulder. "That's Clippers. A miniature horse."

"Ah. Vinnie Swenson's missing critter." There was a pause and he pulled away. "Wait. That thing isn't going to live inside, is it?"

"He's housetrained, if that's what you're worried about," I said, still hiding my grin.

"He'll shed worse than the other two combined."

"Such a nice shade of chestnut, though. It will add to what you've already got going on here." I plucked at a few hairs on his shirt. "But for the record, Jilly would have a fit if Clippers was clopping on her hardwood. Besides, the donkey is bonded to Clippers like you wouldn't believe. That's what started this whole thing. Bocelli, formerly Fred, didn't know what happened to Clippers. I couldn't keep them apart now."

Kellan sucked in a deep breath and let it out slowly. "We'll think about the ark sinking after the holidays."

"Nothing's sinking. Let's just relax and enjoy the tree you saved from a tragic fall."

Neither of us enjoyed it long, however. Within just a few minutes, two humans and two pets were sound asleep in front of the fire.

CHAPTER TWENTY-EIGHT

"Hey there, what are you doing?" Kellan said, from the doorway of the barn the next morning. His hair was disheveled, and his uniform looked the worse for wear under his open coat. It was wrinkled and covered in a thick layer of orange fur. Percy must have done his morning grooming already.

"Mucking out stalls," I said. "The usual."

"But it's Christmas."

I stood the shovel on end, crossed my arms around the handle and grinned. "Farmers don't take statutory holidays. Animals need to be fed and watered every day so they can produce more manure. It's a very predictable cycle."

Also predictable was the slow and deadly stalk of the border collie, who crept around the corner and ambushed from behind. Kellan jumped, turned and swatted all without stumbling. I could never manage that without tripping.

"When is he going to quit that?" Kellan asked, coming over to drop a kiss.

"Less predictable. He's never had a boyfriend before. I think he's excited."

It was nice to see the slow grin spread across Kellan's face. I sensed I was just as big a puzzle to him as Keats was, sometimes. Maybe that's what he liked about me. Hopefully he wouldn't realize there were a few pieces missing until we had the fictional children he was joking about last night. Hopefully that wasn't a joke at all. Although how I'd ever manage to raise kids in my current environment with my side hustle of sleuthing was a bigger mystery still. Maybe by the time that happened, all murder would end in Clover Grove.

Keats looked up at me and mumbled something in a plaintive voice.

"Of course you'll always be my favorite," I told him.

Kellan sighed. "That's what I'm afraid of... that I'll come below not only Keats and Percy but the donkey, the miniature horse and even the emu."

"Never the emu," I said. "I haven't bonded with it yet. Notice it doesn't have a name."

"She needs a name," Kellan said, walking over to her pen. "Even if you don't keep her, she needs a name. It's not fair."

In that moment, with the snow billowing through the wide barn doors, the last remnants of an old glacier melted in my heart. This man who didn't want pets, let alone a veritable zoo, was growing to love mine. Caring about the niceties was going above and beyond.

"You can name her," I said.

"Me? No. That's a big responsibility. What if she doesn't like it?"

"They do have opinions," I said. "Bocelli used to be Fred but he's decided he likes Bocelli, even though he doesn't sing anymore."

"No more singing?"

"Apparently not. I've been running through the carols while I work and not a peep out of him. I guess he's said all he needs to say for now."

The donkey and the miniature horse contentedly pulled at wisps of hay side by side.

"They're a complicated bunch," he said. "I'll give some thought to a good name for a lady emu."

"Some breakfast would probably help," I said. "I've done enough for now so let's go inside and start with some cocoa, and not the instant kind. We're going to have a super full house today. The mayor and her husband are staying on and she's ordered a complete turkey dinner so that Jilly doesn't need to cook."

Kellan raised his eyebrows. "How does Jilly feel about that?"

"Insulted. It was a lovely thought but cooking is how Jilly processes things, just like manure management is how I process things."

"More complications," he said. "Cocoa sounds good."

"Darlings!" Mom hollered down from the porch. "Come inside. I need you."

"On the other hand, maybe you'd like some help with manure management," Kellan said.

"We'll have to go in eventually," I said, laughing. "But the good news is that Mom hates snow. How about we take a long walk later? Just the four of us."

"Don't cats hate snow, too?" he asked.

"Percy's not your average cat." I grabbed his arm as we left the barn. "But he might sleep this one out. There are plenty of available laps right now."

Kellan shrugged. "The more the merrier, right?"

Asher's truck and another car were already coming up the lane. This former introvert wasn't going to get another moment of solitude all day, and I wouldn't have it any other way.

"You're wrong about ranking below the animals, by the way," I said, plodding beside him through the snow. "You're in a class all by yourself."

It would have been nice to savor the moment, but I only caught a quick glimpse of his smile before he fell over face down in the snow. Black, white and orange assailants leapt away and careened around the house. No jackets today. It was Christmas.

Rolling over, he looked up at me through snow-crusted eyes.

"I'm so sorry," I said, trying hard not to laugh and failing utterly. It didn't help that Asher jogged by, laughing too. He was carrying a bouquet and a big bag of gifts.

"Sorry, Chief, I'd help but I've got my hands full," he called.

Kellan reached out, snagged my boot and pulled me down with him. We rolled over and made snow angels in full sight of all the guests at the windows. Keats and Percy zoomed back and made dives at us, leaping away each time we grabbed for them.

There was another shout from the porch. "She said yes! Ivy, she said yes!"

I sat up suddenly. Bronwen ran down the front stairs and stood over us.

"Your mom?"

"She says I can have a puppy. I'm getting one from that breeder you know in Dorset Hills."

"Ah, good," Kellan said, getting to his feet and offering me his hand. "We do like to send business to the Mafia."

"Let's talk about it over breakfast," I said.

"Can I bring the horse inside?" she asked.

"No," Kellan and I spoke over each other and then laughed. On this, we were both the bad cop.

"I meant the miniature horse," Bronwen said.

"Still no," I said. "How about you practice walking Keats on a leash? He'd love to help."

Keats gave me a baleful look with his blue eye, so I scooped him up and carried him like a baby as we walked up the steps. Normally he hated that, but he offered his happy pant in honor of the occasion. Meanwhile Percy had managed to summit Mt. Kellan and perch on his shoulder. Kellan stooped as he went through the door to make sure the cat would be safe.

"I love this place," Bronwen said. "Can we come every Christmas?"

"Absolutely," I said, ruffling her hair with a snow-crusted glove. "The doors at Runaway Farm are always open."

At the top of the stairs, I turned back. A year ago on Christmas, I was at my desk working. I could never have imagined that today I'd be looking down at the gorgeous wreath someone had hung on my very own barn full of quirky animals. I'd been showered with such abundance—home, friends, family, community, and especially the squirming dog in my arms—that there wasn't a single gift under the tree inside that I actually needed. I had everything.

Jilly came out on the porch and linked her arm through mine. "Can you believe all this?" she said. "We hit the jackpot, my friend."

"Aside from the murders and mayhem, you mean."

"Oh, that." She shrugged as she pulled me inside. "It's all part of our story. I wouldn't change a single thing."

Keats mumbled something sassy and panted happily as I put him down.

"Figures," I said, following him into the crowd. "You always get the last word."

Do you want to try my other mystery series? The SECRET series that's hidden in plain sight?

Sign up for my newsletter at **ellenriggs.com/secret-series** to find out how you can read the first in the 11-book series for free. There's a little more romance, a lot less murder and plenty of heart-warming humor.... plus a large cast of mischievous mutts. My newsletter is full of funny stories and photos of my adorable dogs. Don't miss out!

RUNAWAY FARM & INN RECIPES

Mandy's Killer Gingerbread

Cookie Dough

- 1 cup of shortening
- 1 cup granulated sugar
- 2 large eggs, lightly beaten
- 3/4 cup Fancy molasses
- 1/2 cup Blackstrap or cooking molasses
- 5 1/2 cups all purpose flour
- 2 heaping tsp ginger
- 1 heaping tsp cinnamon
- 1 tsp each of baking soda, salt and cloves

Royal Icing

- 4 cups sifted icing sugar
- 3 tbsp meringue powder
- 6 tbsp warm water (use more or less to get desired consistency)

- Colored sugars or candy to decorate

In a large bowl using an electric stand mixer, beat shortening with sugar until light and fluffy on medium high speed. Add eggs and both types of molasses and mix thoroughly until the batter is evenly colored and smooth.

In a separate bowl, sift together flour, ginger, baking soda, salt, cloves and cinnamon. On slow speed, gradually mix into the molasses batter, changing to hand mixing to incorporate all the flour mix as needed.

Separate the dough into 4 discs. Wrap each disc in plastic wrap and refrigerate until firm. (The spices absorb and enhance over time; you can leave it for up to a week.)

Using parchment paper, roll out each disc to about 1/4 inch thickness. Cut out shapes and place on a parchment covered cookie sheet. Freeze till firm. This can be done ahead of baking day and stored in a plastic container in the freezer.

When ready to bake, transfer frozen cut out cookies onto a parchment covered baking sheet, and bake in a 325 degree oven for 12 to 15 minutes, or until the cookies are lightly golden and evenly baked on top. If they are still dark in the center add a minute or two until they are evenly baked, since timing depends on thickness. Keeping cookies on the parchment paper, gently transfer off the hot baking sheet onto the counter until they cool completely. Do not remove them from the parchment paper as they will dry out.

** Decorate the cookies on the same day they are baked or the icing will not attach to the cookie.

Icing

Add icing sugar, meringue powder and water into the bowl of an electric stand mixer. Beat on low speed until the icing sugar is incorporated completely. Increase the speed to medium and beat until the icing comes together and is fluffy, approximately 5 minutes. Fill a piping bag with icing and decorate as you wish. (You can color the icing with food color paste after completing the mixing).

Sprinkle the cookies with sugar or decorations while the icing is still wet to make sure they will stick. Leave the decorated cookies on the parchment paper until they are completely dry, which may take a couple of hours. Then pack in a plastic airtight container and you will have lovely soft flavorful gingerbread cookies.

Author's Note: Many thanks to Cousin Leslie, our family chef, for sharing

More Books by Ellen Riggs

Bought-the-Farm *Cozy Mystery Series*

- A Dog with Two Tales (*prequel*)
- Dogcatcher in the Rye
- Dark Side of the Moo
- A Streak of Bad Cluck
- Till the Cat Lady Sings
- Alpaca Lies
- Twas the Bite Before Christmas
- Swine and Punishment
- The Cat and the Riddle
- Don't Rock the Goat

- Swan with the Wind
- How to Get a Neigh with Murder
- Tweet Revenge
- For Love Or Bunny
- Between a Squawk and a Hard Place
- Double Dog Dare
- Deerly Departed
- Think Outside the FoxMouse of Ill Repute
- Bee All and End All
- Sheep with One Eye Open
- Roo the Day
- Till Death Zoo Us Part

Bought-the-Farm Mysteries - *Boxed Sets*

- Bought the Farm Mysteries - Books 1-3
- Bought the Farm Mysteries - Books 4-6
- Bought the Farm Mysteries - Books 7-9
- Bought the Farm Mysteries - Books 1-10

Mystic Mutt Mysteries *Paranormal Cozy*

- I Want You to Haunt Me
- You Can't Always Get What You Haunt
- Any Way You Haunt It
- I Only Haunt to be with You
- All I Haunt Is You (Novella)
- Do You Haunt to Know a Secret?
- All I Haunt for Christmas

Books by Ellen Riggs and Sandy Rideout

Dog Town *Series*

- Ready or Not in Dog Town (The Beginning)
- Bitter and Sweet in Dog Town (Labor Day)
- A Match Made in Dog Town (Thanksgiving)
- Lost and Found in Dog Town (Christmas)
- Calm and Bright in Dog Town (Christmas)
- Tried and True in Dog Town (New Year's)
- Yours and Mine in Dog Town (Valentine's Day)
- Nine Lives in Dog Town (Easter)
- Great and Small in Dog Town (Memorial Day)
- Bold and Blue in Dog Town (Independence Day)
- Better or Worse in Dog Town (Labor Day)

Dog Town *Boxed Sets*

- Mischief in Dog Town - Books 1-3
- Mischief in Dog Town - Books 4-7
- Mischief in Dog Town - Books 8-10
- Mischief in Dog Town - The Complete Series